The Midnight Lie

About the Author

The Midnight Lie is a first novel by Dr Michael Palmer, a widely-read philosopher, whose previous books have been translated into many languages. A former Graduate Fellow of McMaster University in Canada and Humboldt Fellow of Marburg University in Germany, Palmer was the founding Head of the Department of Religion and Philosophy at The Manchester Grammar School. His *Moral Problems* (Lutterworth, 1991) became a best-seller, selling well over 100,000 copies. Palmer subsequently taught at Bristol University, his lectures available as *Freud and Jung on Religion* and *The Question of God* (Routledge, 1997, 2001). More recently Palmer has published extensively on the philosophy of Atheism.

In *The Midnight Lie*, a gruesome story of a Manchester double murder, Palmer draws extensively on his expertise in philosophy and psychoanalysis. The novel therefore stands within the tradition of intellectual thrillers, such as Eco's *The Name of the Rose* or Rubenfeld's *The Interpretation of Murder*.

Michael Palmer is married, with two grown-up children. He divides his time between homes in Scotland and Italy.

The Midnight Lie

Michael Palmer

Matador
9 Priory Business Park,
Wistow Road, Kibworth Beauchamp,
Leicestershire. LE8 0RX
Tel: 0116 279 2299
Email: books@troubador.co.uk
Web: www.troubador.co.uk/matador
Twitter: @matadorbooks

ISBN 978 1788035 194

British Library Cataloguing in Publication Data.
A catalogue record for this book is available from the British Library.

Printed and bound by CPI Group (UK) Ltd, Croydon, CR0 4YY
Typeset in 10.5pt Aldine 401 BT by Troubador Publishing Ltd, Leicester, UK

Matador is an imprint of Troubador Publishing Ltd

For my family

Foreword

This is the story of the 'Newtown Murders'. These occurred some years ago in Manchester – a double murder in fact, of a man and a woman. The newspapers were full of it at the time, not just the locals but the nationals as well. It got on TV and the BBC did a short piece. So it got a lot of coverage. And I can understand why. Because this was something quite outside the normal run of things. Not, of course, in execution. That's quite rare. After all, there are only so many ways you can polish somebody off: it's a stabbing, a strangulation, a drowning or a poisoning, things like that. Shooting is historically the least popular – for centuries the knife was the weapon of choice – and, by and large, people still don't have easy access to guns, not in this country at any rate. So you soon see that your choice is quite restricted. You can use a sharp instrument of some kind, a rope, a heavy object, put something in their drink, smother them or push them over a cliff. So, as I say, nothing unusual. And that's my point, don't you see? Basically, the actual deed is quite static, it hardly changes, there's little invention. And that, when it comes down to it, is also true of the Newtown Murders. You'll find nothing bizarre about them, nothing particularly inventive about the actual deed, nothing for the connoisseur of method to appreciate. In that sense it was really quite run-of-the mill. And the same, I'm sorry to say, goes for the motive. There was nothing unusual here either. After all, people kill for much the same reasons as they always did. They murder for revenge, greed, lust, ambition or a grudge of some kind. That sort of thing. However far back you go in history, you will always find these same basic ingredients. There are rarely exceptions.

Actually, that's not quite true. The modern world has added something new, which I mention now, if only to get it out of the way. This is motiveless killing. I'm not saying, of course, that this sort of thing never happened before. Caligula drowned people for fun and Alexander of Pherae enjoyed watching men being dismembered by dogs. But these men were tyrants, absolute rulers of their world. So they probably did what they did because they were just bored and looking for amusements. The thing is, we now have ordinary men and women acting in much the same way, treating their victims as so much rubbish to be thrown away. So why kill? I'll tell you why. They're curious, that's what they are. They want to know what it's like to take a life. They spot someone in the street, a complete stranger, and they single them out. So instead of that man over there, the one waiting for a bus, it's that woman pushing the pram. This is "killing-for-kicks" and I'm told it's quite intoxicating, producing a real adrenalin rush. They bear their victims no ill will, they don't care whether they're happy or not, have kids or an old Mum. Here's two examples. In Manchester in January 2013 Imran Hussain spots Kieran Crump-Raiswell waiting at a bus stop and stabs him four times in the chest. Then he drives off in his car, sniggering. Six months later, in Bolton City Centre, a teenager, Eden Lomax, murders a complete stranger, Simon Mitchell, with one punch, then returns home to play computer games. You think I'm kidding you? You think I'm having you on? I'm not. These are real cases. You can look them up, if you don't believe me. So I ask you: what are we to make of these people, all under twenty? They must be mad, you say. Well, the juries didn't think so. They concluded that Hussain and Lomax were quite sane, not psychotic in any way. But surely that can't be right, you reply. Now I understand where you're coming from, I really do. Killing these people was as casual as sneezing or blowing your nose. There was no guilt feeling afterwards, no remorse. They walked away as calmly as you please. So it stands to reason: there must be something wrong with them; there must, must, must be something, there can't be nothing. Well, I don't know. I just don't know. The whole thing seems quite inexplicable to me, quite beyond my reach. I simply can't get inside their heads, you see. I can understand greed and jealousy and desire, but not this. All I can tell you is what Hussain said at his trial: that he just wanted to see what it felt like, to kill someone, it didn't matter who. So perhaps, after all, these young lads weren't so different from those tyrants of old. They were just bored and looking for a bit of fun.

But I digress. The Newtown Murders were not motiveless killings – you can forget that idea straightaway. No, they were quite different. These crimes were meticulously planned and bold in execution. They were not committed just for the hell of it. There was motive, and that motive falls within the familiar categories of revenge, greed, lust and ambition. So what makes the Newtown Murders different? Why the notoriety? Well, I'll tell you. What distinguishes one murder from another – what establishes a hierarchy, so to speak – is how that motive is deployed. Here everything depends on the intelligence of the murderer, on his courage and skill, on his powers of deception, on his skill as a liar. After that it becomes a labyrinthine struggle between two opposing forces – the murderer on one side, the police on the other – in which one watches with fascination as the layers of deceit are gradually stripped away to reveal the criminal. The drama lies in the unmasking. In this regard, I have to tell you, the Newtown Murders were quite exceptional, which is the same as saying that the murderer was quite exceptional.

But this isn't the main reason why the Newtown Murders stand so uniquely high in my pantheon of homicide. Now I like to think of myself as an historian of murder. Murder, you might say, is my thing. So all I do, day in and day out, is unearth gruesome events. In that respect, I depend on the testimony of others. I spend my life in libraries, sifting through court proceedings, autopsy reports, police interviews, trying to resurrect the past. But this wasn't the case with the murders in Manchester. Why? Because I myself was a witness to what occurred. I was there, taking it all in, notebook in hand; and, make no mistake, you see things very differently when you have this first-hand knowledge. The past becomes your present. Memories constantly intrude. You recall sounds and smells, gestures and tones of voice. You never quite escape. Shadows flicker across the retina. Yes, I knew all those involved, all the main characters. And that means I knew the murderer. I saw that person move and speak, smile and laugh, and then saw the mask begin to drop.

And that makes a big difference, I can tell you. Believe me, seeing what I saw had serious consequences for my life.

For one thing, getting to know a murderer made me much more sure of myself. It had a psychological effect. Before I'd always felt that I'd missed out somehow, that there was something lacking. And it was difficult, it really was. Knowing my enthusiasms, people would often ask, "Have you ever met a murderer, got up close?". And what could I say? Nothing! I got fed up. It was a serious omission. But not after the Newtown Murders. Now I could look them in the eye and say, "Well, yes I have…once." Then they'd get curious and ask: "And were they different, different from you and me?" So I'd answer: "Well, of course, they were – they were stamped with the Mark of Cain – but what made them different wasn't obvious at all: it was camouflaged, unseen until the end." Mind you, I sometimes wonder about that. I mean, how far would you go when pushed? Would you lie, cheat, steal, murder perhaps? I do wonder about that, I really do. It's an interesting question.

***

The following account of Newtown Murders is a considerable expansion of a brief entry – no more than half a page – that first appears in my magnum opus, *The Decline and Fall of the British Murder*. This, after many years of sweat, is nearing completion. When finished it will be the most comprehensive and detailed encyclopaedia of murder ever written. My original intention was to make my book truly comprehensive, covering foreign murders as well. But, frankly, I'm over seventy and haven't the time. It's a shame, of course, because I'd love to include, say, French and German murders – particularly the French ones: they seem to have a knack for this sort of thing. But I'm too long in the tooth for a project of that kind. I mean, I'm no Edward Gibbon, who decided to write his history of Rome when he was 27. Still, despite this omission, I can truthfully say that nothing written either before or since can compare with my book in size and breadth. But I am realistic. No publisher will touch it. That I understand. No matter. Plans are afoot to have it privately printed. It will be in two volumes, octavo, in quarter brown goatskin from the Kano and Sokoto regions of Nigeria, with hand-marbled paper sides and end leaves, the spine lettered in gold with one line panels and tooled bands, these too with gilt edges. The title will be embossed on the front cover, with just my initials beneath, thus maintaining my anonymity. So pretty fancy. It is, after all, my life's work.

But you will ask: What got you started? What was your motivation? Why impose upon yourself such a strict rule of life? This is my answer. I'm no fool. I knew from the beginning I was obsessed. But I had a vision. Yes, a vision. And then I heard a voice. And this vision and this voice explain everything, why I live as I do. So I must tell you what happened. Then I'll come back to the Newtown Murders.

My vision came to me when I was nineteen years older than Gibbon. So forty-six. I remember it exactly, where I was, the time of day, the weather, everything. It was a Sunday. I was in London on a theatre-trip. I don't go there much now. I hate the crowds and the noise and being a sardine in the Tube. Anyway, it was a sunny day, really lovely, fresh with a slight breeze. I got out at Charing Cross and decided to walk up towards St Paul's. So I went along The Strand, past the Strand Palace Hotel – my mother lived on the top floor during the Blitz, had a wonderful time – continued up Fleet Street, then past the church of St Clement Danes and the Royal Courts of Justice, and then took a sharp left down Bailey Street. And there it was! The Central Criminal Court, the Old Bailey, the most famous court in the whole wide world! It stands where Newgate Prison once stood, and a little time ago, as a special treat, I was taken down into the basement and allowed to stroll down Dead Man's Walk, a narrow tiled pathway, along which the condemned, men and women, took their last walk to the scaffold, with the crowd outside, baying for blood. It was eerie down there, musty and slightly dank. There's a modern annexe now, housing most of the eighteen courtrooms; but it just doesn't have the magnificence of the old Victorian building, with its ornate main door, over which sit Pomeroy's imposing statues of Fortitude, the Recording Angel and Truth.

Well, there I was, standing there, minding my own business, not doing anything much, just staring up at the famous motto: "Defend the Children of the Poor & Punish the Wrongdoer." Then it was that I had my vision. I don't know what else to call it. With a heavy metallic noise, like the sound of clanking chains, I saw as clear as day the great door open, slowly and all by itself. I scrubbed my eyes. I couldn't believe what I was seeing. But then, almost in the same moment, I heard footsteps to my right. I turned and saw, through a kind of haze, a long row of figures coming slowly towards me, all in a line, one by one. I was rooted to the spot, I couldn't move. Time stood still. And then, coming closer, they came into focus. Then I recognized them – and what's more, they recognized me too, I'm sure of it, bending their heads in solemn greeting. There was Mary Ann Cotton, the "Black Widow" and Amelia Dyer, the "Angel Maker". Then I spotted George Chapman, the "Borough Murderer" and Dr William Palmer, the "Rugeley Poisoner". Then came Dr Crippen, unmistakeable, looking like a little owl, round-eyed through his steel-rimmed specs. Then I saw the trim moustache of Frederick Seddon; and behind him, just over his shoulder, I could see John Christie and after him John Haigh, the "acid bath" murderer, closely followed by that handsome Mr Neville Heath, the "lady killer". After him came Alfred Rouse, the "Blazing Car" murderer, and then, right at the end of the queue, I could just make out Major Armstrong with three more doctors, Cream, Ruxton and Pritchard. And, to my utter amazement, this long line of celebrated murderers, still in single file, trooped slowly through the great door and disappeared. Just vanished, they did! In a flash! Just like that! Well, you can imagine my feelings. My heart was pounding and I felt quite faint but at the same time curiously calm as if in a dream, somehow suspended and outside my body. It is very difficult to describe the emotional intensity of a vision. Anyway, I thought this was the end of things, that I'd wake up. But it wasn't. Because after this group came another, to my mind even more terrible. They were all dressed in the flowing crimson robes and full wigs of Judges of the High Court. Each of them wore the Black Cap, that little square of black cloth put on their heads when passing sentence of death. I shivered with fright. These were heavy men with heavy steps and hooded eyes. Some of them I didn't recognize but I saw Judge Jeffreys – I just knew it was him! – and then Lords Norbury, Alverstone, Darling and Goddard. And as if that wasn't enough, behind them came a final group, quite different. Unlike the others, these men seemed quite cheerful in their flat caps and bowlers, bright and breezy, chatting away, business-like and confident. They looked as if they'd come straight from the pub. There were six of them, all neatly dressed in suits – Billington, Ellis, Berry, Wade and the two Pierrepoints, Henry and Albert. Each of them carried a small leather bag, containing the tools of their trade. These were the hangmen.

That was my vision. It went as suddenly as it came. I was so shaken up that I had to go round the corner and have a cup of tea. I tell you, my hand was shaking as I spooned in the sugar. I sat there for about half an hour, just dazed I was. But it was then, while I was sitting in that café, shell-shocked by what I'd seen, shaking my head from side to side, trying to make sense of it all, that I had my revelation. That's all I can call it: a revelation. It came to me so clearly that I turned round in my seat to see if somebody had spoken to me. It was an inner voice. It told me, quite distinctly, that experiences of this sort are incredibly rare, almost religious and given to very few, that they take place for a reason, and that seeing what I had seen somehow contained a message I could not ignore, and that whatever it was, that message, I had to do what it told me. And what it told me, this voice, was to write my book, to dedicate what remained of my life to writing it. Well, I don't know how Gibbon felt; but I wouldn't be surprised if he'd felt just the same, standing there among the ruins of the Roman Capitol on 15 October, 1764.

My book became my obsession and this long before the Newtown murders came along. I could think of nothing else. It occupied my day-time and my night-time. This could be embarrassing, I can tell you. Take this. I'm at a party or the golf club. Somebody is talking to me, saying something really quite interesting, not boring at all. But I'm not concentrating and they soon see I'm not with them. I get that tell-tale far-away look. Well, they must think me very rude. But it can't be helped. Some little detail had suddenly occurred to me and I have no control over how these things pop up, without warning. So there I am, perhaps sipping a white wine or nibbling on a crisp, when suddenly into my mind comes the vision of two naked feet, dangling over the edge of an iron bath. I am staring at these feet, still dripping, and of course I recognize them. They belong to Margaret Lofty, the last of the three "brides-in-the-bath" murdered by George Joseph Smith, hanged on 13th August, 1915 at Maidstone Prison. According to the famous pathologist, Sir Bernard Spilsbury, Smith drowned them by yanking them up by their ankles. It was a celebrated case. For years they had a waxwork of him in Madame Tussauds. When I was a kid I used to see him there, next door to Dr Crippen, in the section called "The Chamber of Horrors". It was a full scale model, beautifully done: Smith with a towel over his arm, standing beside the bath, staring down at his wife drowning – she's got one leg over the side and you can just make out her face under the water, mouth gaping. Well, anyway, as I was saying, having a sudden idea like that, your imagination working overtime, it's very difficult coming back to reality. But what can I do? I can't very well explain to my friend that I'm thinking of a nude lady in her bath, her face contorted, struggling for breath. Quite understandably, he'd think I was a pervert or something.

I know I'd think the same, if I was in his position. Mind you, mine is not an uncommon condition, not as odd as you might think. To my way of thinking, all artists must be like this, I mean slightly schizophrenic, whether they're writers or composers, painters or sculptors. So I'm in good company, up there with Beethoven and Leonardo. I'm sure they felt much the same, constantly aware of this whirring in the back of their heads, feeling bound by these images or sounds that never let up, that take over your mind, giving you no peace at all. And then, as I've said, when you least expect it, out they jump, these ideas, just like that, without any warning, pushing aside whatever else you're doing or thinking about, demanding attention. You just have to stop and give in. Well, it's all very unsettling. And that's when I'd get my distracted look, when this other part of me takes over. I'm in one place but actually in another. It's like living parallel lives, one bit of you quite normal, the other something else entirely..

You'll understand how excited I was, I mean about my vision. I went home and told my wife. I shall never forget the look she gave me. She tried to understand but she hadn't a clue, not really, just couldn't take it in. By then Janet and I had been married for eighteen years. No children. And it wasn't as if we had other things to do or had much of a social life. We just had each other. I'd hoped for some support, but it never came. To begin with she went through the motions and just put up with things. I'd come home from work, deadbeat, have supper and then I'd be off upstairs to my book. More than anything else, I think she was upset because I had a hobby, because I was happy doing something without her. That's what did it, I'm sure of it. She

xvii

thought I was suffering from some kind of mental illness, that she just had to be patient and I'd recover, that in the end everything would come right. But it didn't. The truth was that she simply couldn't understand what had happened to me, that I was no longer the same man, that my vision had changed me. I now felt under certain obligations, with specific demands and duties, and to my mind these were unconditional, not things that I could just put off, for a few years perhaps, things to return to when retired, like gardening or stamps. When I tried to explain and told her about Beethoven and Leonardo, she just laughed. Well, she'd soon had enough and left. I don't blame her. She was a casualty of my ambition and drive. I really had no time for anything else. And the worst of it was that, deep down, I felt quite relieved when she walked out. With no wife I had no distractions and more time for my work.

***

Anyway, that's how it all started, my writing my *Decline and Fall*. Now I know what you'll be thinking. Didn't George Orwell write something similar? He did, in 1946, for the Tribune magazine. He called his essay *The Decline of the English Murder*, and very good it is too. However, in my own defence, it is a very short piece, totalling just over 1500 words, and so hardly comprehensive. No mention, for example, of the Edinburgh body-snatchers, Burke and Hare, which is, to my mind, the most sensational case of the period, one which really caught the public imagination. Would you believe, they hanged Burke before a crowd of over 20,000? That was on the Lawnmarket on 28th January,

1829 – if you're interested, his skeleton is still on display in the Medical School. However, Orwell does say one thing that is really interesting. He says that the great period of the English murder – what he calls our "Elizabethan period" – is roughly between 1850-1925. Please keep those dates in mind because I disagree with him.

Now I'm not going to quibble with the first date – although remember that the West Port Murders (Burke and Hare) took place over a ten-month period in 1828. No, it's the second I dispute. And here I'd just like to mention a specific month and year – 13th August, 1964 – and two names: Peter Anthony Allen and Gwynne Owen Evans. In case you're wondering, these were the last two murderers to be hanged in the UK, the executions timed to coincide at 8.00 am, the first at Walton Prison in Liverpool, the second at Strangeways Prison in Manchester. Let me be clear. These were the last executions to take place in this country, but they were not the last Britons to hang. That dubious distinction belongs to John Martin Scripps, executed on 16 April, 1996 for the murder of a South African tourist, Gerard George Lowe, whose body parts Scripps distributed around in black bin bags. But this happened in Singapore and so doesn't count.

You'll have guessed my main argument against Orwell. The decline of the British murder coincides quite precisely with the abolition of capital punishment. So 1964 is the watershed. It's not difficult to see why. The absence of the death penalty removed from proceedings the one factor that, like it or not, lifted a trial into an entirely different dimension, taking it quite out of the normal judicial run of things. A life sentence just doesn't cut it. And it doesn't take much to see why. Just use your imagination. Just imagine what it must have been like in the courtroom. As the days went by, as the trial proceeded, everybody must have been thinking the same thing. Would that man or woman in the dock be condemned or not? Would that chap over there, that bloke in the grey suit, with dandruff on his shoulders, actually swing? Remember, these were, by and large, not inhuman monsters but ordinary folk, human beings just like you and me, real people who, innocent or guilty, suddenly found themselves in this living nightmare, standing there, everybody watching, fighting for their lives, with two policemen sitting beside them. The tension must have been incredible and almost unbearable, steady but inexorable, building up to a tremendous climax and ending in those two fateful questions: "Ladies and Gentlemen of the Jury, have you reached a verdict? Do you find the accused guilty or not guilty?" God, I wish I'd been there! A friend of mine was. It was in Leeds. Parliament had already decided to abolish capital punishment, so there was no way the man was going to hang. The court was just going through the motions. Apparently it was nevertheless a terrifying moment, with the chaplain standing there beside the Judge wearing the black cap and pronouncing sentence of death. The poor criminal almost fainted away with fright and had to be stretchered out, and this despite the fact that he knew it was all an act, that he was going down for life, and probably be out in fifteen years. My friend said he felt very sorry for him. Well, just imagine what the real thing must have been like. As I say, the tension must have been unbearable.

And this excitement didn't just exist in the court. Oh, no. It was almost as bad outside. Remember, these were the days before TV dominated our lives. Lots of people didn't even own a telly in those days, and so you mostly relied on newspapers and newsreels. These famous cases were discussed everywhere, at home and in the pubs, going to work, in the park, on the buses, just everywhere. You couldn't escape the publicity, and walking along the street you could hear the newspaper boys shouting out the latest and doing a brisk trade with the dailies. Well, of course, the quality press condemned it all as obscene and prurient, as corrupting and pornographic; but the truth was they were all in on the act, the broadsheets just as bad as the tabloids – the *Daily Telegraph* was particularly notorious for its lurid detail. The journalists, of course, sitting up in the gallery and watching it all, had a field day, building up the tension with enormous headlines: "Waitress Savagely Slain", "Murder Weapon Found", "Murderer Unmasked", "The Jury Decides", "Jones to Hang", and finally "Jones, his Final Hours: The True Story". Things like that. So lots of people, I can tell you, were making lots of money, minting it, they were. The whole thing was carefully orchestrated and circulation rocketed, everybody licking their lips. And on the day of the execution, well it was just incredible. In the old days, when executions were public, enormous crowds gathered – it was a day out. I've mentioned 20,000 at Burke's hanging; but there were 45,000 present for John Holloway and Owen Haggerty in 1807 – with 30 spectators being crushed to death – and 50,000 for Palmer the Poisoner in 1856. The likely record stands at 100,000 for the executions and decapitations of the Cato Street conspirators in 1820. Of course, there's been nothing like that since. But even when things went private, with executions taking place within the precincts of the prison, good crowds were expected, all waiting to see that little framed notice posted on the main gate, certifying that "Judgement of Death was This Day Executed.". A decent crowd of about 1000 was nothing unusual. Sometimes there was quite a party atmosphere – there was, for example, when Crippen hanged, whole families coming along, children in tow. But it was very different with Edith Thompson in 1922 at Holloway Prison or with Derek Bentley at Wandsworth in 1953. Even at the time people thought these were terrible miscarriages of justice – which they were – and I'm told that, despite the fact that on both occasions it was a cold and damp morning, thousands turned up, on their knees praying and singing hymns and booing the police. At Wandsworth two people were arrested for damaging property.

So don't get me wrong when I say that a murder trial was a great theatrical event. What I mean is that it was a dramatic happening, a real occasion, a living drama, something that ordinary people really looked forward to. They enjoyed it, if you get my meaning. It took them out of themselves and away from their humdrum lives. It was thrilling. You may object to my saying this. It just happens to be a fact. But take away the death penalty, and what have you? Nothing much. Everything else becomes, well, pretty mundane really. But keep it in and the trial retains all the basic elements of high theatre in its dramatic effects: mystery, suspense, the police called, the pathologists, the witnesses, the speeches for the prosecution and defence, twists and turns, and then, at the end, the breath-taking finale, which, remember, could go either way. This is why I think Orwell's dating is out by about forty years. Because with that one possibility hovering over it – the possibility of a hanging – a court hearing a murder could never be anything less than sensational, with shouts and screams and sobs. That's why the Press and the general public lapped it up. So I think my main point still stands. Only a capital trial could grab the imagination, get the general public involved and worked up. Nothing else had the same effect. Because, after all, this was no novel or movie, some cheap thrill to be read about in bed or take your girlfriend to. There was nothing make-belief about this. No, this was the real thing, not fiction but a real-life tragedy, involving people like us, their lives on a knife-edge, perhaps with only a few days to go before they faced the rope. And even the setting was theatrical, with the Judge sitting high above the Court, flanked by his officials, the witness box to one side just below him. Then all the solicitors in the well of the court, scribbling away, passing messages backwards and forwards, whispering together. Then the dock with the prisoner and behind that the steeply banked galleries, with the Press and general public, all craning forward, tense, not wanting to miss a word. And what have we got now? Nowadays the stakes are non-existent and the public quickly lose interest. You can't blame them. There's no drama, nothing to grab their attention, no fascinating personalities, no suspense or end result. It's just not the same anymore. There's no intellectual appeal, no appreciation of the finer points. It's sad, it's really sad. The glory days are over.

***

Let's get back to the Newtown Murders. I've already said that watching things unfold had a psychological effect on me, a real impact. I could now hold my head high when asked about murderers because, for once at least, I had actually met one. I got respect. But this experience of seeing things at first hand also had a literary effect. In fact it changed everything. My *Decline and Fall* became less about the theory and practice of killing and more about the motive and character of the killer – I had to re-write large chunks. On my first read-through, it seemed to me that my book was too much like a catalogue of murder, a lifeless dictionary of killing, lacking any real depth or insight into what makes murderers tick. For all the world, it was like leafing through a Hardy Plants brochure, telling you all about the soil, when to plant and prune, but saying absolutely nothing about a flower's beauty. That's when I saw what was lacking: it lacked the aesthetic dimension. What I needed to do was to find a way of breathing life into these people, giving them real shape and weight. As I say, it was the Newtown Murders that did the trick. Because, when you think about it, it's one thing to read about a murderer but quite another to watch them eat and drink and have them shake you by the hand. That alters your mind-set, I can tell you.

But it's very difficult, very difficult indeed, trying to step back in time and make the past alive. I can never quite get hold of it: it seems to change as I change. Certainly it's not static but malleable, not fixed in amber. There I am, sitting at my desk, all the documents to hand. I know everything there is to know about the Newtown Murders. Everything's mapped out – the crime, the pathology reports, the interviews – all in black and white. And then, for no accountable reason, things begin to shift. I don't know why but the landscape changes and I begin to notice new details, little spots of colour on the canvas. Then I'm not so sure. So I look again, closer this time, and another perspective opens up. This happens time after time when I look at a case. Things can become more horrific or less cruel, less calculated or more cold-bloodied. For some reason I begin to see things differently and so set the crime against a different measure. Perhaps compassion creeps in. The murder becomes almost excusable, an inevitability of cause and effect, and the criminal stands as less of a devil, more like you and me, just another pathetic victim of circumstance and bad choices. But, as I say, it can go the other way, with the horror increasing the closer you look.

Here's an example of that, of how the beast emerges. One name: Seddon. I've mentioned him before. Full name: Frederick Henry Seddon. Occupation: District Superintendent of Collectors for the London and Manchester Insurance Company; represented unsuccessfully by Sir Edward Marshall Hall, who described him as "the ablest man I ever defended on the capital charge"; hanged on 18 April, 1912, with a crowd of 7,000 waiting outside for the good news. Generally considered the most unpleasant character in the whole history of British poisoners, a callous, cold-eyed monster, if ever there was one. So a very nasty piece of work, now thankfully buried deep in an unmarked grave at Pentonville. But that's the man I want to resurrect, to bring out into the light. The question is: How do you do it?

Seddon came to trial jointly with his wife, Margaret. The case itself was pretty straightforward and the jury took only an hour to convict. The couple lived in a large fourteen-room house (it's still there) at 63, Tollington Park in the Finsbury area of London. With two sons, three daughters and a live-in father, they were always hard up. So they speculated in property and had a small shop selling second hand clothes. Another way was to let out their second floor. This they did, taking in a lodger, a wealthy woman named Mrs Eliza Barrow. Within a very short time, Seddon had persuaded the poor thing – well, I say "poor thing" but she was a thoroughly unpleasant type herself, mean and slovenly – to sign over to him several of her investments and properties of around £8000 capital value, a very large sum in those days. This was in exchange for a remission of rent and an annuity of about £150 for the rest of her life, which Seddon would provide. Being only 50 years of age, she was likely to live on for many more years, thus costing Seddon money. Well, you can guess the rest. Mrs Barrow became ill; but, blow me, if she didn't make a new will with Seddon as executor just hours before she passed away. He then arranged for a cheap funeral, costing £4.10p, and deposited Mrs Barrow in a pauper's grave and not in the family vault in Kensal Green. The speed of it all aroused the suspicions of Mrs Barrow's relatives, the Vonderahes, who reported the matter to the police. Two months later the body was exhumed and arsenic discovered.

What I'm getting at is this. What more can you say about a poisoner like Seddon? You can give the bare facts, right enough; but these don't bring him back to life. We're no nearer to a living portrait, with very little sense of what he was actually like, in his day-to-day. And, I ask you, how can any decent person understand the inner workings of an ice-man, give mouth-to-mouth to a monster that long dead? I say, start by painting him just like you and me. So there he is: Seddon, a pillar of the community, a lay preacher, respected by his employers but loathed by his subordinates; Seddon the family man with five children and a wife scared of him; then Seddon sending out his eldest daughter, Maggie, to buy a three-penny packet of fly-paper; now Seddon downstairs, counting the money, with Mrs Barrow upstairs dying in agony and Mrs Seddon sitting quietly beside her, looking on; then Seddon's off to the undertaker, quick as a flash, accepting 12s 6d as commission for bringing in new business; and finally there he is with his solicitor, just hours before the hanging, waiting for Mr Ellis as cool as you please, protesting his innocence, refusing to speak about his wife and family, but furious that his car had just been sold for less than he paid for it. And then something entirely out of character. His wife acquitted, Seddon leans across the dock and kisses her full on the lips. In the silence of the court I'm told you could hear the sound quite distinctly.

These details resurrect Seddon. They bring him up close, not as a comic cut-out frightening the children, but respectable and hard-working, someone you'd pass by in the street, unnoticed, a professional man. He comes across almost like you and me, meaner perhaps but hardly different. The reader feels comfortable with him and at first sees nothing wrong. But then things change. It's like looking at a picture of a house at night. You've seen it dozens of times, it's been on your wall for years; but then you notice there's a window open, the moonlight catching a dark shape moving away across the lawn, carrying something wrapped. On the surface nothing has altered, but now you've spotted something sinister within the frame. And it's the same with Seddon. There he is, just as he ever was, but now doing something else, and what he does horrifies you. At one moment he's travelling on the bus to work, listening to clients and giving advice; and at the next he's bending over the sink, dipping the fly-papers into water, carefully siphoning off the arsenic into a small glass jar. See? See what I mean? You've been led down the path of normality, everything bland, and then suddenly you turn a corner and there stands the beast, grinning, scheming, black as pitch. That's how you bring the Seddons of this world back from the dead: by building up the image from the incidentals, a touch here, a touch there, light and shade. I've done that with all my murderers, costing me months, years, of extra work. Well, that can't be helped. There's no point in dedicating your life to something half-baked. So I've put in the hours and in the long run it's been worth it. Because you have to be this single-minded, this focused, if you want to make a real contribution to scholarship. And that's always been my ambition: to make that difference because, believe me, nobody's ever going to repeat what I've done, on this scale, with this compass and reach, buried in the stacks, scouring the records, going to places and writing it up afterwards, spending a lot of money out of my own pocket.

***

I've mentioned Seddon because his history shows you why the Newtown Murders hold such a unique place in my encyclopaedia of murder. Because, after all, unlike the Seddon case, this was no hand-me-down piece of history but fresh in my memory; because, when you think about it, I had one thing that was mine alone, something that nobody else had. This was my memory of personality. I don't mean personality as *described* but personality as *felt*. I mean none of us – not you, not me – ever saw Seddon enter the court and stand in the dock. We never saw how neat he was in his high collar and tie, how polite and incisive, or experienced the chill of that precisely enunciated, high-pitched voice. What's gone is the Seddon *effect*, the experience of the man, how those listening to him reacted in the way they did, not just outwardly but deep in their guts, their feeling of disgust low down in the stomach as they regarded the monstrous thing standing in front of them. We can read about it, imagine what it was like, but we can't feel it; and we can't do that because we weren't *there*. But that's not true of the Newtown Murders. Because I was there, I was a witness of what went on, and I have an excellent memory, believe me. Then it all comes back. As I've said earlier, it's one thing to read about a murderer but quite another to sit down with them and have a chat. Gibbon, after all, didn't know Caligula, whereas I... Ha! Well, I mustn't get ahead of myself. All that's for later.

As you'll see, everything happens in Manchester. I left the City years ago but went back recently to tie up loose ends. It was fun being there again, walking round the place. Almost everything's changed. Two ports of call were familiar haunts of mine. First, out to the police HQ in Boyer Street. In the old days, standing in the Chief Constable's office on the top floor, you could make out the Manchester United stadium way over in Old Trafford. That building's gone now, demolished, the land sold off to help pay for a spanking new HQ out at Newton Heath. Then I went back to the City Centre and the Law Courts. Those remained much the same. I sat up in the gallery of Court No. 3 and heard a couple of Guilty Pleas. Then I caught a bus down to Rusholme and then another one out to Didsbury. That hadn't changed much either, still wealthy, just more so, full of health food shops, cafés and long tree-lined avenues of Victorian semis. Then, finally, I got a taxi out to the Bridgewater Canal. That was a shock. What they've done out there, particularly around the Newtown Estate, is just incredible, really amazing: it's nothing like it was at the time of the murders. It used to be a derelict area of waste ground, covered in litter and syringes, but that's been all cleared away. The Council's done wonders. There's now a shopping precinct, with a maze of designer shops and walkways. I sat outside and had a cappuccino. I felt as if I was in a foreign country.

All in all, I stayed a week, getting my bearings and taking notes. I based myself at *The Sun* pub. I hardly recognized it, now converted into a small B & B, with the bar downstairs. Again, nothing like it was. I used to go there sometimes, years back. It was a real tippler's paradise, almost Irish in its dedication to drink, with no frills, just booze and lots of real characters. I remember Ollie, the landlord, with his gorgeous daughters. He died years back and the girls have all left, except, I think, Polly, who lives quite close. She was a little slip of a thing when I knew her but she's now married with kids. Oh, well! Time marches on! And the thing I most remember? It has to be the rain. Rain and more rain. Those of you who know Manchester will know what I mean. Because there's nothing quite like Manchester rain: that constant, cold, steady, relentless, penetrating drizzle, the sort that soaks you right through, that comes up through your shoes and seeps down through your collar, that just never lets up, that goes on and on, heavy, day after day, week after week, chilling you right through. It was the rain, more than anything, that brought back the memories. Because, as I recall, it was raining on the night of the murders.

So let's take a short step back, a little distance in time, back into a present tense. It's all there, believe me, I've left nothing out. Everything is as I remember it, exactly how it was, with those two bodies, one man and one woman, murdered in the Manchester wet.

Henry on the
Night of the Murders

The Sun pub stands between Dickenson Road and Rusholme Grove, just across the way from the Day Nursery and not far from the Manchester Hospital Schools. Go up Wilmslow Road to the crossroad with Dickenson Road and it's on the left, about three minutes walk away. Just round the corner is the Curry Mile. People come from all over the world to eat there. It contains the largest collection of South Asian restaurants, kebab houses and takeaways outside the Indian subcontinent, over seventy in all. The street never sleeps. The windows are riots of colour, displaying trays of saffron jalebi and balls of glutinous galub Jamun stacked high in bronzed pyramids of soaking sugar syrup; and the dress shops are just as flamboyant, the black-eyed models draped in saris and salwars of blue, yellow and red, their bodies decked in anklets and necklaces of bright gold. But this half-mile strip has another life. It's also the most anti-social street in Manchester, with 260 incidents being recorded in the last year alone. This surpasses the crime rate of other areas of South Manchester, such as Wythenshawe, Stockport North and the student hub of Fallowfield. A speciality of the area is kidnapping, the preference being for abductions from local families.

The Sun attracts a professional clientele: doctors from close-by St Mary's Hospital, staff from the University and UMIST and the large community of barristers and solicitors, who work in the City and who commute down to the more fashionable areas of Didsbury and Chorlton. Grey-bricked, three-gabled and half-timbered on the outside, inside *The Sun* has its original panelling, sells real ale, has no quiz nights, no pub games, the minimum amount of food, and no music. A single bar divides the two rooms: the old tap room or public bar from the more comfortable saloon, with its open fire, always alight, summer and winter. The atmosphere is warm, heavy with the smell of beer and oak. The landlord is Ollie Hickson, a red-faced, jovial man in his late fifties, who prides himself on the variety of his beers. He owns *The Sun*, and for twenty years has managed to keep afloat by working a 95-hour week, by employing his family of a wife and four daughters, and by having a faithful following of dedicated drinkers. There's Arnold, a wiry solicitor with rimless glasses, who comes in every night promptly at 6.30, drinks four pints within the hour, and then goes home to his family without ill-effect. Then, in his corner, sits the Commander, handsome, naval, in his late seventies, a fine baritone. Charlotte comes in most nights, a clumping jolly woman, remembered as a young girl with a full figure; but she has succumbed to drink and now is thick-set, jowled, heavily perfumed, with a loud and phlegmy laugh. Another regular is Mark, a retired librarian, very smart in tweeds and sporting a silk cravat and watch chain, a great drinker, now boring his listener – a middle-aged woman of iron virtue – with stories about himself, his career and conquests. But, all in all, everyone is very happy with themselves, glad to be where they are, in *The Sun's* warmth, and not outside in the freezing wet. The pub is full, noisy, the air viscous with smoke. It is getting late and outside the rain is sleeting down. It has been raining solidly for ten hours. Last orders have been called. Men and women are jostling round the bar, their empty glasses held high, shouting out for Ollie or for one of his daughters, for Jane or Susie or Molly. Some are starting to leave, putting on their overcoats and scarves, steeling themselves against the drenching cold. Others are huddled together, their faces glowing with the heat.

In the corner by the fire sit two men, middle-aged, looking tired and world-weary, attracting little attention. These are well-known fixtures of *The Sun*, sitting in their usual corner and staring moodily at their half-full glasses of Harveys Sussex and Old Hookie. They make a contrasting pair. Henry Fairest is an enormous, heavy-set man, big-boned, dishevelled, wearing cord trousers and a Harris Tweed jacket, frayed at the edges, with leather elbow patches. Terence Waters is small, dapper, bow-tied and dressed immaculately in grey flannels and a V-neck cashmere jumper. They've had enough already and they're not moving. Above them, pinned to the wall, is a framed photograph of the two of them, their younger selves, in the same corner smiling, glasses aloft, and under which someone has scribbled, 'Henry and Terence, with hair and prospects'.

'I'm just depressed,' said Henry, running his finger round the rim of his glass. 'In a few minutes I'll be fifty.

You're older than me, Terence. What are you? Sixty-two? Sixty-three? What then?'

'Treat your body like your servant', replied Terence.

'So how's yours?'

'The bastard's mutinous', sighed Terence. 'But I soldier on. It's just that I get so bloody irritated with everything. TV's rubbish, with all those ghastly cooks, mindless quizzes, talentless celebrities and preening politicians. I don't sleep at night, I pee in instalments, I can hardly see and I'm going deaf. What keeps me going is Spurs, the news, and drink. So here's to you, Henry.'

And he raised his glass and drank deeply.

'And talking of the vicissitudes of one's member,' continued Henry, 'remember Emilia Blond? Very county. Lovely girl, good family, lived just outside Henley. The husband was appalling. Couldn't keep his hands to himself, several illegits. Poor Emilia was just like a sleepwalker, just blind to it. Then he had it off with the char. That was too much for Emilia. Took his beef bayonet off with a Stanley knife. She didn't mean to kill him, of course, but the poor thing knew very little about male anatomy. He bled to death within minutes.'

'Yes, pure ignorance of course,' replied Terence. 'It got her off, as I recall. But it's an interesting phenomenon, how people put up with things for years and then suddenly snap. Remember Dolly Morgan, battered by her husband every day for 10 years? And then one day she sort of woke up, went into the garage, picked up a screwdriver and drove it through his skull.'

'It was a chisel,' corrected Henry. 'And the jury refused to convict. And what about Alan Percy Warbush? Abused by his parents most of his life, slept in a cupboard, treated like a bloody slave, and then, aged 40 odd, put mouse bait in their muesli. They took hours to die and Alan Percy Warbush watched, just sat there, eating a biscuit.'

This conversation was typical. No matter what the topic – God, the failing marriages of their friends, penile dysfunction, sport, insomnia, real ale, and women – Henry and Terence usually ended up with crime and criminals, famous trials and the decisions of the court, matching each other with the gory details. Then Henry said: 'I'm sorry, Terence, but all this talk of passion pistols has had its usual effect. I must go weep a tear for Nelson.'

Henry eased himself out of his chair and walked towards the back door. Although a huge man, fully twenty-three stone and six foot seven in his socks, he gracefully manoeuvred himself through the crowd, swaying slightly but steadying himself on the arms of others, accompanied by shouts of 'Well done, Henry!' 'Many Happy Returns for tomorrow!'

The Gentlemen's loo was the disgrace of *The Sun*: a small dungeon at the back of the pub, across a small courtyard, cobbled, now treacherous with the rain. Henry dashed across, slipping slightly, and went in through a latch door. He entered, holding his breath. It reeked of stale urine and disinfectant. His headache was immediate. The fittings were rudimentary: an aluminium trough for three men. Henry looked down and sighed: 'Bloody prostate!' He waited. Finally, as the pressure increased, a thin stream appeared, falling almost vertically. The relief was not immediate but came incrementally. Just then another man, young, whom Henry had never seen before, dressed in leather and wearing an earring, came in and stood beside him. 'Good evening, Henry,' he said. What Henry then heard was distressing: a gush like a geyser. The man zipped up and left. Henry stood there, ashamed of his thin stream still descending. He looked in the mirror above him, stuck out his tongue, and examined his face.

He had a nickname – "the Bloodhound". It suited him. Henry's cheeks were puckered up in two great folds of flesh, neatly carved on either side of a drooping mouth; and the same descending curve was evident in his dense eyebrows and large pendulous ears. The whole movement was, as it were, downwards: it was as if his entire face had somehow slipped. His nose stood out, bulbous and pitted, with flared nostrils. Even more noticeable, his massive and hairless head was entirely covered with an intricate web of tiny sinuous fissures – it was an etching of corrugated furrows – giving the impression of a skin of clay that had somehow fractured in the sun.

Henry Fairest returned to the bar, to find Terence talking to Ollie.

'Ollie,' said Henry, interrupting, 'every time I go in there it's a bloody nightmare. A young chap came in just now, and it was shaming, Ollie, absolutely bloody shaming. No privacy. I almost got splashed!'

'And the Ladies is just as bad,' cried Charlotte, 'Almost French.'

'What we need, Ollie,' suggested Terence, 'are porcelain cubicles, with their own partitions, something to lean against when tired and emotional.'

Ollie raised his hands. He'd heard it all before. 'Enough! Enough! It can't be done! I've told you before. I've had an estimate. Ten thousand quid, that's what it would cost. Ten thousand! How can I afford that? You tell me! I'd have to put up the price of beer.'

There was a sudden and moody silence.

'OK,' said Ollie. 'I'll have another look. But what we really need is for one of you to die and leave us the money. That would solve the problem. So perhaps you oldies should think about that. But anyway (here turning towards Henry and Terence), enough of this. You two have got to move it. So drink up. Poppy's expecting you in five minutes.'

'That's very kind of you, Ollie. But really you shouldn't …'

'Nonsense, Henry. It's not everyday you're fifty. Five minutes then.'

* * *

Ollie and his wife Poppy and their four daughters lived five minutes walk from *The Sun*. It was still pouring with rain, now even heavier than before. Henry and Terence, wearing mufflers and large overcoats with their collars turned up, walked quickly down the street, leaning slightly forwards, bracing themselves against the cutting rain, which now hit them almost horizontally, stinging their faces. They crossed Dickenson Road and turned left, past Stanley Avenue, Wallace Road, Hall Road, and turned into Birch Grove. This was a road of substantial Edwardian detached and semi-detached houses, each with its three-sided sash windows and dormers, patterned brickwork or geometric tiling, with steep roofs of Welsh slate, some with decorated bargeboards and others with front doors quartered with stained glass. They walked half-way down the road and rang the doorbell of a house on the right, the largest in the street. A florid lady, heavy-breasted, wearing enormous gold earrings and a purple paper hat shaped like a duck, opened the door.

'Henry, Terence!' cried Poppy, and immediately enveloped Henry in a smothering hug and the musty perfume of Madame Rochas. Then Terence was also hugged and kissed; and, taking them both by the hand, she led them through the kitchen and into the sitting room. The entire ground floor was one room, an architectural peculiarity odd even for Birch Grove, like an enormous atrium, topped by a glass dome. Two decorated staircases in Victorian green, one on each side, led up to the surrounding balcony above. The whole area was crowded with about forty men and women, all in fancy dress, and there was a great shout as they spotted Henry and Terence.

'Surprise! Surprise!'

Polly, the youngest of Ollie's daughters and dressed as Little Bo Beep, came up to Henry and placed on his head, amidst much cheering, a Sherlock Holmes deerstalker. For Terence she produced a judge's wig. More cheering. Then the drinking started. Food was provided on a trestle table arranged at the back, and soon there was dancing. But when Ollie shouted, 'Quiet everybody!' there was a sudden hush and everybody listened as the sitting-room clock began to strike. Voices rose in a countdown: 'One, Two, Three....' With the strike of twelve there was a great cheer and a rousing chorus of 'Happy Birthday to You!' and 'Oh why was he born so beautiful.' Henry, by now slumped in a chair, his eyes half closed, rose unsteadily to his feet and made a speech.

'Dear friends. I have to say…yes, I must say this… this is all quite unexpected, quite… And I must thank Ollie and Poppy and the dear girls because I really hadn't a clue…not even an inkling, no, not a glimmer. Such a great secret. Ha! Yes, well, well! I realize, of course, that, given the highly dubious characters I mix with, still consort with, reaching fifty without being murdered is an achievement in itself; and I put my good health down to nothing more than a complete lack of exercise and heavy drinking. (Cheers again). I have as you know…you all know this, it's very widely known…up and down the country…Oh dear, what was it? Ah yes!.. that I have spent my entire life wallowing among the criminal classes…crooks in fact, ne'er do wells and scoundrels…and some of them have become friends, although not all ('Shame!'). This makes seeing so many of them here tonight, celebrating my 50th, a real surprise and treat because I thought most of you were in prison. (More cheers). And need I remind you that

> There are many good reasons for drinking,
> And one has just entered my head.
> If a man doesn't drink when he's living,
> How the hell can he drink when he's dead?
> And so here's to you all!

And with that Henry raised his glass, took a deep swig, and, supported by Polly, went back to his chair. It was a great evening and by 12.30 the party was in full swing. The noise was terrific: there was more dancing, lots of food and plenty to drink. Those not singing were sprawling. It was hot and the faces of the guests glistened with sweat and well-being.

It was at 12.45 that the incident occurred that made Henry's 50th birthday so memorable. There was a ring at the doorbell. Ollie opened the door and was faced by two policemen. For a moment he thought that they were in fancy-dress and had come to the party; but they had a serious look about them.

'Sorry about the noise, officers. It'll be over soon.'

'It's not about the noise, sir. We've come for Henry Fairest.'

'You've come for Henry?' asked Ollie. 'What's he done now?'

'Could you just get him, sir? We really don't want any fuss.'

'Henry!' called Ollie. 'It's the police. You're wanted!'

Everybody heard and the party came to a standstill. Then somebody shouted, 'The bobbies have come for Henry!' and a chorus started: 'Nicked at last! The old crook! Hurrah for Henry!'

Terence went over to Henry and shook him gently by the shoulder. 'Henry, it's the police. They want you!'

Henry woke up. 'What? Want me? Oh, bugger! But it's my birthday!'

He got up and staggered to the door and looked unsteadily at the two young men.

'What do you two want? It's my bloody birthday!'

The two policemen looked uncertainly at each other. 'Well, we're very sorry sir…But you must come with us. Quietly now, sir. It's orders!'

'Oh, bugger, bugger! But it's my birthday! Can't you let me off? Just this once? Can't you do that? It's my birthday! I'm not well! Oh, bugger!'

'It's orders, sir, orders. Please come with us. No fuss now.'

Terence came up and put Henry's overcoat over his shoulders. 'Go on, Henry. I'll see you tomorrow.' And he gently pushed Henry out of the door, watching his friend as the two young policemen, one on each side, their arms under his elbows, escorted a swaying Henry to the waiting car. And that was the last anyone saw of him that night.

★ ★ ★

The police car drove for about fifteen minutes, at high speed, its emergency lights flashing. Henry had no idea where they were going. He sat in the backseat, leaning forwards, his eyes shut, resting his head on the back of the seat in front of him, moaning slightly as he swayed from side to side. The body heat of the three men quickly misted the car's windows, cutting off all visibility. Henry began to feel very unwell. All he could hear was the thrump-thrump of the wipers and the noise of the rain as it lashed against the windscreen. Henry wound down his window and gulped down the air, which buffeted against his face, but he could see nothing. The blackness was impenetrable.

Then the car stopped. 'Where are we, for Christ's sake?' murmured Henry. 'Newtown Industrial Estate, sir.' Henry groaned. He knew the place: it was out beyond Stretford and towards Trafford Park, and backed on to the Bridgewater Canal. It was a sordid area of derelict housing of about three acres, vacant for many years, part of Thatcher's urban renewal, with its gas silos still in place, although these were now in a dilapidated and dangerous condition. To the east was the Sewage Treatment Works, long since decommissioned but still heavily contaminated and left to rot; and to the west was a small area of Council-owned land, most of it unused and ear-marked for future development, although no new building had taken place for fifteen years. All that remained now were the collapsing structures of a previous shoe factory, some storage facilities and the iron skeleton of a petrol station. But Henry could remember a pub here, the *Three Pigs*, which he and Terence had discovered on a real ale hunt many years before: it had served, he remembered, Dark Star and Jennings Sneck Lifter. The Estate's only lighting filtered down from Trafford Road, which ran parallel to it, and from the Canal itself, which formed its northern boundary, its murky water just visible below a steep embankment strewn with litter and sparsely covered with small trees and bushes. All the place was used for now was as a short cut up through Ordsall to the M602, and as a dump for old cars and bikes, some burnt out but mostly just scrap, periodically cleared out by the Council every month or so.

Henry got out of the car and immediately felt the cold air cutting into his face. He shuddered and could feel a slow trickle of water down his neck. One of the policemen came up to him, said 'Excuse me, sir', and removed the deerstalker hat. Henry walked twenty yards and climbed unsteadily over a yellow tape that cordoned off the area. It was like a film set: brightly lit by white light from four heavy-duty flood lamps on tall metal tripods, powered by a small generator whirring in the background. He saw several figures in front of him. They were policemen, standing in small groups, stamping their feet. As Henry passed them, one of them said to other, 'Bloody hell, Jim, it's the Bloodhound!' A plain clothes officer, seeing Henry, came towards him.

'Oh, it's you, Bob!' Henry said. 'This better be good. I'm not well, not well at all. And it's my bloody birthday!'

'Sorry about this, sir, but we had strict orders from upstairs. Happy Birthday, by the way.'

Henry grunted and they moved further down to a lay-by, set back slightly from the road, its surface now scoured by deep puddles of water, furrowing in little eddies of light.

'Ah, Henry', said Dr Stephen Thomas, approaching him with his arm outstretched. He was clothed entirely in green plastic, his cuffs tied at the wrist, wearing yellow boots. They shook hands. 'Sorry to miss your party, Henry. But Happy Birthday anyway. I was coming. I even had my costume. I'm wearing it! Good, don't you think? But of course this happened and so I had to be here. Anyway no need to change, eh?' Dr Thomas had a high-pitched, snuffling laugh, his nostrils quivering at his own joke.

'Well, I don't know why I'm bloody here. Do you know why I'm here, Stephen? It's my birthday, for God's sake!'

'Henry, you have friends in High Places. I heard that the Chief asked specifically for you.'

'At this hour? Why won't the man leave me alone?'

'It's because he loves you, Henry. So come on now, and I'll show you what's what!'

Dr Stephen Thomas led Henry a little further along the lay-by to a car parked parallel to the edge of the embankment, its boot facing them.

'Take a look, Henry. Go round to the driver's side. You won't be disturbing anything. The rain has ruined all peripheral evidence.'

Henry edged his way around the car, steadying himself by holding on to the roof. He heard Dr Thomas calling out 'But be careful, Henry, it's very slip…!' – but it was too late. The bank was soaking wet and as Henry moved along the side of the car he lost his foothold, overbalanced, and slid down fifteen feet on his stomach, his hands outstretched, pulling out the grass in tufts, arriving with a heavy thump against a tree stump. He could feel the mud caking the front of his shirt and trousers, the water seeping through his socks. Dr Thomas hurried round and shone his torch down the bank. He could see Henry, picked out by the beam, white-faced, gently moaning, struggling to get a foothold.

'Well, pull me up, for Christ's sake!'

Dr Thomas turned round to two policemen, standing nearby and staring fixedly at their feet. 'Go on then. Get a move on, you two. Get a rope for the Chief Superintendent!'

A rope was brought and thrown down the bank. Henry was a heavy man and there was a chorus of grunts: Henry groaning as he held on tightly, inching slowly up the bank, and the two policemen groaning even louder as they struggled to bring him up. When he was safely at the top, Henry stood there, swaying slightly, nauseous and furious – 'Oh, bugger, bugger!' Then he steadied himself, moved towards the car, now approaching from the passenger's side. It was an Audi A3, from the number plate about two years old. As far as Henry could tell, it hadn't been in an accident: there were the usual dents and scratches but nothing to suggest a collision. Dr Thomas gave him a torch. Henry clicked it on, opened the passenger door and looked inside. Immediately his stomach heaved and he jerked up, hitting his head sharply on the top of the door frame. 'Bloody hell!' He turned quickly away, rubbing his head vigorously, and leant back against the car, his gorge rising. He breathed deeply. Then he braced himself and looked in again. The smell was unmistakeable and instantly familiar, sickly sweet and cloying. There was a body of a man behind the wheel. He was slumped sideways towards the driver's door, the right side of his face flattened against it but tilted downwards, wedged below the steering column. The left side of his face had been battered to a pulp, clearly a frenzied attack, some teeth dislodged and hanging loose. His left eye, strangely focused, hung down against his cheek, held by one long glutinous thread. The front seats were covered in blood, the windscreen spattered with scarlet rain. Henry straightened up and opened the passenger door. On the back seat lay a green leather shoulder-bag. Henry inhaled deeply and wiped his sleeve across his forehead, now damp with warm sweat.

'Very nasty, Stephen, but I think it's pretty straightforward. He had a passenger, who was sitting beside him, and who whacked him repeatedly with something heavy. Perhaps a woman – there's a bag in the back. But whoever did it would be covered in blood. Perhaps there was a tussle first, a struggle of some kind, but I don't think so. If there'd been a fight, the wounds would have been more diffuse, not just on one side of the head, as here. So my guess is that it was a surprise attack, quite sudden, and the victim didn't see it coming. Anyway, Stephen, you'll be able to tell me more later, after you've had a look at him. But, at a guess, I think I'm right.'

'I think you're right too, Henry,' replied Stephen. 'But there's something else to show you, and it'll explain the lady's bag. And I'm sorry to tell you this, but you're going to have to go back down the bank. Come over here.'

They walked about twenty yards, following the edge of the embankment, and towards a row of burnt-out and battered cars dumped further up the road. Dr Thomas stopped in front of the first of these, an old maroon Vauxhall Vectra, and leaned against it.

'Shine your torch there, Henry,' he said, pointing down the bank towards the canal.

The beam of the torch picked out a small white tent that had been precariously erected on the steep incline of the bank, held in place by four guide ropes, its canvas flapping against the wind. Its interior was dimly lit. Two policemen stood guard in front of it. Poles had been sunk into the ground, with a rope slung between them, so forming a makeshift walk-way. Dr Thomas edged his way down first and waited for Henry, looking up anxiously to watch the heavy figure descending behind him. When Henry had arrived safely, Dr Thomas turned back the tent flap, and stood aside to allow Henry, crouching low, to enter. Inside a police photographer was taking shots of a woman's body. She was lying face down, slumped against a plastic bin bag, her hands stretched out in front of her, the paleness of her bare arms illuminated by a small lamp set up in a corner. She was wearing a plastic raincoat, a brown jumper, with a skirt beneath of light material – it was difficult to see the colour precisely, perhaps pale blue or grey. This was pulled up high, exposing her thighs and white undergarments. Her entire back – her legs, all her clothing from top to bottom – were covered in mud.

Henry waited for the photographer to leave. Then he knelt down beside the body. 'So I suppose we can say,' he said, 'that she's another victim, presumably in the car with the man over there, not sitting beside him but behind, in the back seat. You're right, that explains the bag – she left it there when she ran away. She must have climbed out, tried to escape, running along the edge of the embankment. But she wasn't fast enough. The killer was too quick, caught her and killed her up there at the top. Then either the weight of the blow toppled her down the bank or her killer deliberately rolled her down, to hide the body. So on that score, we have two victims and one killer. Not that difficult to understand. So what's the problem, Stephen?'

'Well, this is the problem, Henry, and I don't know what to make of it. Take at look at this!'

Dr Thomas bent down over the body and gently parted the woman's hair. It fell in long tresses down her back and was thickly matted with blood. 'She's quite young, on the sunny side of thirty, I'd say. I'll have to get her back to the lab, of course. But see this? This wound, as you can see, is at the back of the head. Now, of course, there's nothing strange in that and it fits in with what we've been thinking: that she was killed when trying to escape, the killer striking her from behind. But that's not what's puzzling me, Henry. Look at this. The skull, when you run your finger along it, there at the top, towards the back, is slightly indented, so obviously the result of a blow of some kind, but not generalized, it's specific, with a small impact area, made by something quite small. Perhaps something like a hammer. Anyway something like that. I'm just guessing. But if you look closely, you can see another wound: a similar injury, but this time to the left side of the head, more to the front – see it there? – which may well have been done at about the same time. Either way, I'll be more precise when I've had a better look.'

'So you're saying this, Stephen. This woman was sitting in the back of the car. She sees the murder take place in front of her and runs off. Then she's murdered, her wounds suggesting that she died due to a blow or blows to the head when she was trying to get away: that her killer struck her on the back of the head when she was trying to escape. Then she either fell or was pushed down the bank. Is that right? OK. But that's not all you're saying, is it, Stephen?'

'No!'

'You're also saying that the MO of these two killings is slightly different.'

'Quite!'

'In the first one,' continued Henry, 'we have a frenzied attack, the man bludgeoned to death; but in the other everything is more precise, probably just two blows, the first not sufficient to kill her, the second fatal. There's also the character of the wounds themselves: the man's probably caused by something heavy and blunt, the woman's by something quite different, small, more accurate.'

'Don't you think that's odd, Henry?' asked Dr Thomas.

'I think that's very odd, Stephen,' replied Henry.

Henry Fairest stood up, walked out of the tent, and shone his torch up the slope of embankment, picking out the small trees bending in the wind and the litter being blown around in swirling gusts. He could just make out the outline of the car at the top. He shivered, sniffed the air, took out some aspirin from his pocket and swallowed them whole. Then he returned to Doctor Thomas inside the tent.

'I've seen enough, Stephen. You can turn her over.'

Dr Thomas gently placed his hands under the ribs of the woman and rolled her over. As he did so, her long hair caught behind her and, twisting round, formed a black necklace beneath her open, staring eyes.

Henry looked down at the pale face. The make-up around her eyes was smudged and distended, brown as if bruised, while her mouth formed an inverted u-shape, her lipstick channelled downwards by the rain, curving outwards from her half-open mouth in red streaks.

'What a waste!' said Henry.

He always felt the same when looking at the dead. He'd seen so many bodies: drug addicts and drunks, prostitutes, down-and-outs, the elderly who froze in doorways, suicides, the battered wives. But it was always a shock, this reduction of something living to such a little heap, tucked away in some foul-smelling corner, soaking and discarded. He remembered his first murder. There'd been a violent row and a neighbour had called them in, quite late. The old man was slumped in the corner of the kitchen: stubble-chinned, his head hugging the wall, dressed in a tattered check shirt, pyjama bottoms tied with string, wearing woollen slippers, smelling of beer and nicotine, a carving-knife in his chest. He'd been robbed of his Post Office savings, killed by his son-in-law in a drunken brawl. They

19

picked him up a couple of hours later in a pub just round the corner, spending the money, standing drinks for his pals. He got life. No, up close, there was no mystery to death. And what was true of it was so trite. Death was just a negative, an absence of any spark. That was the shock. There you stood, alive and functioning, gazing down at another human being, a short time before just like you, but now nothing but an empty shell of stretched skin. So you looked, expecting to see one thing, and instead saw something else. You saw eyes that didn't see, flesh that couldn't feel, hands that couldn't touch, lips that couldn't laugh. And so often they looked alive, asleep and as soft as wax, just waiting for the friendly nudge to bring them back.

Henry Fairest left the tent and stood outside in the downpour, buffeted by the wind. He lifted his head, letting the heavy rain wash his face. He felt better. Dr Thomas came up beside him. They stood there for some minutes, oblivious of the weather.

'I've been thinking, Stephen. This is just speculation, of course, just off the top of my head. So try this on for size. This is another sordid little domestic. The driver is the lover, killed by the husband because of an affair with the wife. It could be the other way round, of course – it could be the lover killing the husband – but that really doesn't matter. It's the triangle that counts, with the woman in the middle. They've agreed to meet, perhaps to sort things out. But one of them has something else in mind and carries a weapon, something heavy. Anyway, things don't go well, there's a terrible row, the three of them really going at it, accusations, recriminations flying around. Then, as they near the embankment, the driver, whichever one it is, pulls over. He's had enough and the arguing continues, getting louder and louder. Then, quite suddenly, the husband hits the lover with whatever he's got hidden. The poor girl, sitting behind, is terrified. For a few seconds she can't move. She's in shock, paralysed by horror. Then she comes to her senses, struggles out of the car and runs as fast as she can. But he is too quick for her, catches her up and strikes her on the back of the head. She staggers, now turns towards him, and he hits her again, this second blow killing her. Something like that.'

'Henry,' said Dr Thomas, smiling broadly, 'you're a wonder! And all that on the hoof! But where'd he go after murdering two people? He'd be covered in blood.'

'But what if he's planned the whole thing? Don't you see? It's all been thought through! He's parked his car somewhere, perhaps among the others, just over there, beside the bank. Nobody would notice it. It was there all the time. But hang on a bit…I want another look. Let's go back up.' Calling to the two policemen still waiting at the top, and now gripping hard on the rope, Henry was once more heaved up the bank. Then he walked to the passenger door, opened it, and leant right in, his upper body disappearing entirely.

'Thank God for that!'

'What is it, Henry?' shouted Dr Thomas, clambering up the bank after him.

'I had a terrible thought! But it's all right. Trousers dry!'

'What about his trousers, Henry?' asked Dr Thomas, puffing and out of breath.

'God, I'm really not feeling well at all well. Sorry about this, Stephen. Really my mind's so slow, just not working.

About the trousers. I had a terrible thought. If they'd been wet, then the man got out of the car; and that would have been the end of my theory. But they're not, shoes and trousers quite dry. So I think we're on the right track. He was killed in the car, never got out.'

Henry Fairest was by now feeling quite ill, nausea attacking him in waves. The heavy drinking, the food, the heat and then the cold, the lurching car, going up and down the bank – these had all left him feeling very rough. He felt as if the ground beneath him was moving slightly, a gentle rocking motion, as if on a little boat in a swelling sea. He walked up and down, taking deep breaths, shaking himself, mumbling under his breath. After a minute he returned to Dr Thomas.

'Stephen, do we have a time of death?'

'I should say a few minutes after midnight, say 12.20.'

'My God, that's precise. How can you be so sure?'

'Sorry, Henry, I'm having you on. Of course, I can't be that accurate.' Then turning to a group of policemen nearby, he shouted, 'Inspector Bonfield! Can you come over here a moment? Now, Bob, tell the Chief Superintendent about our witness.'

'You have a witness?' exclaimed Henry.

'We certainly have, sir!' replied Inspector Bob Bonfield. 'Well, not exactly a witness, because he didn't actually see the incident. But he did see the woman alive but injured about midnight and reported in to the station some minutes later'. Inspector Bonfield drew out a notebook, and looked at it. 'Yes, that's right, sir. He reported in at 12.16.'

'Why didn't he report the incident sooner?' asked Henry.

'He didn't have a mobile – doesn't own one – and so had to drive to the station, leaving the woman here, sir.'

'Jesus wept!' said Henry. Then looking at Dr Thomas: 'So Stephen, it looks as if we will have to amend our theory. The two attacks took place at different times. If you're right, it was the second blow that killed the woman; but however it was done, the actual killing, the decisive blow, must have occurred between the time it took our witness to get to the station and the time it took the police to arrive here. How long was that, Bob?'

'We were here in less than ten minutes. The station's not that far away.'

'So let's round it up and say, at the most, twenty-five minutes. That's our window. Within that time, give or take, the murder took place. So where's the witness now, Bob?

Inspector Bonfield looked embarrassed. 'He's gone home, sir. We couldn't keep him, really we couldn't. There was nothing much he could do. H asked to get home to his wife, and anyway he's coming in first thing tomorrow…I mean today.'

'So who is he?'

'He's called Weismann.'

'William Weismann?' asked Henry.

'Correct, sir,' replied Inspector Bonfield, looking again at his notebook. 'A Professor William Weismann.'

Henry whistled. 'Ha! Well, Stephen, I can see now why the Chief called me in! This is no ordinary witness!'

'So who is he, Henry?'

'An academic, really famous. I attended a lecture of his, years ago. Went with Terence. Remarkable stuff. But enough of that. That can all wait until the morning. There's not much we can do now. I've got to go to bed, I really have. Stephen, let me have your report as quick as you can. I'll give you a ring tomorrow. Thanks. Goodnight, Bob.'

Dr Stephen Thomas and Inspector Bob Bonfield watched as Henry Fairest manoeuvred his bulk over the yellow cordon of tape, moving slowly towards the waiting police car, his silhouette black against the headlights. The rain had not let up but was now coming in moaning gusts. There was a flash of silver light, a summoning of thunder. A couple of policemen saluted and Henry nodded back. Then he got in the car and immediately collapsed in his seat. He looked down at his trousers and shoes, both covered in mud, and he could feel the clinging damp seeping through his shirt and the back of his trousers. The noise inside was almost deafening, the rain crashing on the roof, like pebbles on tin. He was cold and depressed. 'Take me home, lad,' he said to the driver.

★★★

Henry Fairest lived in Harley House, a large Edwardian block of flats in Didsbury, across the way from Heritage Gardens. He had inherited it from his parents, antique dealers, and had lived in it all his life. He would never move. It was full of his childhood. It had an enormous corridor, exactly the length of a cricket pitch – so 22 yards long – at the end of which was a door leading into the first of four bedrooms. Looking closely one could still detect the faint outline of cricket stumps, painted by Henry's father, Cecil. Henry was then about seven and almost every evening they would have a game, carefully putting away the photographs and ornaments that stood along the walls. It was one of his fondest memories. On the architrave of another door one could just make out his mother's measurements of his height, carefully dated, and the exclamation mark beside the point at which he had reached six feet. He could remember her, Connie, a tiny woman, climbing on a chair to put it there.

The police car dropped Henry at the entrance to Harley House. It was now well past two in the morning. The rain was still pouring down and he was glad to get inside. But instead of going directly up to his own apartment, No.55, Henry crossed the landing and took out a key for No.53, the flat directly opposite. From behind the door he could hear scuffling and heavy breathing. He slowly opened the door and was almost immediately pushed off his feet by an enormous dog. The dog reared up on its hind legs, put its paws on Henry's shoulders, and began to lick his face, ears, nostrils, with its great rasping tongue. Henry stood there for a moment, burying his face in the dog's neck, breathing in the smell of warm biscuits. This was Lotte, Henry's Scottish deerhound, grey brindle, ninety-five pounds and three feet in height.

'Is that you, Henry', came a voice from inside the flat.

'It is, Twinkie. You still up?'

It was a ritual question. As Henry well knew, Twinkie Schulhoff never went to bed but slept, when she slept at all, on a sofa in her kitchen. Her apartment was identical to Henry's and so enormous; but Twinkie, unlike Henry, lived in just three rooms. She was a wiry little woman, a German émigré in her late seventies, rather cramped and stooping, of sallow complexion. Her thinning hair, tied up in a bun, was in a permanent state of disarray, so requiring constant attention. She loved bright clothes, loved to dress up but had no dress sense, and so always appeared in a riot of clashing colours. This evening she was wearing a woollen dressing gown, pink with embroidered green turtles, multi-coloured socks and bright red chinese slippers, turned up at the toes, which she had spotted in a charity shop in the Arndale Centre. Her eyes had always been her best feature, a brightly-lit flecked brown, her steady and unwavering gaze indicating intelligence and determination. Twinkie looked after Lotte when Henry was out, taking the deerhound for long walks. It was a familiar sight in Didsbury to see the two of them out together. Twinkie could not control such a huge animal but Lotte never misbehaved and always walked calmly beside Twinkie's diminutive figure, in great lopping strides, often turning her head to watch Twinkie gently trotting beside her in little hurried steps.

'My God, Henry!' she cried. 'Look at you! What have you done to yourself? What's that on your face?'

Henry looked in a wall-mirror and could see what Twinkie meant. His face was covered in mud, as were his jacket and trousers, shirt and shoes.

'It's nothing, Twinkie. Don't worry. I slipped, that's all. So…has the lady been good?' he asked, coming up to Lotte and ruffling her head.

'She is always good,' replied Twinkie. Lotte moved back to Twinkie, curling herself up into the smallest possible space beside the sofa. Then settled, head on paws, she looked up at Henry under her bushy eyebrows with a slightly mournful expression, as if to say "Where have you been?".

'And *Alles Liebe zum Geburtstag*, Henry. Was it fun? I heard that there was to be a party. Ollie rang to say. I'm sorry I couldn't make it. It was just too wet and cold. I suppose you saw Terence?'

'I did see Terence, Twinkie, and he sends love. No, I won't sit down. I'm too dirty. Frankly I've had a God-awful night. I'm so tired I can hardly speak. So don't think me rude, Twinkie dear, but I must go to bed. I'm feeling quite unwell. Perhaps I've caught something. So God bless, *meine Liebe.*'

Henry bent down, kissed Twinkie on the top of her head, and moved towards the door. As he did so, Lotte got up and followed him. They crossed the landing together and entered Henry's flat. Henry went into the scullery, got Lotte's bowl, filled it with water, and put it beside her basket. Then he went to the bathroom, changed out of his clothes into his pyjamas, washed his face with cold water, and went straight to bed. He turned off his light and was almost immediately asleep. An hour later, a scratching sound was heard, the bedroom door opened and a shadow moved across the room. The mattress and Henry rose slightly, as Lotte heaved herself up on top of the bed, bending her head towards him, giving him a lick. Then there was a lot of turning and scuffling and yawning as Lotte settled herself down. This happened every night. Henry stretched out his hand, stroked her head, and the last thing he heard was Lotte's profound sigh as she too closed her eyes.

2

William on the
Night of the Murders

The room is large but sparsely furnished, monastic in
its simplicity. There is a deckchair, a small washbasin on
which stands an empty glass, a standard lamp, a small two-
bar electric heater, and, in a corner, an old John Tann safe.
The walls are painted in institutional magnolia, the curtains
grey and un-patterned. There is no decoration of any kind.
One side of the room is taken up by a large Gothic window,
with two casements quartered with glass, through which is
just visible, against the onslaught of rain and the darkening
light, an enclosed quad below and the distant neo-Gothic
outline of the old John Rylands Library. Immediately in
front of the deckchair sit twelve students in three ranks of
four, sitting on cushions, with their writing pads ready in
front of them. This arrangement – of who sits where – once
decided upon in the first term, can never be altered. So any
visiting academic from abroad, however distinguished, has
to make do with a hard chair at the back. The students are
talking quietly among themselves, waiting nervously for
the arrival of Professor William Weismann.

At 8.00 pm precisely they hear footsteps and the door

opens. Weismann is a tall man of middle age, slim, hollow-cheeked, almost military in his rigid straight-backed walk, with a mop of unruly greying hair low on his forehead He is dressed in corduroy trousers, a loose jumper and an open-necked shirt – he never wears a tie – his feet in white tennis shoes. Oblivious of those in the room, he sits down in the deckchair and immediately starts to chew on a fingernail. Then he slumps back and closes his eyes. There is complete silence. This lasts for a full minute. The only sound is the sound of the rain outside. Then Weismann opens his eyes, leans forward, and looks down at the students. He looks at each in turn, making sure they are all sitting in their correct places. His eyes have an unsettling effect, hardly blinking, and shine with a disconcerting focus, raptor-like in its intensity. There is another long silence. Then one black female student, a Canadian, plucking up courage, asks tentatively in a low drawl:

'May I ask, Professor, what you have been thinking about?'

There is a slight pause.

'I have been thinking about…lying. Of what a lie is, its function and form.'

Weismann's voice is light, high-pitched, clipped and precise. There is another silence. The students have now picked up their pads, expectant, their pens poised. Weismann gets up and walks over to the small wash basin. He pours himself a glass of water, takes a sip, and moves across to the window. He looks out at the rain, pinches his nose with finger and thumb, replaces the glass, and then turns back to his students.

'Let's start with a truism. A lie is a deception: its

intention is to mislead. But of course, like all definitions, this is uninteresting, really quite uninformative, as uninteresting as saying that a bachelor is unmarried or that a triangle is a three-sided figure. Indeed, it is a tautology, not non-sensical but picturing nothing. But what does that mean? What does it tell us? It means that there can be no such thing as an unintentional lie. So note. There can be an unintentional *falsehood* but not an unintentional *lie*. Here's an example. Take Schiaparelli's theory of Martian canals. His observations led him to suppose that the surface of the planet was covered by a dense network of linear structures – the famous *canali* – and these channels led in turn to the proposition that there was life on Mars. But this claim was no lie but simply a statement contrary to the facts. It was false but not an intentional deception. We can understand that Schiaparelli wanted to believe that he was right; but the demonstration of falsehood was no *unmasking*, no *revelation of deceit*. This, indeed, is entailed in the nature of scientific discovery, by the potential falsification of its empirical content. And we see it again in the miasma theory of disease or Becher's phlogiston theory or, more recently, in Fleischmann and Pons' theory of cold fusion. But a liar is someone else. A liar is a different beast altogether. Why? Because a liar cannot himself be deceived by the lie. He can certainly be deceived about its effects – that is something else entirely, a miscalculation of consequences – but the lie itself must stand as an incontrovertible instrument of his intention. Yes, in this restricted sense, a lie must be deemed… a truth: it stands as the central fact of his desire, unknown to us but known to him. So the scene is set: to retain the deception and to keep it safe from discovery.

This, of course, explains the whole business of detection and the science of forensics.'

The tutorial continues for another forty minutes. Weismann becomes quite agitated, moving back and forth, sitting then standing, waving his arms about, totally absorbed in himself but oblivious of his audience. The ground covered is comprehensive and swift: lying as omission, lying as distortion, lying as denial, medical lies and the use of placebos, lying to the enemy, lies of necessity, of deception and manipulation, and the lies to self. Then, with a sudden winding down, he collapses back into his deckchair. He looks at his students, scribbling away. Suddenly he remembers something, clicks his tongue and, smiling broadly, leans forward.

'Did I ever tell you that I was once asked to give a lecture at Hendon, I mean at the Police College? No? I wasn't going to go, but then I thought, "Why not?" I expected an audience of about four or five, but in fact it was quite crowded. Lots of people. It was a interesting programme of lectures. It was a series – distinguished scientists, historians, lawyers, doctors, all invited – and you had to talk about a novel of choice. So, because it was the police, I chose Dostoevsky's *Crime and Punishment*, and the great scene between the detective, Porfiry, and the murderer, Raskolnikov. Do you remember it? No? Let me tell you. Raskolnikov has slaughtered the old woman moneylender with an axe. Don't worry! I'm not spoiling the story. His identity doesn't matter. This is a "Why dunnit?" not a "Who dunnit?" Anyway, anyway, the murder doesn't go according to plan because he's interrupted by the old woman's niece, a dim-witted girl. I forget her name. No,

I remember: Lizaveta. So Raskolnikov has to kill Lizaveta too. Now guilt sets in. But that's not the point. The point is that Porfiry genuinely likes Raskolnikov, sees something in him, and only gradually and reluctantly begins to suspect him of the murder. And the clue? The clue – would you believe? – is a piece of philosophy. I love that! It's an article that Raskolnikov has written about the Great Criminal. It's not good philosophy, just second-hand Nietzsche. But who cares? Conrad does just the same in *The Secret Agent.* Anyway, his argument is that some people – a Napoleon, for example, or a Newton – are so extraordinary that they cannot be expected to behave like the common folk, the herd. So this means that they can break laws, do as they like, because in the end their genius will advance mankind. Thus we have two classes of person, the ordinary and the extraordinary: the first group does nothing much but breed; but the second group is the group that changes society, brings new ideas, advances the civilization; and for that they are justified – yes, justified – in wading through rivers of blood to attain their ends. So our culture develops through blood, is mired in blood. Well, you can imagine Porfiry's eyes lighting up when he hears all this talk about blood. He now gets a glimmer, a sniff of a motive. Raskolnikov is obviously a brilliant student. He has the ambition to become a great poet. Perhaps he really does have the talent to become not just any ordinary scribbler but a great man of letters. But how can he ever achieve his goal? He's impoverished, starving! So killing the old money-lender gives him the wherewithal to achieve his ambition, to realize his destiny. Now, of course, Raskolnikov, in telling Porfiry all this, should have masked the truth much better.

But he gets carried away by the ingenuity of his idea, he can't help himself, his philosophy gets the better of him, he wants to convince Porfiry that he is right. So he keeps on and on, and Porfiry keeps asking questions, egging him on in turn, always wanting further clarifications. And then, at the end of their conversation, you know – just know! – that Porfiry has him in his sights. Porfiry has recognized Raskolnikov for what he is. He knows! And you can't help thinking that Raskolnikov knows that he knows and is glad of it, relieved even. So his punishment begins. He has to wait. He has to wait for that knock on the door. He has to lie there on his bed at night and wait, waiting for those footsteps on the stairs, waiting for the man who will come for him, who will finally unmask him, point the finger, and shout "It was you! You are the one! You did it! You're the axe-man!" It's just a matter of time.'

'But all that's bye the bye. I'm not interested in the details of Porfiry's interrogation of Raskolnikov, wonderful though it is. That's not important. Set that aside! No, what I was interested in was the *process* of revelation. It was this that I wanted to discuss with my Hendon policemen. Now the more questions Porfiry asks about the theory of murder, circling, always keeping things very generalized, the more he unravels the motive. And the motive illuminates the murderer, brings him out of the shadows. This is Porfiry's brilliant trick and by it he gets what he wants. Not a conviction but – and here's the difference – a confession! This is what Porfiry wants because by confessing Raskolnikov shows that he was redeemable, that he was a fundamentally good man, despite his terrible crime: that he's criminal but not a crook. Well, that's Dostoevsky's religious conservatism for you! But I'm not religious. There is no God for me. So I'm not after a confession. What I want is a conviction, somebody behind bars, locked up! In a word, I want to act like a proper policeman.'

'So let's go back. As I say, the motive for the murder reveals the murderer. Nothing unusual there, that's a commonplace. And of course every detective is faced with a whole host of motives, all different. So how does he tell them apart? How does he get hold of the *right* motive? Or rather: what do we know about this right motive, so that we can *identify* it, distinguish it from the rest? What do we know about it that *must be true*? Well, what we know is this. The motive, whatever it is, will be expressed in the language of lies. The path to truth will be paved with lies. For whatever else he or she wants, the murderer wants to point the Porfirys of this world in the wrong direction, away from the truth. So our goal is to decipher this language of deception; and for that we must learn the syntax of lying.'

Here Weismann pauses, cataloguing his thoughts. He continues:

'Now the language of lies has a specialized vocabulary, identifying the use we make of it. All language is like this: the use determining its notation. In that sense, language parallels music. The black dots on the stave tell us about the sounds, and we can move from the one to the other. So once we learn about these dots we can hear, actually hear, the music. All language, whatever its variety, has this form and this function. We distinguish one language from another and confusion arises when we mix them up. Think about it! We have the language of love, with its own private dialect, with nicknames and jokes, little bits of inside information, born of intimacy and known only to the lovers themselves. Between lovers one spoken word or look can trigger a whole history of memories. Look at old couples, if you don't believe me, those together for years, those whose silences speak. But all languages are like this, all with different uses, their own verbal dances: not just the language of love but of hate too, of ridicule, of envy, of disgust and compassion, of forgiveness, and so on. Language, indeed, is like a garage full of junk. Open it up and you will see different things – hammers, chisels, screwdrivers, a wheel-barrow, a spade, a whole assortment of objects, all with different functions. And language is like that. And just as you wouldn't use a screwdriver instead of a chisel to carve a statue, so you don't use one kind of language in place of another. So a lover doesn't speak the language of biology: it would be considered crude and inappropriate, even though technically it might sometimes be accurate. In these senses, then, language betrays the activity. If you can read the language, you will go some way to revealing the secret messages. And so it is with the language of criminals. As I have said, this is the language of lies, the language of deception, of covering your tracks, of placing the blame elsewhere. And this is what I told my Hendon policemen. Become versed in the language, know the syntax, and you will begin to unearth the hidden motives of crime.'

'But I also told them this. You policemen have one great advantage over the rest of us. You are constantly in the company of criminals and by this connection you get to know the territory, you become familiar with it. So associate with them, don't avoid them but watch and study them, get to know their ways and habits and, above all else, learn their language, their cryptic signs, their morphology. That way you will begin to know what they know, of how words conceal and deceive, of how they camouflage greed, ambition and desire. This is the way of the great detectives, of Holmes and Poirot, of Sergeant Cuff and Alphonse Dupin. They mix with criminals so often that they can enter their mind-world, learn their tunes.'

'But now look at the other side of the coin. Move from the detective to the criminal. What of him? What does the criminal know of you? Here we find a critical asymmetry, which, make no mistake, provides the fulcrum of detection. Criminals know a certain truth about themselves. Their intention is to deceive and thus, as we have seen already, they cannot know that they are not lying. But there is, for all that, something that they do *not* know. What they do not know is that, while their lies are certainly encoded – a code that they believe protects them from detection – the code itself has a hidden music, with a notation that is readable; and that you have read the score, that *you can hear the melody*. So, like Porfiry, you hear a tune, perhaps muted, perhaps nothing more than a disturbance of the air. But that is enough. So, by the slightest gesture or hesitancy, by what may be nothing more than a flicker of an eye or a slight movement of a hand, the music sings out and you hear it; and by this method what was thought concealed has been made known to you. Thus is the criminal unmasked.'

'We have all had experience of this. How many times has someone looked you in the eye and said something that you know, just know, to be untrue? Another person believes them – perhaps everybody believes them – but you don't, you know they are lying. The lies of politicians: "I did not have sexual relations with that woman," "I didn't inhale", "There will be no whitewash of the White House". Most familiar are the lies of sex and seduction: "I'm married but getting a divorce", "I'll call you later", "Of course I respect you." Some of these are small lies, often harmless; but they get bigger, so big that the liar begins to believe the untruth. He has worn the mask of deceit so long that it has meshed with his skin. They escalate up, ending at the summit of lies, Hitler's *Große Lüge*, a lie so unbelievable that people believe it and it changes the world. So the little lie expands and goes on to create a whole universe of lies, a whole domain of deceit, with the criminal as creator, drawing others in. But you – you! – you still don't believe them! And why not? It is because you have heard the hidden, the underground music.'

'A final example. Let's take a scene from domestic life. A husband and wife are in the kitchen. The woman has been having an affair. She has kept her secret, never said a word. But the man knows...oh yes! he knows. But he says nothing. So silence. Silence from him and silence from her. But listen, put your ear to the ground. Do you hear it? Do you hear it? There's a music playing, unmistakeable and persistent. What is it? It is the melody of an unspoken truth: that she knows that he knows; and moreover, that he knows that she knows that he knows. So the tune plays on, getting louder. And then comes the overwhelming need to confess. She has had enough, she can't carry on, she must speak, the deafening silence is breaking her. And now the desire for truth becomes overwhelming; and, just like Raskolnikov, she yearns for redemption and forgiveness. Her guilt speaks. So she begins: "I must say...I have to say… I want to say…" And he knows what she will say. Make no mistake, he knows! But he puts up his hand and covers her mouth before it is too late. "Stop!" he shouts. "Say nothing! If you say it, the thing exists!"'

'Do you get it? Do you see what is happening here? He has heard another tune, getting louder, more insistent, a discord, jarring his senses, creeping in like a worm in the ear. And this he cannot live with! He can live with suspicion but not with knowledge. He can live with the deception but not with the unmasking of the lie. Why? Because the lie contains the smallest grain of hope. After all, it may be true that all is well, that his wife is still faithful, that she still loves him and will never leave. But what he cannot do is live with the lie unmasked, the truth told.'

'So what do we take from this little commonplace drama, so often played out within the everyday life of domesticity? It is this. That it is often by saying nothing that everything is said; and that this silence – without sound but gorged with memory – has the power to entrance and appal; and that, when this melody sings out, our listener may well find it unbearable, cover his ears in terror, and shriek out loud at the horror only he can hear.'

Weismann is now standing by the window. All the students are looking at him, wondering if more is to be said. But Weismann makes a gesture of the hand, a slight turning of the wrist, almost a dismissal, and they know that the seminar is finished. So the students gather their papers together, stand up, and without a word leave the room. A few minutes later they will reconvene in a student room – there's a rota of sorts – and there, drinking coffee, they will go over their notes together, reviewing and discussing what has been said, preparing a definitive version. This will then be copied out and distributed round the group. Many years later, these notes, scribbled down in cheap exercise books of different colours, will be bought up by the University of Texas for an enormous sum.

But the ritual of a Weismann seminar is not yet over. As the group is leaving, Weismann calls out, picking a student at random:

'Crispin, where are you off to?'

'I'm going back to my digs, Professor,' replies Crispin, bracing himself for what comes next.

Weismann moves towards him and takes him by the elbow. 'No, don't do that! Come to the flicks! Do you know what's showing at the *Duke of York's*?

'I've checked, Professor. It's a double bill: *Now Voyager* and *The Lady of the Camelias*.

'*The Lady of the Camelias* is a terrible film, all treacle and crinolines. But Garbo's death is worth waiting for! But *Now Voyager* is something else. Have you seen it? No? You'll love it, just love it! "Oh, Jerry, don't let's ask for the moon. We have the stars." And the scene when Bette Davis comes down the gangplank – wonderful! Oh, I can't wait! You'll love it, Crispin, you really will. Come on, off we go!'

So Professor Weismann and Crispin leave the seminar room, hurry down the staircase and get into Weismann's car – a white Jaguar XK 150, Weismann's pride and joy, which he drives at breakneck speed – and soon the two of them are sitting in the front row of the stalls of the *Duke of York's*, only a few feet from the screen, drinking Coke and munching pop corn. The Garbo film has almost finished but they're in time for Garbo's death scene. Crispin sometimes glances sideways at Weismann. He has never seen anyone watch a movie with such absorbed concentration. He sits there, intense and straight-backed, perched on the edge of his seat like a little boy at the circus, his eyes wide open in the flickering light, mouthing the dialogue from *Now Voyager* which he knows by heart. "These are only tears of gratitude – an old maid's gratitude for the crumbs offered…You see, no one ever called me 'darling' before." "May I sometimes come here?" "Whenever you like. It's your home too. There are people here who love you." The credits roll but Weismann doesn't move. His face is awash with tears. The show finishes at 11.30 and the lights come up, and people begin to leave. Still Weismann doesn't move. Then he gets out a handkerchief, wipes his face, and mumbles, 'That was fantastic. Wasn't Henreid great? God, I feel better. So come on, Crispin, let's go! Time to take you home.' And with that, Weismann jumps up amidst a spray of pop corn, and dashes out, Crispin hurrying behind him. The rain is still pouring down and they run to Weismann's car. Then Weismann drives Crispin back to his digs, waves him good night, and turns his car homewards, ready for the journey back, taking his usual shortcut through the Newtown Industrial Estate.

3

Henry and William on the Day after the Murders

The next morning, promptly at 9.00, Professor William Weismann entered the divisional Headquarters of the Greater Manchester Police at Chester House, an eleven-storied cube of glass on Boyer Street in Stretford. It was still raining heavily and Weismann was glad to get inside. He was wearing a broad-rimmed Borsalino hat of brown felt and a pale cream French-style trench-coat with broad lapels, its belt tied at the waist. These he took off and shook out as soon as he entered, spraying water around him in a fine mist. The girl at the central desk signed him in and asked him to wait. A few minutes later a man walked up to him and introduced himself as Inspector Robert Bonfield. Weismann was then escorted up to the second floor and taken into a small room, where he was asked to fill out a Witness Statement.

★★★

WITNESS STATEMENT OF WILLIAM JOACHIM WEISMANN

Criminal Justice Act 1967, S9 Magistrates Courts Act 1980, SS5A(3)(a) and 5(B) Criminal Procedure Rules 2005, r 27.1

NOTE: only this side of the paper to be used and a continuation sheet to be used if necessary. All additional sheets are to be consecutively numbered. If statements are to be typed please use double spacing.

Case Number: 92B

Statement of (name of witness): William Joachim Weismann

Age of witness (if over 21, enter "over 21"): Over 21

Occupation of witness: University Professor

Address: Pullovers, St Ann's Road, Prestwich, Manchester M25

Home Telephone No.: 0161 773 9121

Business telephone No.: 0161 306 6000

Contact point (if different from above): None

This statement, consisting of… 3…pages, each signed by me, is true to the best of my knowledge and belief. I make it knowing that, if it is tendered in evidence, I shall be liable to prosecution if I have deliberately stated in it anything which I know to be false or do not believe to be true.

1. My name is William Joachim Weismann. I am a Professor employed in the Department of Philosophy at Manchester University. I have been a member of the University for 15 years. I am also a Visiting Professor at the Universities of Chicago, Leiden and Marburg and a Fellow of the British Academy.

2. The incident to which I refer took place yesterday evening. As usual on a Thursday night I held a seminar in my room for research students in the Department of Philosophy in the University. The seminar ended shortly after 9.00 pm. I then went to the Duke of York's cinema in Old Trafford, accompanied by a student of mine, Mr Crispin Campling. The film ended at approximately 11.30 pm, after which I drove Mr Campling back to his home in Whalley Range. I then prepared to drive home to Prestwich.

3. In order to avoid traffic, I take a short cut to the M602, crossing the Newtown Industrial Estate. I entered the Estate shortly before midnight. As usual, there were some old bikes and three or four cars on the south side, just beside the embankment which leads down to the canal. Visibility, however, was appalling due to the weather. I was travelling at about

30 mph. Suddenly a woman ran out from behind a car on the canal-side of the road – I had to swerve to avoid hitting her. She seemed quite dazed and for a moment stopped right in front of me, shielding her eyes from the glare of my headlights. She then lurched off to the right. I presumed she had been in a crash or injured in some way. I stopped my car, got out and approached her. She was clearly distressed, weeping uncontrollably. I asked if I could help. There was no response. Coming closer, I saw that her face was covered in blood. I tried to get nearer to her but she turned away, moving further across the road. She seemed completely disorientated, crying and stumbling about. I tried again to come up to her but she kept her distance, running away from me. She was clearly in a state of shock. Then she turned and slumped on the ground, holding her head in her hands. She then said: 'Help me!'

4. I do not own a mobile phone. I knew, however, that the police station was only a few minutes away – I pass it every Thursday. I told her what I was going to do, that I was going for help. She said nothing, just nodded. I therefore ran back to my car and drove to the police station at Pendleton, near Broad Street.

5. There I reported the accident to the sergeant on duty. He immediately logged the incident. I stressed the urgency of the case and was informed that the police and an ambulance would be at the scene very shortly. I then asked if I could leave as my wife was waiting at home. The sergeant suggested I ring her first. This I did. I informed her what had happened and that I would be delayed getting back. I was then told to report to the Pendleton station the next morning. When I said that I worked at the University of Manchester, the sergeant told me to report instead to the Headquarters of the Manchester Police in Stretford at 9.00 the next day, where I would be required to make a statement.

6. I left Pendleton police station at approximately 12.25 and arrived at my house in Prestwich at approximately 12.50 am. I understand that my wife is to confirm my time of arrival in a separate statement.

Signed: William Weismann (signature appended)
Witnessed by: Inspector Robert Bonfield (signature appended)
Place taken: Headquarters, The Greater Manchester Police Authority, Manchester M16 0RE

★★★

After completing his Witness Statement, Inspector Bonfield escorted Weismann back to the central lobby, where he was asked to wait. He was assured that he would not be waiting long and that, in a few minutes, there would be a short preliminary interview. This would be a purely routine check going over the details of his statement. The Inspector then left. Weismann sat down and thumbed through a copy of *The Police Journal*.

After twenty minutes Bonfield returned, this time accompanied by a man of enormous height, wearing a grey double-breasted suit. Weismann noticed that he had a strange walk, a kind of swaying gait, with the top half of his body inclined at a forward angle, so creating the impression that he was in the grip of some motor malfunction, some inner propulsion over which he had no control. Weismann noted also that his face had an expression of extreme melancholy, hang-dog even, that it had the texture of cracked parchment, and that his drooping eyelids created an impression of permanent weariness. For a reason that Weismann could not explain, he felt intimidated, that he was about to be given some terrible news; that this giant would look down on him and say in mournful tones, 'Professor, the prognosis is not good' or 'Your sentence will be heavy.' So Weismann braced himself, pulled his shoulders back and lifted his chin. But the man stretched out his hand and introduced himself: 'My name is Fairest. Chief Superintendent Henry Fairest. I am so pleased to meet you. I am a great admirer.' And with that the drooping eyelids suddenly lifted to disclose watery eyes of green, of a penetrating dark intensity, all the more disquieting because of their sudden disclosure.

Then, without speaking, Henry Fairest, with a gesture towards the elevator, escorted William Weismann back upstairs, Inspector Bonfield following behind.

The interview room, to Weismann's surprise, seemed quite domestic: prints on the wall, a large rug of geometrical pattern, a rubber plant, two sofas facing each other, and a couple of chairs. There was a small Ikea sideboard, on which stood cups and a large plastic jug. One entire wall was of glass, with a view out towards Old Trafford.

'Coffee?' asked Inspector Bonfield.

'Yes, thank you,' replied Weismann. Inspector Bonfield poured one cup and placed it on the small table between the two sofas. That done, he moved towards a small tape recorder fixed to the wall and pressed a button. A light flashed from red to green. Bonfield said, 'Interview with Professor William Weismann, conducted by Chief Superintendent Henry Fairest. Also present: Inspector Robert Bonfield. The time is 9.41 am.' That said, he sat down on a chair by the door.

William Weismann sat down on one sofa and Henry Fairest lowered himself down on to the other, facing opposite him. He had Weismann's statement in his hand.

'First I must say, Professor, how very grateful I am to you for coming in so promptly. I hope this has not inconvenienced you in any way. No lectures or seminars cancelled, I hope?'

'I have a lecture this afternoon. But generally I can come and go as I please. That is one of the few advantages of being a senior member of the Faculty.'

'This is really routine, Professor,' continued Henry. 'I just want to go over your statement.'

'Well, I hope it was useful. There was very little to say. Events moved very quickly, and I couldn't have been at the scene of the accident for more than about three minutes.'

Henry looked up. 'You assumed it was an accident?'

'Yes, I did. The place was deserted and I just guessed that there had been a crash of some sort. Why, was I wrong?'

'We'll come to that later, if you don't mind. May I ask you whether you saw anything else that, on reflection, you think was unusual or out of the ordinary? I mean something that you might now want to add to your statement, perhaps something you may have forgotten.'

'Chief Superintendent, I am an extremely observant man, and I can think of absolutely nothing to add. The weather, you will recall, was atrocious and so it was very difficult to see anything clearly.'

'But you saw some cars parked to the left of the embankment?'

'Yes. But I wouldn't use the word "parked". They're usually there, just dumped, scrap really."

'How many were there?'

'That's difficult to say. Three or four. Perhaps more.'

'As indeed you mention in your statement. Can you describe them? Their colour or make?

'I am sorry, I can't recall anything like that. It was very dark.'

'Quite so. But do you think, for example, that they might have been occupied?'

'Hardly! I'm sure there was nobody there. Admittedly, I wasn't looking very closely. I was driving, after all. But, as I've said, cars are often left there, also old bikes, prams, supermarket trollies, that sort of thing, just left there to rot, usually not many. The Council clears them off eventually. But I'm sure I didn't see anyone. Of course, I have to accept the alternative: that there may have been someone there that I didn't see. I am sorry I can't be more helpful.'

'No matter. Let's move on. I want now to discuss more precisely what you did see. You saw a woman, whom you describe as lurching across the road.'

'Yes, that is correct. She was quite visible in my headlights. She jumped out right in front of me. I almost hit her.'

'That must have been quite a shock, seeing her like that. When you use the word "lurching", what exactly do you mean? Could you be more precise?'

'I thought, Chief Superintendent, that I was being precise enough. I could have used other words. I could have said that she was swaying or reeling or staggering. Certainly she was neither walking nor running but, as I have described her, "lurching". By that I mean that she did not seem to know where she was going, she looked somehow lost, moving from side to side, dazed even, in a state of shock. If it hadn't been for her hands, I'd have said she was drunk.'

'Her hands?'

'She was clutching her head with her hands. It was this that made me think that she had been hurt in some way.'

'So you stopped your car, got out, and went over to help?'

'Correct.'

'What was she wearing?'

'A plastic mac. I couldn't see what was underneath.'

'Where was she now? In the middle of the road? In front of your car? Where exactly?'

'She had moved off to the right, not far, no more than thirty feet at the most. It's difficult to say precisely. But she was clearly in great distress. I think the glare of my headlights must have frightened her because, as I got nearer, she continued to stumble away from me, further to the right and away from the embankment. I had clearly panicked her.'

'But you followed her?'

'Yes. But I couldn't really get near her. As I approached her, she was always moving away. It was like trying to trap a bird.'

'But you spoke to her?'

'Yes. I can't remember exactly what I said; but I'm sure it was something like "Can I help?" "Are you all right?" The usual things. But whatever I said, it was of no use. She seemed completely disorientated and distressed. Then, all of a sudden, she slumped to the ground, just sat down, bent forwards, doubled over, her head almost in her lap. That's when she spoke. She just said, "Help me!"'

'How did she sound? Did she speak clearly?'

'No, not at all. Her voice was muffled, guttural, it came from deep inside her throat. It was actually quite difficult to make out what she was saying; but I'm pretty clear in my own mind that she said what she said.'

'So she said "Help me!". Did you go up to her when she said this? I mean, how did you respond to her cry for help?'

'Well, I moved towards her, but that seemed to upset her even more. She started wailing. She raised her hands in front of her face, covering it, as if she was warding off something. I think she must have thought that I was going to do something to her, to injure her in some way. So I backed off.'

'Or perhaps she thought you were her assailant returning?'

At this remark, Weismann leant forward and looked sharply at Henry Fairest. 'Do mean to say, Chief Superintendent, that she was not the victim of an accident but of an assault?'

'That is correct, Professor Weismann. And that would explain why she was so terrified of you. She had just been attacked and she might well have thought that you were her assailant and that you were going to attack her again.'

'Good God! Are you sure about this, I mean about her being assaulted?

'Quite sure. Now her face, you say, was covered with blood? Is that right?'

This new information – that this was no accident but an attack – had clearly shocked Weismann, who lost concentration for a moment and asked for the question to be repeated.

'Was her face covered in blood?'

'Yes.'

'Again, Professor, could you be more exact?'

'Well, I've thought about this. It was blood, I'm sure of that. But blood at night doesn't look like blood, does it? I mean, it's not red, there's no colour to it. It's almost black. So it looked like her face was covered in…well, it's difficult to describe…let's say molasses. It was as though her face had been somehow dipped in treacle. There was a shine to it, streaked, sticky, something cloying. It's difficult to describe.'

'But at least it was clear to you that her injury was severe?'

'Yes. I was pretty certain about that. But the trouble was that I had no mobile, I had no means of calling for help. I explain that in my statement. I felt quite helpless. The thing is, I never carry a mobile. I'm useless with them. I know that sounds odd, but there it is – and I'm afraid I completely forgot to ask her whether she had one. But anyway I couldn't get near her. So I thought the best thing to do was to drive off and get help. I knew where the police station was. I pass it every week when I go to the *Duke of York's*. So I thought that was the best thing to do.'

'Did you explain this to the woman? I mean, did you make it plain to her that you were leaving her to get help?'

'Yes, I made that quite clear. I said something like, "I'll get help. Don't worry. Stay there! I'll be back in a moment." Something like that.'

'So then you left her by the roadside, on the opposite side to the canal. Is that correct? How far from the embankment was she when you left her?

'Well, the width of the road and a bit more. I should say no more than 40 feet. No more than that.'

'So to be more exact – and I'm sorry to ask this again, Professor, but this is very important – the woman was some little way from the embankment and on the right hand side of the road when you left her. So some distance away from the slope down to the canal. Is that right?'

'Yes.'

'Did you at any time go over to the other side of the road, I mean to the edge of the embankment?'

'No.'

'Did you see anything on that side of the road?'

'Yes, a parked car. It was the car that made me think there'd been an accident.'

'Why did you think that?'

'Well, I assumed it was hers. It was parked a little away from the others. It clearly hadn't been just dumped there.'

'Did you go over to have a look at it?'

'No.'

'Why not?'

'Because I was preoccupied with the woman, trying to help her. There was really no time for any kind of vehicle inspection, no time to check where there had actually been an accident or not. I just wanted to get help as quickly as possible.'

'Quite so. And then, as you say in your statement, you got in your car and drove to the police station at Pendleton, where you reported the accident. There you spoke, I believe, to Sergeant Will Little, the officer on duty; and it was he who arranged for you to call your wife and allowed you to go home. He also made this morning's appointment. Is that correct?'

'Yes. I knew my wife would be worried if I wasn't back at the usual time, even though she's quite used to my being late on Thursdays. Anyway I rang her from the station, just to put her mind at rest. I believe my wife is coming in later on today to make a separate statement about all this, corroborating what occurred.'

'And we are very grateful to you both. You've been a great help, believe me.'

Henry Fairest stood up, walked towards the window, and looked out. Despite the rain the Manchester United Stadium was just visible in the distance. Weismann, thinking the interview was over, also stood up. But Henry turned to him, 'No, please Professor, do sit down again. We haven't quite finished. Just a few more questions, really just odds and ends, quite informal.'

★★★

Henry Fairest moved towards the sideboard, poured himself a coffee, went back to the sofa, and sat down opposite William Weismann. 'Of course, Professor,' he said, glancing down at his cup and placing his spoon carefully in its saucer, 'you are something of a professional when it comes to lying!'

Weismann felt a sudden sense of unease, of panic even, as he looked up and saw the heavily-lidded eyes fully open, unblinking, watching him.

'What? You think I'm lying? I really...'

'Oh, no, Professor,' said Henry, interrupting, 'you misunderstand me. I'm not talking about your statement. That's fine, I'm sure. I'm talking about your book.'

'My book?'

'Yes', continued Henry. 'This book.' And he drew from his pocket a small blue volume, well thumbed, and showed it to Weismann.

'Oh! That book!'

'Yes, this book!' Henry opened it and read: *"The*

Hendon Lectures, subtitled, *Novels in the Art of Detection*; authors various, Cambridge University Press. A selection of essays delivered at Hendon Police Academy." You must remember!'

'Well, you may not believe this, Chief Superintendent, but this is really an extraordinary coincidence. Quite astonishing! I was talking about this only yesterday. At my Thursday seminar. What are the probabilities of that? How amazing! I remember that lecture very well.'

'So do I', said Henry. 'I was there!'

'You were there!' exclaimed Weismann, leaning back and holding up his hands in surprise, obviously delighted. Then he leant forwards: 'May I look? I lost my copy.'

'Of course,' said Henry, handing over the book. 'I remember those lectures quite vividly, but unfortunately I couldn't go to them all. But the lecture I particularly remember was, of course, yours on *Crime and Punishment*.

'Porfiry and Raskolnikov', said Weismann, leafing through the book. 'Here it is: beginning on page 93. I called it "Porfiry's Trick"'

'Yes, that's it! The immortal duo! I'm a great fan of Dostoevsky. I've even done the tourist thing and gone to St Petersburg. You should go, Professor. But go in June, when you get the White Nights.'

'Yes, yes, well, well. I might go one day, when I have time,' replied Weismann, hardly able to contain his impatience. 'But may I ask, Chief Superintendent, what you thought of my article? I mean from the professional viewpoint.'

'I found many things of interest, Professor, many things to think about. I've just read it again. I particularly liked your analysis of what you called "the harmony of lying" and the "counterpoint of deception". You certainly have a way with words.'

'Well, being a word-smith is, I suppose, part of my job. And your job, Chief Superintendent, is to catch criminals. So may I ask you again? Did you find what I said useful? Words, after all, mean nothing unless they have a use, a function. So did my article have any practical application?'

'Hardly any, I'm sorry to say.'

'I beg your pardon?'

'Let me put it like this, Professor. Your essay was the work of someone who had never actually participated in an interrogation. It lacked knowledge of how a real interview proceeds. You were, if I may say so, obsessed with the philosophical idea but ignored entirely what I might call the practicalities of lying. I'm sorry to be so blunt.'

Weismann's eyes glittered with excitement, but he held himself in check and studied Henry with a look his students knew well: his face showing no emotion, taut, drained of feeling, impassively staring at his opponent. Henry was well aware of this reaction but, shifting his buttocks on the sofa, carried on regardless.

'You say, for example, that lying is moored in the truth, that it is this truth that must be hidden from the likes of me, from the Porfirys of this world. So the criminal conceals the truth by lying. But what you failed to mention, Professor, was this. You say that a lie is based on a remembered fact. True. But that fact is not fixed but shifts, it's malleable: it conceals itself the more lies you tell. Strange but true. Let me explain. A man comes in charged with some offence. To cover his tracks, he invents something, he lies. At this point, of course, I don't know he's lying. I may think he is – I may hear, in your words, a certain dis-harmony – but I can't be sure. So I ask questions, more and more questions. I go on and on. And the more questions I ask, the greater becomes the distance from the truth – for the liar, I mean. To give credibility to his lie, he must layer his lie with more lies, constantly invent more detail. And then what happens? He gets to the point where he can't quite remember it all, how it all fits together. Do you see? Do you see what I mean? To be a really good liar, you have to have a phenomenal memory, of Olympic standard. And you must never panic, never be off guard. In the old days, of course, this could be a matter of life or death. You hanged if you made a mistake! Let me give you an illustration. Let us suppose that it was you who attacked this woman. So all that you've just said to me is a pack of lies. Nothing's true. You've lied to me. It's as simple as that.'

'But that idea's outrageous, Chief Superintendent? Do you really believe that I am the criminal, that I assaulted this woman? Is that what you are saying?'

'Please, let me finish, Professor! Now in your witness statement you've given us certain details: when you left your seminar; when you went to the cinema; how long it took to get home. You were quite exact. So two of my officers will check your story, trace your route for themselves. This is quite straightforward, a mere formality, purely routine, nothing to be anxious about. Speaking for myself, I think you've been telling the truth. But I do not *know*. You take my meaning? Now suppose my lads come back to me and say, "Well, he couldn't have done the journey in that times. That's quite impossible!" So I question you again.

And your heart sinks – you're the one who assaulted this woman, remember. Have you overlooked some detail, left something out, perhaps something quite small? Is there something you've missed, a trace left behind for us to find? So you lie. So you say something like: "Oh, yes, it did take me longer to get home, yes, I was late back because…. because…(here you are thinking madly)…because the traffic was heavy or I lost my keys or I forgot a book and had to double back. So I say: "Fine. We'll check. We'll question your neighbours, there's CTV in the area etc. etc." This makes you very nervous. Now you panic. Your mind seizes up. And while you're trying desperately to remember how it all goes together – this complicated jigsaw of lies – there I am boring you to death with my questions. You just want me to shut up, to have a small breathing space. You just want to think without this blathering background noise. But there I am, talking, talking, just like Porfiry, and all you can do is sit there with me droning on. Do you see what I'm getting at, Professor? You have now so overlaid the truth with lies that it is no longer the truth you're worrying about but the lies themselves. The actual truth has faded away and you have *to make these lies your truth*. The only way to save yourself is to an invent a past *that has become real for you*. The fiction has gained a life of its own; and it is that – that! – that you must, at all costs, protect.'

'So you see, Professor, we catch criminals not so much because they lie but because *they replace one truth with another truth that has become true for them*. That is an important distinction. We catch them through boring repetition, by the constant demand that the same story be told. Because every time they tell their story, they add something. They embellish, they tell us something new, something they will later forget, perhaps something they included in a previous version of the same event but which they now can't quite remember. And of course I am keeping a tab, and I'm always quick to point out the little discrepancies, the little differences between one story and another. It's very simple, really. That's why we ask suspects to go over their statements again and again and again. They think it's boring – and so it is – boring for them but not for us. We have to be on the alert, wide awake. And there's no magic in this, no hidden music, no subtle trick. For the fact is, Professor, that the more you tell a false story, the more it gradually disengages from the truth. The truth becomes a distant memory, the lie your reality. And, by and large, that's how we catch them.'

Weismann leant forward. 'I have a question. What if the truth is never verbalized but concealed by silence? What then? Suppose, for example, a marriage is breaking down? Suppose both parties know why that is. It's quite clear to them both. There's been a deceit of some kind, perhaps a debt concealed or an affair. But they never speak – it's a conspiracy of silence – because to talk about it would ruin everything. The truth would kill all hope. One could never go back from that. I don't think this is at all uncommon with couples, it's part of the hinterland of intimacy, this knowing when not to speak. But suppose one of them has other ideas? Suppose one of them is unforgiving and full of hate. Then what? Now silence has a different meaning. Saying nothing now conceals consequences, it lulls the victim into believing that silence is the same as forgetting or forgiving. But it may be something else, something else entirely. It may be the first step towards a terrible revenge, to a murder even.'

'That's true, Professor, that's true enough. But don't forget the criminal still has to act, to come out into the light. He can't just think someone dead. He still has to wield the knife. And, remember, whatever he does will always contain his reason for doing it. And he will have to lie about that reason, conceal his motive. And that's where I come in.'

Here Henry Fairest paused. 'But may we move on? I'd just like to go back over the events of last night and add into the mix one or two extra details. You tell me that you are an observant man. I am sure you are. But, for all that, there were things you didn't see, not because you are unobservant but simply because you didn't look. Not your fault, of course. For example, I asked you about the position of the woman when you left her, the exact distance from the road. I also asked you whether you had gone towards the embankment, looked at the car parked there; and you said that you hadn't. That is correct isn't it?'

'Yes, that's right.'

'That's a great pity, it really is. Because if you'd done that, if you'd had a closer look at that vehicle, you'd have saved us an awful lot of trouble. It was an Audi A3. And I can tell you, it hadn't been in any crash – you were quite right about that – there was hardly a scratch on it. But what we would have loved to know is this. Was that car occupied just after midnight, at the time you said you were there? Because it was certainly occupied at 12.25 or thereabouts, when my men arrived. Then, at that later time, if you'd been with my lads and looked more closely, you would have seen a man slumped sideways in the driver's seat. And if curiosity had got the better of you, and you'd looked in, as I had to do a little later, you'd have seen that this man, the man you didn't see, had been battered to death in a frantic attack, his head beaten to a pulp with a heavy object. Yes, no wonder you're surprised, Professor. Appalling, isn't it? I felt quite sick myself. But there it is. Not you fault. You couldn't have seen him from where you were standing. He was face down against the driver's door. So invisible to you. And that's not all. When my lads turned up at the scene, shortly after you left the police station, the woman you say you saw was not where you had last seen her. She was not on the right side of the road, a few feet away, where you said she was, but on the other side, on the left, at the bottom of the embankment, wedged against a rubbish bag. And she was dead, too, Professor, lying face down in the mud. I'm sorry, another shock, I know. Yes, she was quite dead, killed by a blow to the head, not frantic in this case but precise, measured.'

Weismann was silent, white-faced, staring at Henry Fairest, trying to take in what had just been said.

'And we're not finished yet, Professor. As I say, these were things that you didn't see. But there's more. Because for me the really disturbing thing about this – what makes this case so very peculiar – is that a preliminary examination revealed that the woman died from the second of two injuries. Yes, two! She had been hit with a hard object of some kind. And this makes me think. This poor woman was alive when you left her but dead when the police arrived. So if she was not where you said she was, then I think we can begin to understand why she was so frightened when you approached her. Think back! Remember how appalled you were when I suggested that she may have mistaken you for her assailant returning? I now think that she was fully justified in being terrified when she saw you, coming out of the night like that. She might well have thought you were her attacker returning. There is, however, another alternative.'

'What's that?'

'This is much more plausible and much more sinister. If you were not the murderer and somebody else killed her, then she was killed between the time you left and the time the police arrived. We know that much. Which means that in all probability the killer was waiting for his chance, waiting for you to leave, so that he could finish what he had started. So you and this poor woman were being watched and the murderer was hidden, hidden perhaps behind or in one of those old cars. Remember, I asked you whether they were occupied. Well, I think one was! He was there! And as soon as you drove away, he came out of his hiding-place, and the woman saw him coming and ran away from him, now running back towards the canal, trying to escape. It was a chase, a run for life. But it was no good, he caught her and hit her again, this time fatally, and she fell down the bank. Either that or she was rolled down. Anyway, that's what I think.'

'I was being watched?'

'Yes, I think you were being watched.'

'By the murderer?'

'Yes, by the murderer.'

'So all that time I was with this woman, her attacker

was only a few feet away, looking on? Is that what you're suggesting?'

'Yes, that's what I think. I don't know, of course, I'm only guessing. But if I'm right, then her situation becomes really terrifying, doesn't it? As you were trying to help, she was watching him watching her. For all I know, she might have known who it was. Perhaps all she could see was a face, a blurred image behind a shattered windscreen or the shadow of someone crouching behind a car. I don't know. But I think it must have been something like that. So she tried to run away. She was certainly frightened of you, suddenly appearing like that, but she was far more terrified of him, this other one. It hardly bears thinking about, it's nightmarish. But when you left, he seized his chance and went after her. She must have known what would happen; and what she was dreading did happen. He killed her.'

'But why on earth didn't she ask for my help?'

'But she did, Professor, she did!'

4

William and Marietta on the Day after the Murders

'Just as I was leaving, he told me who they were. They're called Kelly. Richard and Maddy, quite young, in their mid thirties. Apparently there's no doubt about it. Anyway formal identification will take place in a couple of days. The man's sister is coming down from Dumfries. Then he asked me whether I knew them, whether I'd even heard of them. Well, of course, I hadn't. I didn't know them from Adam. He seemed satisfied. Have you ever heard of them? No, I thought not. They're also checking on the cars, the cars by the canal, although I can't imagine they'll get anything from them. They're just heaps of junk.'

'What's this Henry Fairest like?'

'Oh, didn't you meet him this morning? I thought he'd be there when you made your statement.'

'No, he was out.'

'Did it go well?

'Yes, yes. I didn't have much to do. I just wrote down when you got home. There was somebody there called Bonfield.'

'That's the Inspector. But it's a pity you didn't meet

Fairest. I'd love to have known what you made of him. A good case-study. I thought him clever, deceptively so. I've asked around. He's quite a celebrity, often in the news, with important friends. I wouldn't want him after me, I can tell you. He'd never give up, just keep on going. Do you know he has a nickname? Bloodhound! Quite ridiculous. But I can see why. He looks rather like some monstrous dog, with heavy jowls. His face reminded me of Auden's, all cracked. And then, at the same time, I couldn't help thinking of Marlon Brando in *Apocalypse Now*. That awful baldness, the glistening head, and that feeling of enormous power, reserved, all suppressed. He was rather like that. People must find him intimidating.'

'Did you?'

'No, no, of course not! Why should I? I mean, physically he's a towering hulk; and because everything's big about him, everything in proportion, it's only when you're standing next to him that you realize how really big he is. I hardly came up to his chin! So he must be six feet six or seven at least. But he also had a rather comfortable, crumpled look about him, rather engaging really. So certainly impressive. He has a funny walk, as if his head's too heavy for his body. But as I said, clever. Yes, certainly clever.'

'So Willy, this Fairest, you think he'll find the murderer? That he'll find out who did it?'

'Oh, he'll find him all right. No doubt about that. He's on the scent, with that great nose of his, like a dog's. He'll never give up. It's just a question of time.'

William Weismann was sitting with his wife, Marietta, in their kitchen, with a bottle of Rioja between them.

The kitchen was enormous: it filled the entire basement of the house, with steps up to a narrow garden, a staircase to the rooms above, and a door leading straight into an adjoining double garage. His wife was an excellent cook and the kitchen deluxe, with a central island with whicker baskets, French copper pots hanging from ceiling hooks, and, most striking of all, a great array of Aîné and Perrier Sebatier knives, fifteen in all, displayed in a row above a butcher's block: cooking knives of various types and sizes, two oriental cleavers, a ham knife, a bread knife, and others for paring, boning, carving, filletting and slicing. Weismann enjoyed helping his wife. He always set the table. This could take up to an hour. Everything had to be measured – he had a small ruler for the purpose – so that the distance between the knives and forks, between the place mats and glasses was always exact. The slightest deviation made him feel unaccountably anxious, fearful that something terrible would happen, that the meal would be ruined. So, if he wasn't satisfied, he would start again. He knew this was obsessive behaviour; but his wife didn't mind, was used to it after so many years of marriage, and always made a point of complimenting him on the finished result.

Weismann's obsessions were a constant of his character, apparent when he was quite young. As a child he had always searched his room before going to sleep for fear of intruders. This had left him an incurable insomniac. He could not sleep on his right side but only on his left, facing the door. At his boarding school he would wake up in the night and count the strikes of the college clock: an even number meant happiness the next day, an odd number unhappiness. He would make extensive lists of things to do, setting a strict timetable. He would rewrite his homework again and again, not because it was wrong but because it looked untidy. He suffered from a permanent state of anxiety, of doubts, and had a nameless fear of contamination, which could only be kept at bay by extreme cleanliness, by constant washing, by the silent incantation of private words and phrases, by always sitting with the same people at mealtimes and in the same place in class, and by the neat arrangement of his bed, his room, his books, pencils and pens. He was sure that the back of his head was deformed in some way and so could not pass a mirror without checking. He had favourite numbers and favourite colours. He was oversensitive to light and the noise of crowds. The only time he felt completely happy was when he was performing the day-to-day rituals of his life. Then at least he achieved some kind of peace and security, having now, he believed, ensured himself against any outside threats. The one thing he lacked was any form of religious mania. This was because from an early age he regarded religion as a neurosis of the uneducated. Oddly enough, he attended the school Chapel regularly. He liked its neo-Gothic magnificence, the performance of unchanging ritual, the music of the choir and the organ; but the content of religion he dismissed as entirely vacuous.

The other side of the coin was his intellectual precocity, quickly spotted by his teachers. He had an extraordinary memory, an extensive vocabulary, enjoyed wordplay and puns, crosswords and jigsaws, could rattle off the batting averages of famous cricketers, knew all there was to know about dinosaurs, Tolkien, the cathedrals of France, the Sherlock Holmes stories, the London Tube and Land

Rovers. His teachers regarded him as a prodigy. But despite this array of gifts, which easily distinguished him from his peers, he was not unpopular. His peculiarities were not merely tolerated by his classmates but regarded with some pride. They pointed him out to their parents as the resident genius, on a par with those other heroes of the school who excelled at sports or were simply very rich. He was never bullied but left alone. Among his many interests, one stood out. He loved the movies. He would devour all the relevant magazines. As a boy he had a private order for *Picturegoer* and *Sight and Sound,* and in adult life subscribed to *Entertainment Weekly, The Hollywood Reporter, Total Film* and *Empire.* He knew all about the film stars, all the gossip, who was in and who was out. He knew the names of the directors, the designers, the script writers, the film's date and foreign distribution. Some scripts he knew by heart: *Citizen Kane, Casablanca, White Heat, Kind Hearts and Coronets.* He could imitate the voices of Cagney, James Stewart, Bogart and Cary Grant. He was no snob. He would watch anything, from Disney to Bergman. He started up the school's film society; and many years later, when he was famous, he became its President, an honour that delighted him more than the Honorary Doctorate from Cambridge awarded in the same year.

He met his Austrian wife, Marietta, at a party at the University of Marburg in Germany. He was spending a sabbatical year there as the Humboldt Fellow, on leave from Bristol University, putting the final touches to his book on Martin Heidegger, who had taught at Marburg during the 1920s. The Humboldt Foundation gave a reception for the new Fellows – there were four in all – in

the *Landgrafenschloss*, the 13ᵗʰ century fortified castle which
overlooks the town. There was to be an entertainment and
a small troupe of five actors were to perform two tales –
Little Red Riding Hood and *Rumpelstiltskin* – written by the
most famous of Marburg's sons, the Brothers Grimm.
William was enchanted with the performances, and could
only wonder at the kaleidoscopic skill of the actors as they
switched from part to part, seamlessly adapting their voices
and physical shape to their characters. Afterwards and still
in their costumes they mingled with the guests, chatting
away, accepting the congratulations of their audience with
professional reserve. William spotted the young actress
immediately. She, unlike the others, had gone off to change
and she returned to the hall wearing a trouser-suit of blue
corduroy and a flat cap with a little bow at the back, of the
same colour but darker, from under which billowed out
a mass of golden curls. He thought she was the spitting
image of Marlene Dietrich, the young Dietrich of *The Blue
Angel*, having the same curved and narrow eyebrows, high
cheek bones, full lips and hooded, sleepy eyes, of a bright
and quite startling iridescence. What was their colour? And
she even moved like Marlene: a long-legged stride, with
a turn of the hips, balletic in its natural poise, but manly,
androgynous even, with the head held high, haughty
and self-possessed. So it was not surprising that the first
words he said to her were, 'You look just like Dietrich!'
And she knew it, of course, indeed had cultivated the
resemblance, but was still surprised by the frankness of
his remark. His concentration on her was unswerving and
she felt uncomfortable. He drank her in. He discovered
that the next day the troupe of actors was to move on to

the university town of Giessen, seventeen miles away, and that they would be performing the same programme at the *Stadttheater*, but adding two further Grimm stories, *Rapunzel* and *Hansel and Gretel*. So he followed her there, attending the five evening performances, sitting in the front row, holding a flower – sometimes a rose, sometimes a carnation or little crocus pinched from the municipal gardens – which he gave to her after each show. When the troupe moved on to other neighbouring universities and *Hochschulen* – to Wetzlar, Friedberg, Bad Wildungen, and as far as Siegen – he was there again, following the same routine, with a flower in his hand. By this time the other actors were teasing Marietta about her besotted admirer. They were all curious about this strange, gangly young man, with the unruly hair and black eyes, whom they all could clearly see, night after night across the stage lights, staring up at Marietta from the stalls.

What did she make of him? At first she was startled, embarrassed and irritated by his attentions; but when he didn't turn up one night, she wondered why and was surprised at her own reaction the next day, relieved when she saw him again. She thought him very good looking, with an intensity of expression which she found disconcerting but hypnotic. Eventually she found herself forgetting the audience and acting only for him, even turning her body slightly towards him so that he could take in her every gesture and movement. But he was admittedly very odd. He hardly spoke when he came back stage, just said "This is for you" and gave her the flower. Inevitably she got curious about him and asked him questions: about his work, about how he came to speak such excellent German, where he was living. He seemed too shy to ask her out, so she asked him. She thought nothing would come of it, but she was intrigued, bored with touring, and he seemed harmless enough; and he was, after all, very handsome. She took him to a little *Bierkeller* in Siegen, just behind the *Apollo* theatre where they were performing, a student bar, down some steps and poorly lit. They sat in a cubicle: she had wine, he drank *Alt Bier*. She told him about her family: of her parent's life in Vienna before the war, and of how her father, as a young student, had helped Freud escape from the Nazis, travelling over to Hampstead with his books and artefacts.

She noticed that he was immaculately dressed, that his clothes looked almost new, crisp and clean. He was colour-coordinated, wearing an open-neck yellow shirt, a brown pullover, tan trousers and, incongruously, tennis shoes – these latter, she was to discover, being an almost permanent feature of his wardrobe. His head was a mass of black curls, each prematurely tinged with silver, with a great quiff at the front falling across his face. He was a man in constant movement, fidgeting with his drink, the table mats, pushing his hair back, shifting in his seat, constantly looking over her shoulder to watch the other customers come and go. He had the sunken cheeks of an ascetic and the full mouth and curving lips of a voluptuary. At first his eyes seemed to have no colour at all, creating the unsettling effect of black unfathomable hollows, inky pools in the face; but looking closer Marietta saw that they were in fact of the deepest brown, with an inner light of sudden flashes, revealing an intelligence that was intense and penetrating. When laughing, his eyes seemed to change to a paler colour, emitting a twinkling gleam that was both sardonic and humorous.

She of course seduced him, and there lay the great, overwhelming surprise for Marietta. In later years their marriage was to be the constant focus of gossip, the speculation being among those who knew them that it was a *mariage blanc*, a union unconsummated but convenient for them both, the consensus being that they were both homosexual. But such was not the case. Admittedly, they never had children, nor did they desire any; but in the early days of their time together their sex lives followed the familiar pattern of other young couples: sex was frequent, spontaneous, funny, caring and passionate. William's love-making was a revelation to Marietta, a concentrated act of romantic giving that overwhelmed her. But their sexual appetites for each other were weak and their sex lives gradually dimmed and petered out, becoming finally routine and intermittent. To them the acts of sex seemed quite unnecessary to confirm or reinforce the acts of love; and they quickly realized that for those of their temperament binding affection was more clearly demonstrated through shared interests. Nothing was ever said, but the transition from the emotional intensity of the bedroom to the more placid and comradely comforts of everyday living brought great happiness to them both. William loved Marietta, of that there was no question. For the first time his compulsive personality could focus exclusively on another human being. She was all he wanted and she was all he would ever seek. But did Marietta love William? That is more difficult to say. The answer lies in the beginning.

Marietta left the troupe and returned with William to

Bristol at the end of the academic year. They were married a few weeks later. Marietta got a job teaching Drama at Clifton College; but she soon found this unrewarding – she'd had enough of acting – and so took a degree in Psychology at the University, eventually getting a position as an assistant in the Medical Sciences Division of the Department of Psychiatry, researching into eating disorders among the young. To begin with they kept themselves very much to themselves. Then everything changed with the publication of William's book on Heidegger. As a complete reworking of *Sein und Zeit,* it created a sensation, generally hailed as being fully the match of the original, better written and without the jargon. William's fame was quite sudden and unexpected, the book sold well and he made money. So they moved into a larger house, an Edwardian three-storey in the Clifton area, and it was here that Marietta discovered her love of cooking. The kitchen was completely refurbished and both Marietta's and William's friends from work and the university were often invited over. It was their reaction to him that made her look at him afresh. She now saw him through their eyes and became increasingly astonished at what she saw and heard: how people approached him, often quite timidly, how they talked about him, sought him out, how they were intimidated and dazzled by him, and how they unashamedly confessed to having never seen his like before. Even William's colleagues seemed, to Marietta at least, without envy. One day the retired Head of the Department, Professor Denys Halvorsen, came into her kitchen. In his late seventies, as a very young man he had known Wittgenstein. Now, putting down his glass of wine, he confessed that 'Marietta, my dear, I have never known

73

anything like him, no never. I can die happy. I have seen Mozart.' But she still did not understand and could only ask herself, 'What have I married?'

So she attended some of his lectures. He knew she was there, sitting quietly at the back of the crowded lecture hall. Some of William's colleagues also attended, discreetly out of sight. There were about two hundred students present. William spoke without notes. The formal part of the lecture lasted about forty minutes. Then William took questions. His manner was courteous and patient, his answers clear and to the point. But gradually the questions began to falter and finally stopped altogether. Marietta looked round to see what was happening; but she soon realized, from the expectant faces, that everybody had been waiting for this moment. William was no longer interested in the questions being asked and seemed quite oblivious of his surroundings. He seemed to have entered some kind of trance-like state, communing only with himself, alert only to his inner ear. So began a virtuoso and dazzling display of philosophical extemporizing, in which William, without any sense of embarrassment or affectation, entered into a dialogue entirely with himself, a duet for solo voice. It was then that Marietta realized for the first time that this man she shared her life with, whom she knew so intimately in his everyday ordinariness, was, at this precise moment, completely strange to her, another being entirely, a creature even more extraordinary than she had imagined. She felt that she was face to face with some elemental force, hypnotic and uncompromising, and that before her stood a verbal magician of charismatic power.

There was one lecture that Marietta would not forget

until her life's last hour. William was discussing the Danish philosopher Søren Kierkegaard and his analysis of Christian love in his *The Works of Love* of 1847. Christian love, says Kierkegaard, is on a much more exalted plane than erotic love because neighbour-love, the love of the Good Samaritan, is selfless and outgoing, without poetic yearning or sexual attraction. Here the person you are required to love may be the person next door, the stranger that happens along, the individual for whom you feel nothing. Contrast this with the young girl dreaming of her future and looking at the men walking by and wondering which of them is her destined lover. But for the Christian things are much simpler. The person to love may be the first person encountered, precisely the stranger walking up the path, unknown to you and undesired. This is an act of divine duty without reward, all-forgiving because freely bestowed.

But William did not agree.

'Forget Kierkegaard's theology. We know that God is dead, buried beneath the laughter he provokes. So simply ask: Is Kierkegaard right? Is he right about this, about love, about what most of us hold to be the supreme human emotion? Do we really think that love can be so selfless, that it can be generated through a sense of duty? I deny this! We only have to look inside ourselves to know what rubbish this is. No one, absolutely no one, can create love in another. That is why love torments us, why it tears flesh. The lover may certainly assume that loving presupposes love in the other or that somehow by his own love he will ignite the flickering candle of devotion into a living flame. He may believe this, he will certainly desire this. But he may, for all that, have deceived himself and merely carved out from his own desires a mannequin of marble.'

'So love creates, but not in the way that Kierkegaard thinks. This is Christian nonsense. Set it aside! But then, as an antidote, remember Stendhal. Ha! Now here's a different tale. Recall that in the summer of 1818 Stendhal goes off on holiday to the salt mines of Hallein near Salzburg. He's with his friend Madame Gherardi – his 'la Ghita'. These salt mines are famous for one peculiarity. It's this. Towards the end of the winter season, the miners throw bits of wood down the shafts. Anything will do, boughs, branches, little twigs. So down they go! And then, a couple of months later, up they come! These bits of wood, saturated with salt and now dried out, have become completely covered with crystals. Even the tiniest twig no bigger than a tom-tit's claw is encrusted with these dazzling little diamonds. The original wood is unrecognizable: it is now something else entirely, an object of beauty, which the miners then sell on to the tourists. Now comes the interesting part. On one of their trips to the mines, Stendhal and his lady friend are introduced to a Bavarian officer. He takes a shine to Madame and soon shows all the symptoms of love. He attributes all kinds of perfections to her, excellences that, for the life of him, Stendhal can't see. He coos, for example, over Madame's hand, even though it's been pock-marked since childhood. Madame Gherardi is, of course, quite oblivious of all this, of what is happening here, of the meaning of these attentions. So Stendhal puts her right, and as he does so he notices that she is toying with one of these little bejewelled twigs, a leafless piece of hornbeam. And that gives him his idea, his famous theory of crystallization, because what has happened to the twig is precisely what has happened to Madame Gherardi. She too, like the little bit of wood, has been covered with diamonds, been endowed with all sorts of qualities she does not possess. She has undergone a metamorphosis generated entirely by the force of the lover's love. And this metamorphosis, make no mistake, is no delusion. No, no, it's real for him. Our love-sick officer really does believe that this woman before him, however plain and uninteresting in reality, is the fulfilment of his desires. This is certainly his truth, even if it's nobody else's.'

'Well, I have to say this – this is all too cynical for me, perhaps just a symptom of Stendhal's own amorous disappointments, of his own unrequited love for Mathilde Dembowski. We know all about this, it's well documented. But it's not difficult to see the direction Stendhal wants us to take. For the crystals melt, yes, they melt away. Then another form is revealed, at first gradually, drop by drop, the ice falling away to uncover something else. No diamonds now but the original carbon, jet black, hard, and dirty to the touch. What then of our poor officer? All he can do is stare at what is left, shocked and repelled. He beats his head against the wall, tears his hair, and cries out that he has been a fool, a dupe, that he has been deceived somehow, that it is not his fault but hers. How could this have happened to him, to him, to such an intelligent man, talented, always kind and generous? How could this be? What has he done to deserve this? He is at a loss. So then another metamorphosis occurs. His pity for himself now transmutes into hatred for her. How happy he would be without her. If only she was not here but somewhere else, anywhere would do, just away from him. Then he would achieve something. It's never too late, after all. Well, not for him anyway. So he dreams on, with this woman snoring beside him. And in the end he plans her destruction, his only pleasure imagining the pain he will one day inflict. And for that he must dissemble, smile, never let her know. And the deceit works. She knows nothing, is unaware of her fate, never hears the dissonances of deception, seems content, happy with her home, her domestic chores, her children, the company of her friends. She is always making plans for a future, but it's a future she will never see.'

'But I ask: Is this really the case? Domestic assassinations occur, of course they do, but they're not that common. In general couples just make do, settle down into their humdrum routines, two twigs shackled together, content with those endless repetitions of life, which are the only things left to them and which will be quite sufficient to see them out. They don't want to delve too deeply into the past, they don't want those old emotions resurrected, it's too painful, too disturbing to look back on the choices of youth, on the alternatives they never took, on what might have been, on what they might have become. So perhaps in the end unlucky in love is lucky in life. Because, after all, nothing can disturb the superfices of unimagined living.'

'So where have we got? Kierkegaard's neighbour-love is impossible, perhaps deliberately so, but that can't be said of Stendhal's. No, not at all. Cynical maybe, but not impossible. But, you know, for my money even that doesn't matter. And I'll tell you why. It's because crystallization, for all its concentration on desire, is not really about loving at all but – and this is my point – it's not about love but about the death of love, about its dying, why it dies: it traces out love's final trajectory. We know the end in the beginning. We know right at the start, from the way Stendhal talks about twigs and bits of wood, how matters will end, that it will end with revelation, disappointment and disgust. But I ask: Is this the inevitable price of falling in love with your own imagination? Must it be that all crystallization has to offer our Bavarian soldier is the memory of an adolescent spasm? Must it happen that one day, years later, when he has recovered from this peculiar illness and made his sacrifice to Asclepius, he will look back on his younger self with nostalgic disbelief, perhaps even with contempt at his youthful passion for an ideal now revealed as entirely false? Is there, I ask, no other alternative to accepting that sightless sight is the oxymoron of love? Well, I think there's more to be said. For just imagine this. What if our Bavarian officer isn't blind? What if, as he stoops over that little hand, he looks open-eyed at that pock-marked and disfigured skin? What if it was that, precisely that, this slight deformity, that set him off?'

'So this may be how it is. And I've just remembered something! I once asked a friend about his wife. So, David, I asked, what attracted you to her, I mean, right at the beginning? And do you know what he said? Her teeth! Yes, her teeth. *L'Amour des Dents*. And we both laughed because, really, her teeth weren't that good, they were slightly skewed. Ha! But, you know, it could have been something else, anything really: a slight squint, a hare-lip, the way she hides her mouth when laughing, her half smile, the swaying walk, the toss of her head, the fullness of a lower lip. Yes, it could be anything. And you, standing there, looking at her, you're in no doubt. You know them by their effect, by that unmistakeable inner tension that rises up within you – unbidden, inexplicable, sudden and intoxicating – this sensation that grips you, that makes your mouth go dry. You really can't explain why the slope of a nose or the willowy form or the curls under a little cap should work this magic. But why should these emotions necessarily melt away? After all, our officer has imagined nothing. What he sees is the bare wood, unadorned, perhaps its very simplicity operating as the catalyst for the inimitable effect. I know the opposite happens. Of course it does, and things may turn out as Stendhal predicts. It may even be the case that this happens more often than not. But I don't think it's inevitable.'

'And I say this because of something else, a test, if you like. Remember, Stendhal believes that the tragedy is in the unmasking of the truth. That's true. But it is also true that tragedy lies in knowing the truth too well. Remember Somerset Maugham's *Of Human Bondage*? Published in 1915, I loved this book, it spoke to me. Here he is, Philip Carey, an orphan with a club foot, obsessively in love with the selfish and vulgar Mildred. But the triggers are there all right: "The greenish pallor of her skin intoxicated him, and her thin white lips had an extraordinary fascination." That's what he says. I'm quoting. So no diamonds here. He knows she is a parasite in his heart, feeding off his blood. She is a worthless creature, who ends in prostitution. But he sees all this. He's in no doubt. He sees her for what she is. But when she leaves him he is wretched, and when she returns he despairs. And he could have escaped. He could have married Norah, a decent enough girl, but he chooses otherwise. I quote again: "He did not care if she was heartless, vicious and vulgar, stupid and grasping, he loved her. He would rather have misery with one than happiness with the other."'

'Well, what are we to make of this? And here's another example: the case of Mariana Alcoforado, a 17th century Portuguese nun, living in the convent at Beya. Her letters may not be original, some think they're fiction, written by Gabriel de Lavergene. We don't know. But let's assume her story is true. Aged about 25, Mariana is seduced by a young aristocrat, Nöel Bouton de Chamilly, later a Marshal of France. He then deserts her. In 1699 her famous letters are published, the book becomes a notorious bestseller, so unblushingly frank that the term *lettres portugaises* becomes a synonym for such blunt and amorous revelations. Her passion for him is absolute, hysterical even. But she still sees him for what he is: mediocre, faithless, deceitful, base. These are her adjectives. Believe me, this is exactly how she describes him. Yet she still loves him. She says that she would prefer to endure the terrible unhappiness he has wrought upon her than never to have seen him, never to have loved him at all. She says – and I quote again – that "willingly, and without a murmur, I consent to my evil fate."'

'What is wrong with these people? These are sensible men and women, after all, quite sane, not children or adolescents but individuals of intelligence, cultivated and well-educated. And yet they place themselves in these positions of degradation, seem to feed off their misery, becoming in their own eyes cheap and soiled. Are they mad?'

'Well, this is what I think. There comes a moment in the life of every person, man or woman, when, perhaps without warning, they hear the grinding of time's mill. They look in the mirror and see with horror the unmistakable marks of age etched upon their bodies. They see the watery eye, death-spots on the flesh, gravity exerting its pull on the sagging breast. Their days shorten, years seem like months and months like weeks. Time speeds up. There's nothing they can do to halt this this tramp, tramp, tramp of heavy boots towards oblivion. The clock still ticks away. It seems now quite impossible that they were once objects of desire, that this little hand could ever have been anything other than it is, withered and pock-marked. But so it was all those years back. Then is our Bavarian officer remembered, entering through memory's door. And don't you see? This single recollection transforms everything! For while Stendhal may be right and such passion dies – it may even be the first to die, dying long before the body dies – its mortality doesn't make it any less valuable, something to be dismissed because so light and fragile, a feather on the wind. In fact the opposite, the exact opposite is true. For like a mother's love for a child who lives only a few hours, this love, precisely because it is so short-lived, becomes not the least precious but the most precious thing of all, never forgotten but re-lived, never disappearing from the landscape of the mind but encased in lead within the memory. I tell you, it is this – this! – that everybody seeks. Don Juan seeks it, but this is not what I mean. He is sensuousness personified, the seducer of ice tallying up the numbers, never pausing in his conquests, giving nothing of himself, terrified of one thing only: to be bored, to yawn through life. What I mean is something else. What I mean involves the experience of abandoned unselfishness, of selfless giving, when the world drops away and all that is left is an ego now outside itself, dissolved within another flesh. I tell you, this is what the young girl dreams of as she sees the strangers pass. This is what places her alongside Philip and Mariana. Like them she longs for this one moment, it's all she can think about. She too is happy to pay the price, however terrible that may be. With a fierce desire she longs for these simple things: to feel her heart on his, the same pulse and intake of breath, to touch and be touched, to know in him what he knows in her, and to be finally safe, at home, two bodies entwined together. At any rate, that's how I see her, waiting at the garden gate, watching the men walk by. Which one is it? Which one will it be? And so she sits there, hoping and waiting for the inviting look. And if it that glance comes, beckoning her, at whatever age, young or old, why, then, the carousel's music begins. Things may or may not work out as Stendhal predicts. But that is all irrelevant now. She at least has something to feed off, enough to remember, the little that will sustain her as the years pass on. Her withering skin has been anointed by memory. She is not to be pitied as the one who missed out. No, no! She at least has felt the magic touch, Plato's divine madness, the delirium of mutual possession. No, don't pity her. Reserve your pity for the others, who regard erotic love as beneath them, as undignified, animal, messy, the basest form of love. These are the ones who become the cold-eyed monsters, unloved and unloving, who have never been the objects of desire, who do not know what desire is, have never desired anything, never felt the coils of passion, and who accordingly dry up from within.'

As Marietta listened to William her mood changed. At first she felt astonished, mesmerized, elated even, by this extraordinary and seamless flow of thoughts. She was used to the stagecraft of actors, she had known performers who could hold an audience by gesture and voice, by the alchemy of their physical presence. But she had never seen anything quite like this. Here the magic lay in William's effortless construction of a kind of intellectual labyrinth, his restless mind moving his listeners through an infinite maze of cascading words. But a bell rang to mark the end of the lecture and the students quickly left, chatting amongst themselves. The spell was broken and William walked off.

She saw what others saw in him. But her own feelings were now quite different. She felt a gripping chill around her heart. It was hard to breathe, she felt dizzy, there was an odd tingling sensation in her fingertips, her forehead became damp with clammy sweat. And she knew why. It was all this talk of erotic love. She began to feel increasingly uneasy. She looked round at those sitting near her, at William's students and colleagues, but there were no sidelong looks, no embarrassed half-glances, nothing to suggest that they knew what she knew: that William had been speaking directly to her. She was certain of it, laying bare for all to see the inadequacies of their own intimate life. She felt she had been undressed in public, her nakedness exposed. Had he simply forgotten she was there? No, he knew, she'd told him. Then how could he do this to her, humiliate her like this in front of all these people? Was he simply unaware of what he was saying? Not only that, this was not just a misunderstanding. This was something else, worse, a betrayal even. Because hadn't everything been said between them? Hadn't he agreed with her when she'd said that companionship could be just as potent as youthful desire? She remembered the conversation, she remembered it almost word for word, because it had been such a relief to know that he felt as she did, that there was nothing to worry about when passion faded. But here he was, acting like some romantic schoolboy, belittling a life without desire as somehow a lesser life, half-lived, something always to be regretted as you looked back. So had he changed his mind? Did he really believe this? Did he now deny what they had once agreed about? In which case, he'd been lying all the time, deceiving her, pretending to be happy when all the time he'd been the opposite: unhappy, dissatisfied with what had been, frustrated by her lack of sexual need. And where was her fault? She had never pretended otherwise. So how had he expected her to change? By an effort of will? Of course, she had always known the difference: that what was lacking in her had been more potent in him. But surely there was nothing odd in that, it was just how things were with most couples, with one side always more demanding, more aroused than the other. This was an imbalance that everybody knew about, something that could never be corrected because it was organic, a physical thing that could not be changed, like the colour of eyes or the texture of skin. So why, then, was William attaching blame, dismissing her as a creature to be pitied because she had never known what he had known, never felt for him what he had felt for her? Had he already forgotten what he had just said: that you cannot generate love in the object of love, that the passion on one side does not necessarily transfer to the other? Why, then, was she to be pitied? No, it was the other way round. He was the one to be pitied, not her, because all along he had desired something he could not have, something he must have known he could never possess, known even from their first days together, the one thing she could not give, everything else perhaps, but not that.

It was after this lecture that Marietta realized that she did not love William – well, not in the way that William loved her. She admired him, she cared for him, she led a contented life with him, but he had never been the object of her need – perhaps of appetite when she was young – but not of this sexual desire desired by William, felt by him for her. How, then, could she mourn the loss of something she had never had? So perhaps, after all, she was the exception to Stendhal's rule. She lacked the inner longing to crystalize anything. And anyway what she held in her hand had no need of transformation. The bare William didn't need it because the real William had a glitter all his own. He possessed no encrusted diamonds ready to melt away but retained in himself a hard and singular brilliance quite impervious to heat.

★★★

That was all such a long time ago. Their lives together had continued along an even path. Yet Marietta never forgot the lecture on Kierkegaard. Her feelings for William had not really changed, not substantially, nor, she knew, had his for her. For many years now she had been entirely reconciled to her situation, as she believed him to be with his. For her part, she could not miss what had never been. So there they sat, William and Marietta, with the bottle of Rioja between them. When she looked at him she saw the same good looks. He was slim and beautifully dressed, there was still the full head of hair, although now almost white, the famous quiff, the same agitated restlessness, the same deep-set, almost unblinking eyes in the concentrated face. She admired him intensely, was proud of him, basked in his fame, and could not help but be thrilled when, in front of others, he deferred to her, always wanting to know her opinion, treating what she said with deep seriousness. Even when she wasn't there, he would often remark, "I must ask Marietta", "I wonder what Marietta thinks." And as for William, when he looked at her he still saw the living focus of his passionate nature. She had never been conventionally beautiful. Yet all these years of marriage had in no way dimmed his love of looking at her, his pure aesthetic enjoyment of her singular looks. She was still angular, lean like a thoroughbred. Her eyes retained their slightly hooded, languid look. He didn't like the fact that the billowing curls were gone, that she had cropped her hair like a boy's; but even that only served to accentuate the upward slant of her eyes and the incisive lines of her jaw and chin. He loved the way she moved and the way she dressed. She was always elegant, poised like a dancer, and still walked like an Empress.

'Well, I'm off to bed,' she said. 'Are you coming?'

'I'll just put the rubbish out and then I'll be up,' he replied.

For years they had slept in separate rooms – William's insomnia made this necessary and Marietta had much the larger of the two, a double bedroom with a bow-window looking out across the park. It was full of memorabilia of her time as an actress and family souvenirs: framed costume designs, signed programmes, a gilded *servetta muta* mask from Venice, a photograph of her parents skiing in the Alps, an ancient teddy bear, and, in a separate cabinet, her collection of scent bottles. By contrast, William's bedroom was tiny, no more than a box room, just enough for a narrow single bed and a bedside table, piled high with books, his reading through the night. It was without decoration, except for a small 18th century etching of the Marburger *Schloss*.

Marietta did not take off her clothes but lay down on her bed exhausted. She looked up at the ceiling without expression. Then she got up, went to the bathroom, returned, switched the light off, and undressed. Quite naked she stood in front of the large window, then opened the right-side casement. She liked a cold bedroom and the evening breeze entered immediately, flowing over her. She shivered, crossed her arms, and rubbed herself down. She felt the goose-bumps on her skin and the friction of her hands warmed her slightly. She stared out through the glass. Far off, she could just make out lights twinkling through the darkness. These belonged to the houses on the far side of the park. She looked across at them, at the rooms illuminated from within, at the shadows moving behind. What did she know of them or they of her, of their lives and loves, this secret world of other people? She took a deep breath. Then she drew the curtains, turned to her bed, and lay down. The slight draught in the room moved the cool air around her, gently caressing her bare flesh. She lay there for some minutes, staring into the darkness. Her mind was numb, all her senses becalmed, alert only to the rhythm of her breathing. She stretched out her arms beside her, placing her hands palm down on the quilted bedspread; and then slowly she raised them to her face, moving them delicately across the surface of her body, feeling the stubbiness of her cropped hair, then down across her eyes, to her lips and neck, kneading the bunched skin beneath her fingers. Her hands moved on, further down to her breasts, which she cupped in each hand, caressing the hardening nipples. Then down again to the flat stomach and the small mound of fine curled hair and to the silken crease beneath. Then her hands moved up again, back along the contours of her body, feeling the shape of her hips and the texture of her skin, then back to her face, now wet with tears. She turned her head into the pillow, muffling the sobs that mounted up through her aching lungs. Then she took deep breaths, trying to control the hysteria that was creeping up through her throat. But her jaw opened of itself and she could feel the screams coming. So she fisted her hand and rammed it into her widening mouth, her teeth drawing blood on her knuckles. Her body arched up as if electrified, her muscles locked in spasm. Then, just as suddenly, her body relaxed and she fell back against the cushions. She was now drenched in sweat and breathing in short, panting bursts. Her whole body ached with longing, a physical sensation she now knew well, a churning of nerves deep in her lower belly, her insides melting. Then she sat up. She had heard a sound. She turned towards the door: beneath it, just visible, was the light from the hall. It was William coming up the stairs. She could hear him clearly now, the floorboards creaking. Then she heard the opening and closing of doors, the noise of water running. Then silence. There was not the usual "Goodnight" from him – he could see that her light was off. He would be reading now, perhaps for an hour. The pattern of his nights never changed. He would sleep, wake up, and then read some more. He could read a book a night. But Marietta said nothing – no greeting from her either – it was better he thought her sleeping. She remained motionless, sitting bolt upright, staring in front of her. Then, quickly, she shifted her body, turned the covers of her bed down and moved beneath them, pulling the heavy blankets up to her chin, then over her head. She burrowed down, curled up under the weight, bringing her knees closer to her face. She must not think! She must put everything behind her, let her mind go blank! She longed for oblivion and the increasing warmth made her feel drowsy. But she knew there would be no sleep, not for her, not this night. She knew she would lie awake until morning. She knew that all night she would lie there, listening to the ticking of her bedside clock, counting the hours as they slowly passed. She knew this because, persistent in her mind and never releasing its hold, was one nagging question, ever-present, which would kill all sleep: "Does he know? Does he know?" So, facing the night's darkness until dawn, she huddled into herself, deep within the womb of blankets, clasping her hands in fear and despair, whimpering into her pillow.

5

Henry, Terence and Twinkie
One week after the Murders

That night Marietta had treated William to Beaufort Sole with Oysters, followed by *Crèpes soufflées au Grand Marnier* – both recipes copied from her favourite *Lady Maclean's Cookbook*. A week after the murders Henry and Terence were tucking into an evening meal prepared by Twinkie: toad in the hole followed by treacle tart and a selection of cheeses: Wensleydale with cranberries, Stinking Bishop and Cornish Yarg. Terence and Henry provided the wines, mostly German in homage to their hostess, with beer and schnapps to finish. These lengthy meals, with Terence of necessity staying with Henry overnight, were a regular feature of their lives, held whenever their busy schedules allowed. They were the highpoint of Twinkie's life, full of bibulous fun. Henry looked rumpled and tired, even more hang-dog than usual. Lotte, sitting beside him in her basket and sensing his exhaustion, had her shaggy head buried in his lap. Terence had come straight from the Crown Court in Crown Square and propped up against his chair was a suitcase of brown leather, containing all the regalia of a Queen's Counsel. Twinkie was wearing a brightly coloured Mexican dress, with billowing underskirt, and an enormous necklace of seashells.

Then Henry told them about the Newtown Murders.

'I don't know what to make of this case. I'm exhausted by it. We're a week in but it's getting more tangled the deeper I dig. And to make matters worse, the Press have got hold of it. So the pressure's on. Well to begin. Terence, you'll remember that my birthday party came to a rather abrupt end when I was hauled off by two of my lads. And you'll remember, Twinkie, when I came back here, very late that night, and how dead tired I was, covered in mud. And no wonder! I'd been dragged out to the Newtown Industrial Estate, a truly God-awful spot, on special orders from our Chief Constable, Jock Pringle. He does this sort of thing to me, and I wish he wouldn't! Anyway, the weather was absolutely bloody, freezing, belting down. Stephen Thomas was there already, all kitted out like a plastic gnome. He was clearly puzzled as well. He showed me two bodies, one in a car near the embankment: a man, battered to death, nasty. The other was a woman at the bottom of the bank, near the canal, hit on the head a couple of times. All straightforward, gruesome but clear-cut, since confirmed by Stephen in his autopsy report. The woman had been a passenger: her bag was on the back seat. So not unreasonably my first idea was that this was some crime of sexual passion, a case of Milton's "injured lover's hell", with the usual triangle: the husband killing the lover or the lover killing the husband. So not a problem or so I thought.'

'So a *crime passionnel*?' asked Twinkie.

'Not quite that, Twinkie,' continued Henry. 'Because, as I've just said, we are dealing with two murders not one.

And although the killing of the man might well have been a *crime passionnel*, given the nature of the wounds, which certainly suggested somebody out of control, the killing of the woman was clearly premeditated. Because not only did she try to escape but – and now comes the first sensational detail – the murderer was interrupted. Yes, astonishing, isn't it? And I know this because we have a witness, someone who saw the woman after the first attack, running across the road, bleeding from what he took to be a severe head wound. He thought she'd been in a car crash. Quite understandable. So he drove off to get the police but by the time they arrived at the scene the woman was dead. And Terence, guess who the witness was?'

'Go on, then…Who?'

'William Weismann!'

'You mean the philosopher, the Dostoevsky man, who gave that lecture we went to?'

'That's him!'

'What on earth was he doing on the Estate?'

'Every Thursday he passes through it. He's a movie nut, and every week goes to the *Duke of York's*, usually with one of his students from the University. Then he drives home, taking the M602 short cut up to Prestwich.'

'Who is this Weismann person?' asked Twinkie.

'A famous philosopher', explained Henry, 'made his name writing a book on Heidegger. I haven't read it but I gather it's quite astonishing. Anyway, to carry on. Where was I? Ah, yes. These two murders were odd in other respects. The first peculiarity was that the weapons used in them appeared to be different, the first one, used on the man, heavy and blunt, the second one, used on the woman, something lighter, more precise, like a small hammer. Well, that's what we thought. But now Stephen's not so sure. He now thinks it could be the same weapon because even something quite small could do terrible damage if the man was beaten long enough, say, in a sustained frenzy. So the first oddity may not be so odd after all. The second oddity is… But hang on a bit, I won't be a moment.'

Henry hurried out of Twinkie's flat and went back to his own. A couple of minutes later he returned, carrying a large brown envelope.

'Now see what you make of these. These are some of the photographs taken at the crime scene. I won't show you the pictures of the man, Twinkie, they're too gruesome, but these will do.'

Henry put the photographs on the floor. There were ten of them. Each was numbered in the corner with a blue marker pen. Henry laid them out in a line across the carpet. Then he went down on his hands and knees and knelt in front of them. Terence and Twinkie came over to look, craning over Henry's shoulder. Then they too crouched down beside him, the three of them now leaning forward together, their backs bent in a row like three pilgrims at prayer. They stared at the pictures for some minutes. The first one was of an Audi A3, a side view, taken from about twenty feet away; the others were of the dead woman.

'The picture of the car,' explained Henry, 'confirms what Weismann said he saw – that is, nothing at all. The body's in there but you can't see it because it's slumped inside. That's why he thought the car unoccupied. It's these other photos, of the dead woman, that are more interesting.

Come on, you two, what do you think? Is there anything odd about them? I think there is. But can you see what I see?'

'Yes,' said Twinkie, pursing her lips in concentration, 'I think I see something. But first let me get this straight. You said, Henry, that this woman – oh! how young she looks, poor duck! – that this woman, when Weismann saw her, had already been attacked and was bleeding from her injuries. So he thinks she's been in an accident. In fact, as we know now, she hadn't been but was probably just dazed from the first attack, only saved because Weismann turned up. Then Weismann goes off to get the police, and while he's away she's killed: her killer finishing what Weismann interrupted, this occurring between the time Weismann left and the police arrived. And the poor thing ends up at the bottom of the bank, wedged against a bin bag or whatever that is. That's right, Henry, that's what you said, isn't it?'

'That is exactly what I said,' replied Henry.

'Well, in that case,' continued Twinkie, 'I find the position of her skirt very strange.'

'Go on, Twinkie, go on!'

'Well, I mean, if you're running away from someone and they hit you and you fall down, your skirt wouldn't be like that – would it? – not hitched up that far, almost above your knickers. And it certainly wouldn't be like that if she crawled forwards, away from her killer, and it's hardly likely that she crawled backwards. And I think that her skirt wouldn't be that high up even if she rolled down the bank or just fell. So I think we have to say that she was dragged somehow, dragged by the feet, and maybe over

95

some distance. Yes, that would have to be it. That explains the skirt. Was that what you were thinking, Henry?'

'Yes, that's it. Twinkie. It's just a little detail, but it could be important.'

'But I don't think that's all, Henry. No, I can see something else.'

'Now you've lost me, Twinkie. Go on.'

'Well, let's agree that the murderer dragged the woman to the bank and rolled her down. Let's say he probably pulled her by her feet, on her back, dragging her along. I'm sure we're right about that. I'm sure that was how it was. It explains her dress. But then I ask myself: if he was at pains to hide the woman, why didn't he hide the man while he was at it? Why leave him there for all to see?'

'Well, presumably,' said Henry, 'because he thought the man was already well hidden, that nobody would see him where he was. Weismann didn't see him, after all. Or perhaps he was afraid of being interrupted, of another car coming along. So he had to be quick.'

'Of course", replied Twinkie, 'you may be right. Our murderer was in a rush and was scared of being seen. That's always a possibility. For all we know, perhaps another car really did come along and he had to hide and so didn't have time to do anything about the man's body. But all the same, it still seems odd to me. I mean, an Audi's quite an expensive car, not like any of the others, like those other ones dumped by the canal – and it's also some distance away from them. It stands out like a sore thumb. So I think it would be quickly spotted. I mean, in the morning, as soon as it was light, somebody would have seen it, they could hardly miss it. So they'd have stopped to have a look. That just seems common sense. They'd be curious. Then they'd have seen the body. But that doesn't seem to interest our murderer. He's not worried about that at all. He doesn't care if the man's found. No, I think he cares more about the woman's body. She's his priority. She's the one he's got to hide, not the man.'

'Well, all right, Twinkie, I'll accept what you say. You may be right, but I'm not so sure. But I'll think about it. You may be on to something. Anyway, we'll have to wait and see,' said Henry, collecting up the photos. Then the three of them got up and went back to their chairs.

'Now for some more details,' continued Henry, settling himself down, 'and it's these that take the case well out of the ordinary. The couple were called Kelly. We know this because the man had a driving licence on him and the woman a Co-Op card in her bag. So the killer made no attempt to hide their identity. Also odd was the absence of any mobile phones. That might be something and nothing; but I still think it's strange – young people nowadays are lost without them, it's the one thing they can't do without. So my guess is that the killer took them because otherwise the numbers could be traced back to him. Well, anyway, they're gone and probably destroyed. But the third detail is much more important. Stephen has established that the woman was pregnant, about three months. Yes, terrible I know. Yet it seemed to confirm what I had originally suspected: that this was a tragic triangle, with the woman at the centre. She was pregnant by one of them and the killer killed them both in a jealous rage. Anyway, something like that.'

'So the pregnancy's the key? Is that what you're saying, Henry?' asked Terence 'That the woman was killed not just because she witnessed the murder but because of her condition – that she was going to be killed anyway, that this was always the plan? Man No.1 batters Man No.2 to death, with the pregnant woman looking on. But being pregnant won't save her. Some killers might hesitate but not this one. It makes no difference to him. Of course, it may be that he didn't know she was pregnant. There's always that possibility. But let's just suppose that he did know, and knew well in advance what he is going to do; and that what he did he did quite deliberately in front of her. That was the whole point. Remember the case of Sidney Pewsey, Henry? Did just that, slit his throat under the Palace Pier at Brighton, in front of his mother! So it's like that here. He wants his theatrical moment, for her to see what he can do. He wants her to see and then to know that she's next. He wants her terrified, to know what's coming. Get what I mean, Henry? She's being punished for what she's done, punished and then executed.'

'So the three of them are in the car together,' continued Twinkie, enthusiastically. 'They've arranged to meet, they've phoned ahead. Yes. So off they go. And it's pouring! But that's good – good for our murderer, I mean – because the rain covers the evidence, and the Estate is a wonderful spot, isolated and deserted. Perfect. So the killer gets the other two there, there they are, he knows the layout, everything has been thought through. And all the time he has some concealed weapon on him, perhaps hidden under his coat. Then he kills the man and tries to finish off the woman but she runs off. So he chases after her but misses his chance because Weismann arrives. Then he hides and waits, still keeping his eye on her. And when Weismann leaves he comes out from wherever he's been hiding and finishes her off. Terrible! What a monster!'

'And now add this into the mix, another extraordinary detail,' said Henry, smiling. 'A couple of days ago Richard Kelly's sister came down from Dumfries. Actually his half-sister, a Mrs Penny Eustace: they have the same mother but different fathers. I was a bit surprised to see how young she was, a good ten years younger, at the most twenty-two or three. So she identifies the body. Of course, half the face had to be covered up, just the right side visible, but still pretty nasty. But it was enough. She's obviously upset, of course, very weepy, as you'd expect, poor thing. But then she said something really interesting. I was standing beside her and heard her say quite clearly. "Oh Dickie, you were warned. Why didn't you listen?" That took me back a bit. So I ask: "What were you afraid of, Mrs Eustace? Do please tell me. You never know, it may help. Did Richard say anything to you? Was it perhaps a marital problem of some kind?" I was thinking of the pregnancy and guessing that he might have confided in her. But then she drops the bombshell. "Richard wasn't married! What made you think he was?"'

'I felt like hitting myself over the head. What a bloody fool I'd been. I just assumed they were husband and wife. I mean, of course we'd have found out sooner or later, really in no time at all; but I was still kicking myself. Such a stupid, stupid mistake. But then I had a terrible thought. So I asked her, "Mrs Eustace, do you have a sister?" "Yes," she says. My heart sank. So, there and then, I arranged for a second identification, and of course Mrs Eustace immediately identifies her. It's her half-sister all right –

Maddy. The poor girl's now in a terrible state, completely hysterical, and collapses. She had to be taken to hospital, heavily sedated.'

'Well, you can imagine how we all felt. Terrible. It was a tremendous shock, real heartbreak. Anyway, this morning I went to see her. I kept things short. She was still in a bad way but was now thinking more clearly and tried to answer my questions as best she could. I wanted to know, of course, why she said what she'd said when identifying her brother, why she'd been worried about him, what she thought he'd been up to. She told me what Maddy told her. He had been a tough character, a heavy drinker and sometimes violent, somebody you wouldn't want to meet on a dark night, always on the edge. She was very forthcoming about this. Her sister had clearly had a hard time of it, living with him. He'd dropped out of school, done a bit of stealing and dealing, nothing really serious, but evidently a young man mixing with some bad people. The only constant in his life was Maddy. She could manage him to some extent and they really only had each other. The three children shared a mother, who, reading between the lines, was a thoroughly unpleasant character. Richard and Maddy were the children of her first marriage; but the husband couldn't stand her, he scarpered off, leaving her to bring up the kids. Then when they were about ten and eleven, the mother married again and soon had her third child – Penny, our Mrs Eustace. The second husband was much older, well into his fifties, wealthy and was quite prepared to take on his two step-children; but the mother wouldn't have it and farmed the two kids out to some foster parents up north in Salford, which was cheap and out of sight, paying for their keep, but always only the absolute minimum. There was always trouble getting money out of her. So while the mother lived in some luxury – a large flat in London, a place in the country – the two kids were near the poverty level, virtually disowned. So the three children hardly ever saw each other, Penny down south, the silver spoon, private schooling, Richard and Maddy up north largely fending for themselves in a very tough neighbourhood, semi-educated. Well, to cut a long story short, the step-father died leaving comparatively little money – keeping his wife in luxury had cost him a fortune – and then a few years later the awful mother died, moaning and spoilt to the end. So now it was just the three of them. The brother was still a problem, but the two half-sisters, despite their very different backgrounds, got on and became quite fond of each other. Mrs Eustace got married recently, to a Scot; but they still telephoned each other regularly and could swap stories about their monster of a mother. Maddy was happy to have a shoulder to cry on, and Penny soon learnt what a problem the brother was, going from job to job, never staying long, often on benefit, the usual depressing story. He tried his hand at a lot of things, but I gathered from Mrs Eustace that, when he put his mind to it, he was in fact quite hard-working, and would sometimes come home with money, cash in hand, most of which he handed over to Maddy without complaint. His most recent job was as a driver. He'd been at it for some time, a decent living. And he really did know something about cars, was quite a good mechanic, had a natural gift for it, and he really enjoyed driving people about. He seemed to have settled.'

'But why, then, did Mrs Eustace say what she said,

about warning Richard?' asked Twinkie. 'That doesn't sound as if she was just generally worried about him. It sounded more specific than that, something that Maddy must have told her, something he was doing that might actually be dangerous. So what was it, Henry?'

'Hang on a bit, Twinkie, I'm coming to that. But first, let's go back a bit. Here we have a couple, both in their mid-thirties, with not much money between them; and there they are driving a two-year old Audi A3, a car they couldn't possibly afford. But the fact that Kelly, as we now know, was often employed as a driver would explain that: if it wasn't his car, then it was probably borrowed from a garage or private owner. Anyway, it was easy to check. So we did. The registration number led us to a small fleet owned by a car-rental company called Western Hire Cars. So Bob Bonfield rang them up. And yes, they confirmed that Dick Kelly was often employed by them; and, oddly enough, what they said about him wasn't what we'd expected. They said he was a reliable, nice lad, quite shy; and yes, he was sometimes allowed to take the car back home, particularly when he had a late call, after hours, when the garage was shut. So it was quite all right for him on some nights to keep the car, bringing it back the next morning. They knew about that and it happened quite often. So Bob asks: "Did it happen last Thursday night?" "Yes," they said, "it was a regular one out to Alderley Edge, quite a trip." Then Bob asks, "Do you have the name of the client for that night?" "Oh, yes," says they, "He uses us almost every day, our most regular regular, lives in a whopping house, near all those footballers." "So what's his name?" So they tell him and poor Bob can't believe his ears. He bloody nearly has a heart attack, nearly falls of his chair. The passenger for that night was – wait for it, Terence! – a certain Thomas Seda …'

'Slide!' exclaimed Terence, turning his head quickly towards Henry. 'You're kidding me, Henry! Not Slide, not Monty Slide!'

'Yes. The very same!'

'Dear God! Ha! Well, that changes everything. Monty Slide! I can't believe it! Monty Slide! You're into the big league now, Henry! Twinkie, sorry, but I need another drink'.

'I'll have one too,' said Henry. Terence crossed the room to a small crystal decanter of whisky, filled up two large tumblers, brought Henry his, and then returned to his seat, sitting down heavily and whispering to himself, 'Monty Slide! Bloody hell! Monty Slide!' Then, turning to Henry: 'Does Jock Pringle know?'

'I've told him and he's as worried as hell. But it's too early to tell at the moment. It might just be a coincidence. Let's hope so anyway.'

'There are no coincidences where Slide is concerned,' mumbled Terence, looking intently into his glass.

Henry and Terence remained silent for some time, moodily sipping their whiskies. This was too much for Twinkie. She looked from one to the other, expecting some reaction, but none came. There they sat, morose and grim-faced, occasionally looking furtively at each other, clearly uncomfortable.

'Excuse me, boys,' she said, 'but who is this Monty Slide? He's obviously reduced you two to quivering wrecks.'

'We make no apologies for that, Twinkie,' replied Terence. 'Henry and I know Monty Slide of old, probably know him better than most. Believe me, this is no joking matter. And I'll tell you something else. He'll also know all about us, what company we keep. So he'll know about you too, Twinkie. We'll be catalogued in his head: background, education, career, cases, dates – they'll all be there, neatly tucked away, to be fished out later when he needs something.'

'So why haven't I heard about this Slide before?' asked Twinkie. 'Presumably he's a crook? Otherwise you two wouldn't know him. And why's he called "Monty"?'

'That's a nickname,' explained Terence, 'given to him because he's a fanatic for military history. Also a major donor to the War Graves Commission! Ha! But everybody knows him, up and down the country. There's only one "Monty". He's a one off. His real name is Tomas Slas, a common enough name in Lithuania, son of Vladas and Ruta Slas, born in June 1945, in Vilnius. The parents got out a couple of years later and settled in…'

'Chiswick', continued Henry. 'and "Tomas" became "Thomas" and "Slas" became "Slide". "Seda" is the name of the father's village, where the family came from. So Monty kept that part. And they were a clever family, hard-working, did well, a chain of flower-shops, doubling up as off-licences, but all their hopes centred on their bright son. So off goes "Thomas Slide" to Grammar School – I think it was Latymer's – and there we get the first hint of things to come. We'll never know exactly what happened, but he drops out and never did his A Levels. Odd, because he was a really clever lad. Then he went into business on his own, still only a teenager, probably financed by Dad. It was a simple scheme: buy a house, rent it out, and with the money buy another. What set Monty apart was the remarkable success he had with people who didn't want to sell. One moment they were telling him to push off, and the next they were gone, selling out for a low price. Well, what we know about our Monty *now* makes clear what happened *then*. He was threatening them, making life unbearable; but there was nothing to be done because nobody complained: everyone was too frightened to speak. A wall of silence. If they left their homes, they were spat at in the street or there was some oaf shouting abuse. Graffiti on doors, super-glue in locks, drains blocked with dead cats, that sort of thing. And if you still didn't sell up, then Slide went up a notch. There were physical threats; and it didn't really matter whether you were young or old, you still got the Monty-treatment. And he never went for the house-owner directly – he was too clever for that – it was always the nearest and dearest. If you had an elderly mother, she was targeted, jostled in the street or her handbag nicked; if you had a child, that child went missing for an hour, not long, just enough to terrify the parents. And it worked. By the time he was twenty-five, our Monty was a millionaire. Before long he had one of the largest property portfolios in London. Then he had another bright idea. Why employ a builder when you can buy the company? So he did. And it was the same with architects, with plumbers, electricians, even the solicitors doing the conveyancing. Now all working for Monty. And there he sat, in the middle of this bloody great web, gathering in the dosh.'

Henry took a gulp of whisky and Terence took up the story.

'Then Monty came north and did much the same up here. Property was cheaper, after all, and Manchester was on the up and up. So he started diversifying: not just properties but clubs and restaurants, gambling and, through intermediaries, a couple of plush brothels. The only thing to be said for Monty was that he didn't do drugs – well, not that we know of. But this wasn't a question of morality. He didn't care one way or the other. He stayed clear because druggies were unreliable, they weren't good business men, couldn't be trusted, and there was far too much violence, they were always killing each other. Anyway, that's the story. And the legal profession came across Monty Slide – indirectly, that is – all the time. Still does. I've seen people in court for comparatively minor crimes – burglary, that sort of thing – and they turn up with a solicitor way out of their league, charging 500 quid an hour. That's Monty. So these guys get off, it's still happening, and from then on they're in his debt and so always obey Monty. Yes, Monty looks after his own all right. So what Monty wants, Monty gets. But woe betide anyone who crosses him. Those that do have a habit of disappearing.'

'Anyway, there you have it, Twinkie,' said Henry. "That's Montgomery Slide. And so I don't think it's unreasonable to suppose a connection between Slide and the Kelly lad, that it must mean something. If he was in danger in some way, as Mrs Eustace seemed to think, then that danger will come from Slide. Make no mistake. I'll bet my pension on it. There'll be something there. I don't know what,

106

but it'll be the key to everything. These murders will have something to do with him, I just know it.'

'So what will you do now, Henry?' asked Twinkie.

'We do what we always do. We wait. There's nothing magical in police-work. There is no great *Columbo* moment, with everybody gathered together, while the scruffy detective unmasks the murderer. It's never anything like that. That's fiction. In reality all you need is patience. In the end, as Terence knows, it usually comes down to one of three things – money, sex and power – and more often than not it's a combination of the three. With Monty we have the money and the power, and perhaps, with Richard's sister Maddy, with her pregnancy, we have the sex. We shall see, Twinkie. So I'll just wait. In the end, something will give, somebody will say something or some little detail will come to light. It'll be something like that and it'll get back to me. But now, Twinkie dear, it's 2.30 in the morning, and Terence and I have early starts.'

'Keep me posted, won't you?' said Twinkie, getting up with them. 'I want to know what happens. But do be careful with this man Slide. He sounds horrid.'

'He is,' confirmed Henry. 'But don't worry, Twinkie, I know what I'm doing. I know him and he knows me. So I doubt he'll take me on.' And with that Henry and Terence kissed Twinkie goodnight, and then crossed the landing from Twinkie's apartment and entered Henry's, Lotte following behind.

'Monty Slide,' mumbled Terence. 'I still can't get over it. You know, Henry, I sometimes think that if Slide had been dealt with, all those years ago, the crime rate in Manchester would have dropped by a good 20%!'

'If not more!' confirmed Henry. 'Anyway, bed-time. I'll have gone before you're up, Terence. So will you be at *The Sun* tomorrow? About 8.00?'

'I'll ring first, Henry. I might have to go to Preston for a nice little case of a Vicar stealing the collection; but I'll let you know.'

So they went to bed: Terence as usual in the spare room, Henry in his own, and Lotte in the scullery. But Lotte was restless. After a few minutes, she left her basket, sniffed around the hall for a while, then went to see if Terence had settled in. He was in bed, had turned off his light, but was expecting her. He reached out and gave her a biscuit from the table beside him, kept ready for her in a little bowl. He ruffled her head and she licked his hand. Then she left and went back to her basket. An hour later, she was on the move again, pushed open the door into Henry's bedroom and settled down next to him, her head by his feet, the two of them snoring loudly through the night.

6

Monty Slide

In March 1980 Monty Slide saw this advertisement for a property in Over Alderley in Cheshire:-

Tenure: Freehold
Price: £350,000
'St Edmund's': A charming and recently refurbished & extended detached country dwelling, believed to date from 1791 and in the same family since 1940. It offers spacious versatile accommodation with the highest quality of materials and fittings, retaining many original features. Extensive mature grounds to approx. 2.2 acres or thereabouts enjoying open views beyond. Reception hall, drawing room with vaulted ceiling & library above, dining room, living kitchen with double oven Aga, family room. Five bedrooms, 2 bathrooms en-suite and 2 shower rooms, utility room & laundry room. Double garage and substantial outbuildings.
Call our friendly team.

Monty knew the area – a wooded escarpment looking over the Cheshire plain, with fine views and walks and he could see himself settling down there, like a Victorian cotton baron from Manchester, in a substantial villa set back behind a heavily tree-lined street with a spacious and private garden of its own. So Monty Slide visited *St Edmund's*, met the vendors – a couple of retired vets, who had decided to down-size, now that their three children had left home – and immediately bought the property for the asking price, which delighted them. The money was in their bank within three working days. Then they went abroad for two month's holiday, visiting relatives in South Africa. On their return they were horrified to discover that during their time away Monty Slide had bulldozed the entire property, leaving nothing but rubble: their family home of many years had been flattened. One or two of their former neighbours protested but Monty was never on site. Then, to add insult to injury, they watched with increasing anger the construction of an eight foot wall round the entire property, the main access now being across a cattle grid and through an electric double-fronted iron gate of Palladian proportions.

Monty's house was to be in the Georgian style, based on James Gibbs' *Book of Architecture* (1728), a folio-sized pattern-book with magnificent plates, which Monty had bought many years before on a trip to Bath. This builders-manual became Monty's Bible, the inspiration for his new home in all its essentials: in its rigid symmetry, box-like form, classical proportions and external features. The interior, however, was to be much less traditional, stylish and modern, with an immense corridor of light oak going back the full depth of the house and leading to a large drawing-room, panelled in sage green, with floor-to-ceiling windows looking out on to a south-facing conservatory-cum-hothouse, containing exotic plants, whose heady perfume infused the whole building. In the basement was a bar, a cinema room, a Finnish sauna, a gym and a guest bedroom en-suite, a cork-lined study for Monty, and a massive 80 square meter heated swimming-pool, with a relaxation area and small kitchen. The interior was to be stylishly decorated and Monty was well aware of the investment potential of modern art. He had already ordered large canvases by Hockney, Bacon and Frink. The centrepiece, however, extending down the whole length of the central corridor, was to be two enormous murals by Gerhard Richter, chinese in effect. On the outside there was to be a separate garage for six cars, with the house protected from view by extensive plantings, shrubs and manicured lawns.

Within a year Monty's house was finished, and he was delighted with it. He often had people to stay – business associates, local politicians, magistrates, one or two MPs, lawyers and TV personalities. His hospitality became famous. He held parties by the pool, gambling nights, wine tastings and opera galas in a marquee set up on the lawn. A lot of money was raised for good causes – the local Hospice was a particular beneficiary – the champagne flowed, contacts were made and deals done, and there was always an endless stream of pretty and accommodating girls specially bused in from the clubs in Manchester. He was a popular and generous host. But his neighbours were outraged. They disapproved of the late nights, the noise, the screech of cars, the laughter, the sheer fun of it all; but above all they hated, absolutely loathed, his house. They said it was tasteless and over-blown, out of all proportion, in the wrong brick, an architectural nightmare. But Monty didn't care. And anyway, these neighbours were all hypocrites. They soon shut up when the footballers arrived. Then they were quick to sing to another tune, only too happy to move out, to sell their precious family homes for outrageous sums of money. And then, of course, the footballers did what Monty had done. Once the house was theirs, they demolished it and built something more suited to their athletic lifestyle and millionaire status. Soon the indoor swimming-pool, gym and sauna were no longer luxuries but accepted as the everyday necessities of life in the country. Within ten years the area round Alderley Edge, Wilmslow and Prestbury became the golden triangle – "Gold Trafford" – with chic restaurants, designer shops and speciality food suppliers. The house prices rocketed, there was nothing unusual in seeing Aston Martins and Porches parked outside *The Alderley Bar and Grill*, and tourists flooded in at weekends, like explorers on safari, hoping to catch a glimpse of their favourite soap star in the latest Versace or a celebrity chef in his suede baseball cap. Soon there were more millionaires here, more champagne drunk here, than anywhere else in Britain. And all this was due to Monty Slide, the first of the many.

The routine of Monty's working life hardly altered. During the week a car came to pick him up from home and drove him into Manchester. It was a different car every day – he had a pool of them at Western Hire: Mercedes, BMWs, Audis, Jags, all at his disposal. His car was his place of work, it was much safer that way, and so he was always on the move. And anyway he liked being seen about, seeing to invoices and receipts, meeting the staff, letting them know who was boss. He had two bodyguards – Ben and Matt, serious thick-set men in their forties, who'd known him since they were lads. To see Monty, you had to go through them. And then, in the evening, Monty loved returning to *St Edmund's*: the quiet drive back, work over, Ben and Matt following behind, then past the security guard, a wave of the hand, the gates slowly opening, feeling the crunch of gravel on the drive, the slow turn round the large flowerbed of rhododendrons and azaleas, then up the steps and in, and then perhaps some lemon tea, Channel Four News, and a light supper, usually fish, cooked for him by his housekeeper, Mrs Hamilton. Then a final hot drink, a book, and bed by 10.00.

Monty's delight in his house never diminished. Grander houses were built around him, larger and more ostentatious; but *St Edmund's* was his retreat, a place where he could get away from the pressures of work, well-guarded and safe. And it kept him fit. He loved swimming in his pool. Almost every night, with Ben and Matt looking on, he would bob about in a pink rubber dinghy, with a little portable radio on one side and a glass of orange juice on the other. He did his thinking while floating. Those visiting him would often have to stand on the edge of the pool, their voices echoing across the water, watching carefully as he paddled away and drifted off. Then, at other times, visitors had to wait outside the sauna, lounging about on the chairs and sofas, taking a drink at the bar, waiting for Monty to emerge, his normally pale face now quite pink, wrapped in a heavy-duty bathrobe of imperial purple. Although in his early sixties, he was the picture of health.

a small, slightly corpulent but dainty little man, fleshy, well-scrubbed and sweetly-smelling of expensive cologne. If his Lithuanian origins were visible at all it was in his cue-ball head and slightly flattened face, in the splayed nostrils, high cheekbones and wide forehead. He had three distinguishing physical characteristics. The first was a noticeable swelling of the upper eyelid, which gave his light grey eyes a rather hooded, owl-like appearance. The second was his hair. When young he had been very blond, almost platinum, but now he had gone quite white; and although bald on top, he wore his hair in long tresses on either side of his face, carefully groomed and tied back in a pony-tail, his eyebrows so light in colour as to be hardly noticeable, so giving his face an almost bleached effect. The third characteristic was his hands. Monty suffered from arthritis and all his fingers were slightly curved, giving a claw-like appearance, the joints gnarled and often painful: in winter he wore finger-mittens to keep them warm. His voice was soft, well-modulated, clear and precise, its tone by nature conciliatory.

Monty Slide was a man at ease with himself, enjoying to the full his position in life, reached, as he always said, solely by his own industry, by his ambition, imagination and intelligence. These were the qualities he valued most in others.. He was not a man of pretence or show; but, then, there was no need for that. Everybody had heard the rumours, those myths of power that circled him about, stories of ruthlessness and sudden violence. But looking at him these things were so difficult to believe. He was such a moderate man in his personal habits, teetotal, invariably polite and concerned for his subordinates, knowing all the names of their family members, asking after their children and their general health. That he was called a criminal by others he dismissed as no more than an expression of a moral code different from his own, one generated by a herd-like majority, adhered to by those incapable of decision and envious of success. For him there were no absolutes of conduct, no criteria of right and wrong. Everything was a matter of pragmatism, of doing what was necessary to achieve a designated goal, and achieving it became its own justification. So to cause pain and to terrorize others was quite wrong when done solely for its own sake – these were the actions of psychopaths, actions that Monty deplored – but they were not wrong when applied to achieve an objective. Cruelty, accordingly, was only valuable if surgically applied to obtain a result. For this reason Monty Slide believed himself to be entirely straightforward and above-board in all his business dealings.

This philosophy of life derived from Monty's study of war. His obsession with all things military was well-known and it gave him his nickname. He disliked it himself – thinking Field-Marshall Bernard Montgomery, the general of El Alamein, a second-rate commander – only Mountbatten was worse. But the nickname had stuck. There was nothing he could do about it now: he would always be "Monty". The library at *St Edmund's* was festooned with pictures and framed autographs, with signed letters from Patton, Rommel, Zhukov and Slim ("the greatest of the British generals"). Then, on another wall, he had portraits of those he considered the great captains of history. It was an eclectic choice: some predictable – Hannibal, Alexander, Caesar and Napoleon

– others less so: Marlborough, Cromwell, Robert E. Lee, General Giap. He had made a special study of Hannibal and had learned a lot from his campaigns. The famous deceptions and feints, the traps laid, the march across the Alps, hiding an entire army among the reeds of Trasimene, the battles of Trebbia and Cannae – all had demonstrated that morality had no place on the battlefield; that if you wanted to win, to defeat your opponent, then everything was permitted. And it was just the same in business, there was really no difference. And then there was Hannibal's legendary cruelty: those tales of mutilations, crucifixions, the destruction of whole towns and villages, women and children slaughtered. Most of it was untrue. In reality Hannibal was no worse than any of his contemporaries: it was just that he had let the legend stand, fostered it and let is spread. And there he proved himself the master psychologist. For in warfare reputation was everything. To terrorize the enemy *before* a battle was a great art. You had to let their imaginations work overtime, you had to get them thinking about the terrors to come, how they would be treated in defeat. This could break their resistance right from the start. Monty did the same. He was not a cruel man, he hated physical aggression and pain; but it was necessary that people believed in his cruelty, that he was pitiless in his desires, that what he would do to his enemies and their families would be measured and persistent. Sometimes, of course, Ben and Matt had to be unpleasant, had to demonstrate that it wasn't all show. That couldn't be avoided. But then word spread and people came to see that Monty wasn't a man of empty threats. So, yes, there was no question about it: it was much easier doing business with people who were afraid. Then, by and large, they told you the truth.

★★★

The day after Henry's meal with Terence and Twinkie – so eight days after the murders – there was a meeting at *Tonino's*, a well-known Manchester delicatessen and pizzeria. It took place in a tiny box room at the end of a corridor stacked high on either side with wooden crates of fresh vegetables and various types of dried pasta and herbs. Overlaying everything was the delicious and heavy aroma of coffee and new-made bread. Matt stood guard outside the room and inside were Monty, Ben and a man nicknamed "Smudge". There was just enough space for two straight-backed wooden chairs. Monty sat on one and Smudge on the other, no more than two feet away. Smudge was very fidgety, constantly rubbing his hands together, sometimes looking up nervously at Ben standing by the door. Monty leant forward, placed his hand on Smudge's knee, and gave it a slight squeeze. Smudge looked down and shivered to see Monty's mittened fingers resting lightly on his trousers.

'Now, Smudge,' Monty began, 'relax, there's nothing to worry about. I only want to ask you a few questions.'

'If it's about the money, Mr Monty, I can explain.'

'Well, I must be honest with you, Smudge, it *is* about the money. But it's not just that. Now you owe me...how much is it?'

'It's 200 quid, Mr Monty. I've got about 100 so far, but it's taking a bit of time to get the rest. Business has been

117

bad, very bad. Nobody wants decent tailoring anymore, they all buy off the peg. I explained all this to Ben.'

'He did, Monty', agreed Ben, reluctantly, looking down at Smudge as something better scraped off his shoe.

'I know business is bad, Smudge,' continued Monty. 'I understand, I really do, and I still wear the suit you made me. Nice tweed. But times, Smudge, are hard. You know that. And you also know that I'm always ready to help. But I'm not a charity, Smudge, I have my overheads. So while I'm quite happy to lend money to my friends, they quickly cease to be my friends if they don't pay me back. You understand me? I feel cheated, betrayed, Smudge, and I really don't like being let down like that. I feel disappointed. But then you said something else to Ben, didn't you? You said that you had something to sell, something valuable, something that would clean the slate. That's what you said, didn't you, Smudge. I haven't misunderstood you, have I?'

'No, that's right, Mr Monty, I did say that.'

'And then, Smudge, you used a magic word. You said it to Ben. Now what was that word, Smudge? You tell me.'

'The word, Mr Monty, was "Bloodhound". That's what I said to Ben there.'

'Yes, that's what he said, Monty,' confirmed Ben.

'And when you said that word, Smudge,' continued Monty, 'you were not of course referring to dogs, were you? Not to our canine friends, Smudge, but to something else. Or should I say to *someone else*?

'That's right, Mr Monty, it was the copper I was referring to.'

'You mean Chief Superintendent Henry Fairest?'

'Yes, that's right, Mr Monty, the big feller.'

'So what you've got to tell me, Smudge, is something to do with this officer, something you think is valuable. That's right, isn't it? Just nod your head. Good. So we agree. And you know, of course, that Fairest and I go back a long way, a very long way. And I have to tell you, Smudge, that I'm not fond of this person, he's not among my favourites, because he's sometimes got in the way of business. And that's something I hate. Why, only recently I had a nice thing going with some lovely nuns, charming girls, but that had to stop because of this man and I lost quite a bit of money. So I wasn't happy and I have to admit that I'm still not happy about it, not at all. I wasn't happy, was I, Ben?'

'You were very unhappy, Monty. I've never seen you so unhappy.'

'Well, I wouldn't quite say that, Ben,' said Monty smiling broadly and rocking back in his chair. 'No, that's going bit too far. I wasn't heart-broken, inconsolable, but I was certainly upset. Anyway, let's just say my plans didn't mature and we'll leave it at that. So you see, Smudge, I'm always interested to hear anything to do with this particular person, anything at all. And I reward people who tell me things about him. So if what you tell me is useful, then I'll let you off the 200 quid and we'll call it quits.'

'But, Mr Monty, how will I know whether it's useful or not? I mean, if I tell you and it's not useful, then I'm back where I started.'

'Not quite,' said Monty, leaning forward and lightly tapping Smudge's knee. 'Because I now know (tap! tap!) that you know something that I don't know (tap! tap!) and that's a big difference, to me at least (squeeze!). So, I'm sorry, Smudge, you're going to have to tell me. Now what was it?' And then there was the slightest shift of Monty's eyes up towards Ben, standing at the door. Smudge turned round in his chair, saw Ben staring impassively down at him, swallowed hard, and changed his mind.

'Yes, well, it's like this, Mr Monty. We all heard about your driver, Dick, him being done in. And I was very sorry to hear that, course I was, very sorry. And then there was the sister, a pretty girl, Maddy, knew her slightly, down the clubs. Now there's this friend of mine, works in the hospital, a kind of porter, wheeling the bodies about, chucking out the body parts. He's been there for years. Nobody takes any notice of him. Which is good, 'cos he hears things. And then one day, in comes the big feller, and he's chatting with Dr Thomas, the Doc who's in charge of the case, see, the case of Dick and his sister, I mean he's the one who's opened them up and had a look inside, and anyway my friend hears them talking, about the case I mean, the murders…'

'Get on with it, Smudge, we haven't got all bloody day,' says Ben. 'Just tell us what they said.'

'I'm getting to it, Ben. I'm trying. So there they was chatting, with my friend listening, and then the Doc tells Fairest that the girl, Dick's sister that is, was in the family way, three month's gone, she was. My friend said that, when he heard that, the big feller went quite white and swore. That's all I know, Mr Monty. I'm sure nobody else knows, so I thought it best to tell you. And that's why I contacted Ben. And, honest, that's all I know, Mr Monty, it really is.'

'Smudge, I'll tell you this. I didn't know that and, yes, that's useful, and a deal's a deal. So I'll let you off the money. Now you do something for me. Tell your friend that there'll always be something in it for him if he keeps his ear to the ground and keeps in touch. You know Ben's number, so give it to him, to this friend of yours. OK, Smudge?'

'That's great, Mr Monty, really kind. Anything to be helpful. Yes, I'll tell my friend. I'm sure he'll...

'Fuck off, Smudge,' said Ben, opening the door.

When Smudge had left, Monty turned to Ben: 'What do we know about the girl? Was she one of ours?'

'She was, Monty, part-time, but that was some time ago.' said Ben. 'She worked in the parlour on Duke Street, couple of times a week, but no complaints from Susie, who runs the joint. Kept her hours, good with the customers. In-calls and out-calls, the usual thing. Then she left, and Susie heard that she's at the bar at the *Imperial Hotel*, making quite a nice little living off the business-types, them coming up for a night or two. So a whore, Monty, but a tough tart, knew what's what, kept her nose clean, a pretty girl but hard, wanted to get on, up to anything for readies.'

'Who's the barman at the *Imperial*? Did he run her?'

'I'll get the name, Monty; but the word is she was freelancing, on her own; but he must have got a percentage, some kick-back, giving the nod to customers and then the free drinks, the usual thing. So there'll be something there, Monty. Want me to check?'

'Yes, you do that, Ben. Go and have a word. Take Matt. Discreetly, mind. No frighteners. What I want are some names, the names of the men. There'll be some regulars. And tell me, Ben, what about our Dickie? Did he know about his sister, what she was up to?'

'I don't think so, Monty. Might have done, of course, but I'd be surprised. He was a simple lad, a bit backward, if you ask me, just loved his cars and driving you about.'

'Well, he was good at that. Very quiet. I liked him, nice boy. Never said anything about his sister, not a word. But the pregnancy's the key here, Ben. So let's take it from there. I want some names, Ben, it's the names that'll get us in. Yes, let's do it before Fairest gets there! Because I know him, he'll be there soon enough. Understand me, Ben? Before him! Then, who knows, we might have some fun and make some money!'

Monty got up from his chair. Ben opened the door for him and followed him out, past Matt on guard outside. The three of them went through the back exit and entered an alley behind the pizzeria. Here Monty's car was waiting for him, his car of the day, a Jag, his new driver, Rob Sharpe, leaning against it, a cigarette cupped between thumb and forefinger. Seeing Monty, he took a quick drag, flicked the fag on to the pavement, scrubbed it with his foot, and opened the door. Monty got in the back seat and the car drove off. Ben and Matt hurried further down the alley to a black BMW, jumped in, and accelerated fast out of the back street to fall in behind Monty's car.

★★★

The Imperial Hotel, just off Mosley Street, was always one of Manchester's grandest hotels: a Victorian building, its splendour still visible in the heavy mahogany panelling, ornate brickwork and arched windows. But ten years ago it had a complete make-over. Go there now and it is hardly recognizable. The central lobby is dominated by an enormous chandelier of pink Murano glass hanging from a domed ceiling above a polished limestone floor, with deep armchairs in heavy leather on either side of a pillared colonnade, at the end of which stands, discreetly to one side, the reception desk. To the left is the Hotel restaurant and to the right the bar. The bar is the main attraction, said to be the longest in the City, seventy feet in length. The atmosphere here is chic and deliberately retro, catering for middle-aged men on large expense accounts, overworked and overpaid, with nothing to do in the evenings and ready to play away from home. This explains The Imperial's main attraction: that scattering of girls along the bar, sitting on high stools, sipping their drinks, looking bored and disdainful, but in reality dressed up and ready for work.

On the evening of Monty's meeting with Smudge, Ben and Matt arrived at *The Imperial Hotel* at about 10.15. They sat together on two stools and studied the menu of drinks. The barman came up to them and asked for their orders.

'What are you having, Matt?' asked Ben.

'I think I'll have a Whisky Sour,' replied Matt.

'And I'll have an Old Fashioned,' said Ben, putting the menu back on the bar.

'So two bourbon lovers!' said the barmen, smiling.

'That's us,' said Ben. 'Nothing fancy.'

A little later the barmen returned with their drinks and stood in front of Ben and Matt, cleaning glasses with a white cloth, watching them as they sipped their drinks. He was a slim man in his forties, Italian-looking, with slicked-back corrugated hair gleaming with gel, neatly dressed in black, with a tie-on bow tie and dark green silk waistcoat.

'You two gentlemen just in for the night?' he asked.

'That's right, my friend. Business and bored.'

'Very bored,' sighed Matt. 'So bored I could die of it.'

'What are you in, then?', asked the barmen.

Ben looked up at him. 'Waste Management. Doesn't sound much fun, does it? But you'd be surprised how much money there is in rubbish. People are always throwing things away.'

'That's the trouble with a consumer society,' said Matt, 'it's a throw-away culture.'

'You're right there, Matt, absolutely right. It wasn't always like that. My Mum kept everything, old clothes, newspapers, everything. But then she went through the War!'

'So she did, Ben. I remember that, she never threw anything away, a real horder your Mum was. But things was different then, Ben. They all pulled together under Winston. All gone now.'

'So where are you two from?' asked the barmen.

'Bolton,' replied Ben, looking down at his drink.

'Bolton?' said Matt, looking sideways at Ben. 'Oh, yes, Bolton! Ha! That's right. From Bolton. You ever been there…? Sorry, what did you say your name was?' he asked the barman.

'Brian. No, I've never been to Bolton.'

'Well, my advice, Brian, is steer clear of Bolton. There's nothing there, it's a bloody desert, bleak, dirty, but full of rubbish.'

'So tell me, Brian,' said Ben, leaning confidentially

across the bar, and dropping his voice. 'Those ladies over there. They looking for company?'

Brian grinned. 'Well, they might be. You want me to ask?'

'Hang on a bit, Brian, not so fast. We must finish our drinks first, get ourselves in the mood. But just let me say, to put your mind at rest, that my friend and me, we travel around, stay in lots of places, usually very nice, we can afford them. And we always try to be where there's a little action, we being sociable types. So, Brian, I have to ask, being a business man: How much? Do you know? I mean, that redhead over there, she's lovely. A hooker, right? How much she'd be then?'

Brian looked under the bar and brought out a pad and pencil and scribbled something down. Then he pushed the pad towards Ben.

'500 quid!! You're kidding me! That's a hell of a lot for a night, Brian?'

'The hour!' whispered Brian.

'500 quid for an hour! Bloody hell, Brian, what the fuck do you get for that? A bloody gymnast?'

'Calm down, Ben,' said Matt, patting him on the shoulder. 'I warned you. I told you it'd be expensive. I told you, remember? But we can afford it and we're only here for the night. So let's make the most of it. And don't forget, Ben, Brian was recommended.'

'Recommended?' asked Brian.

'Well, not of course by name,' continued Matt. 'I mean our friend didn't know your name was Brian, Brian. No, all he said was "See the barman at *The Imperial*."'

'So, gentlemen, may I ask, this friend of yours, the one who recommended me, what was his name?'

'His name, Brian, is Monty Slide. And he was quite particular. He said that when we got here we was to mention his name to you, and that when we mentioned it you would look after us. That's what he said, Matt, wasn't it?'

'Yup,' replied Matt. 'He was very precise, always is. Speak to the barman at *The Imperial*. He'll see you right. That's what Monty said.'

Brian the barman had stopped cleaning glasses, had put his cloth down on the bar, and was now fixing them with a steady look. 'Monty Slide. No, sorry lads, never heard of him. We gets lots of gentlemen in here, of course, so I may have met him without knowing. But I can't remember anybody of that name.'

Ben raised his hands in astonishment and looked at Matt. 'Did you hear that, Matt? Here's a bloke never heard of Monty Slide! Well, well! Well, I never! Have you ever heard of such a thing, Matt?'

'Never heard of Monty! I can hardly believe it, Ben. What's the world coming to? All we need now is for the sky to darken and the bloody Four Horsemen of the Apocalypse to appear and that would really make my day. Never heard of Monty indeed. I don't believe it. I can hardly take it in!'

'And what's more,' continued Ben, now reaching across the bar and gently prodding Brian's green waistcoat, 'this Monty, our friend you don't remember, not only told us about you, Brian, but also about one of your girls, a girl that he said we should certainly look up, that was often here of an evening, real friendly, if you know what I mean. What was her name, Matt?'

'Her name? Now you ask me. What was it? Madge? Maisie? Madonna? Moira? Oh, it's terrible this, I'm always forgetting things. It must be my age. And I tell you, it's getting worse. Why, sometimes I get up in the morning, look in the mirror, and ask myself "Who the fuck's that?" And that's the truth! I should see a doctor, get treatment. Hmmm…Melody? Margaret? Marion? No, I've got it! Maddy! That's it, that's her name. Maddy her name was.'

'That's no good, Matt. Can't you remember her surname?'

'Her surname? Oh, God, Ben, really this is too much, it's like being on bloody *Mastermind*. Now what the bugger was it? But hang on, it's coming to me, it's there, I can feel it, it's just on the tip if my tongue. I've got it! I've got it! Her name was Kelly. That's it! Maddy Kelly. Monty said she was a pretty little thing, always ready for a laugh.'

Brian had now gone quite pale. He said, 'No, sorry, lads, no, I don't know anybody by that name. Sorry I can't help. Now, if you don't mind…I've got other customers over there. So nice talking to you… but I've got to get along.' And he started to move further down the bar; but Ben caught his hand and held it in a vice-like grip, making Brian wince.

'Well, we do mind, Brian, because we haven't finished yet. You may have missed what my friend Matt was saying about this Maddy. Perhaps you missed the past tense. Matt said she *was* a pretty thing. *Was*, Brian, *was*! And that tense is very appropriate because, as we speak, our poor Maddy is lying in a steel drawer in a hospital mortuary, all shaved and scrubbed clean, with half her innards missing. And because our friend Monty was so fond of this Maddy, just like a daughter to him she was, he wants to know why this has happened, why his little girl ended up like she did, on a slab, all naked, with doctors poking around her parts. And he thinks, and I think, that you might know something about that.'

'No, sorry, lads, as I said, I don't know anything about this, really I don't, you've got the wrong bloke there. Now, if you'll just let me get on...' But Ben gripped his hand harder, so hard that Brian could hear his knuckles cracking, bringing tears to his eyes. Then Matt walked slowly round the bar, came up behind him and patted him gently on the back. 'Do you know you've gone quite pale, Brian, really quite peaky. Are you sure you're OK, old cocky? You don't look good to me, not good at all, really poorly. Feeling unwell? What do you think, Ben?'

'I think he needs the bathroom,' said Ben. 'He looks as if he could faint, quite done in. It's the shock, of course, hearing about all these old pals he's never heard of. I think we should take him to the toilet and help him out. He looks ready to puke. Don't you think that's a good idea, Matt? Yes, let's take him to wash his hands. Otherwise I'd be worried about him and wouldn't sleep nights.'

'So where's the Gents, Brian?' asked Matt. 'Ah, yes, I see it, over there, in the corner. Come on, then, I'm sure we can sort you out and you'll feel ever so much better after. There you go. Excuse us, ladies, passing through. Now that was easy, wasn't it, Brian? Oh, I like this: lovely room, clean towels, soap dispensers, proper porcelain, smells of lavender. Shut the door, Ben. This won't take long. Now let's have a little chat, Brian, about our mutual friends, the friends you know nothing about.'

★★★

128

'I'm sorry, Monty, it took longer than expected, and Matt here, God bless him, got quite carried away. Anyway the little toe-rag will be off work for a couple of days, nothing serious. A & E will soon fix him up.'

'I couldn't help myself, Monty, and I apologize. But after all (here turning to Ben and grinning broadly) that's what boys from Bolton do!'

It was 8.30 the next morning and the three of them were sitting outside Monty's sauna, drinking coffee and eating croissant. Monty was in his purple dressing-gown, reading from a little black book.

'And this is the list? You're sure this is it?'

'Oh, it's the list all right, Monty,' confirmed Ben. 'He was just a poncey little creep. Shitting himself with fright, he was. Lucky we were in the Gents, that's all I can say. Anyway, he had his little book close by. Kept it under the counter, in an ice-bucket. On each page is a girl's name – Scarlett, Rowena, Tania, Sasha, Desireé, Lorraine, lots of them, fourteen in all – and then below the names are lists of initials and telephone numbers. Average about twenty each. So quite a little stable of ladies. You'll see that our Maddy has fifteen. So those'll be her regulars. Brian was very confiding in the end, desperate to help he was. The punters ring him to say what night they'll be staying, and then the silly sod rings back with the room number and time. The gents then arrive, go to work, visit their clients or whatever, come back and pay the girl for the hour or night, with Brian getting his cut. It's a simple arrangement. But these guys must be classy, what with those prices. 500 quid an hour, Monty! That's a lot of money for a shag.'

'That's nothing, Ben,' replied Monty. 'There's a place

I know down in London, a really posh service, with girls charging £3000 a night, usually for chinks or Arabs, and that doesn't include the dinner and drinks. Solicitors, doctors, teachers, you'd be surprised at the types, well-spoken and educated, good talkers with nice manners, can take them anywhere, lovely girls. But, anyway, even if this Brian was taking a low cut, not a pimp's usual 50% – let's say just 10% – he'd still be in the money. Four girls working would make him £200 a night, and that's probably very conservative, what with the weekends and the odd overnights. So knocking two grand a week. A nice little earner.'

'So what do you want to do, Monty?'

'We'll take the business over: it's too good to miss. When he's recovered, Ben, you go round and see him. Tell him we take 75% from now on, with us providing the usual insurances and safeguards. If he says "No", tell him he'll be out on his ear in a week. But he won't refuse: he'll still be making a good living from the left-overs.' Then Monty tapped the little black book. 'But I want names for these initials. I want to know who these guys are.'

'For all of them?' asked Ben.

'No, just for Maddy's lot. I don't want to kill the business. So just her names. And then, when we have them, when we know who they are, why then I'll make a few calls. Because, lads, don't forget, one of these punters may well be our boy, the boy who did for our Maddy. And I bet it's some important chappie, with a reputation, with a big job, responsibilities, kids and school fees. That's my guess. And I'll tell you something else…' – here Monty bent down over the little black book, sniffed at it and then breathed in deeply, his nose almost touching the paper

– 'I smell money! I can smell it, it's there all right. I can always tell.' And he sniffed again and licked his lips. Then he stood up, placed the little black book on a table, took off his dressing-gown, undid his pony-tail, walked to the edge of the pool, got hold of his rubber dinghy, threw it in and, taking careful aim, jumped on top of it. When he'd squeaked himself in, he started to paddle, faster and faster, towards the middle. Then, drifting to a stop and leaning back, he started to sing in a light tenor voice:

As some day it may happen that a victim must be found,
I've got a little list – I've got a little list
Of society offenders who might well be underground,
And who never would be missed – who never would be missed!

Monty could hardly contain himself. He was laughing out loud and wriggling with pleasure, splashing the water on either side with the palm of his hands. Ben and Matt stood up and were now standing by the pool's edge, grinning back, delighted to see their boss so full of fun. Monty shouted back at them: 'Look at me, boys! Look at me! I may be floating but you take care! I'm the Lord High Executioner, that's who I am. So chop, chop, and off with their bloody heads!' And with that, Monty Slide, his normally pale face now glowing with happiness, quite flushed pink, steered himself further across his pool, hitting the water hard with each beat of the song, and singing out:-

And apologetic statesmen of a compromising kind,
Such as – What d'ye call him   Thing'em-bob, and

likewise -Never-mind,
And 'St-'st-'st – and What's-his-name, and also You-
know-who -
The task of filling up the blanks I'd rather leave to you.
But it really doesn't matter whom you put upon the list,
For they'd none of 'em be missed – they'd none of 'em be
missed!

Ben and Matt were now doubled up with laughter, bent over, giggling like schoolboys. Straightening up, they pumped the air with their fists, and started to dance, arm in arm, pattering their feet in a little vaudeville routine, like some end-of-pier double-act – right leg forward and left leg back, left leg forward and right leg back – pirouetting about in little circles and clapping their hands together above their heads. Then, with their lower-pitched voices echoing across the pool, they joined in unison with Monty and sang out the chorus:

He's got 'em on the list – he's got 'em on the list;
And they'll none of 'em be missed – they'll none of 'em be
missed.

7

Monty, Henry and
Reginald Lockyer, M.P

Monty Slide was right. Henry Fairest was fast closing in and soon knew what Monty Slide had just discovered: that Maddy Kelly had once worked as a prostitute at the *Belles* parlour on Duke Street in Manchester. It was a well-known brothel, one of the few tolerated by the police as part of their policy to stop curb-crawling and to get the girls off the streets. Susie, who ran the place, had been quite forthcoming. Maddy had been hard-working and honest, never cheating on her or her customers. Susie said nothing about *The Imperial Hotel.* She was a sensible girl: that was information reserved for Monty. So she played dumb. All Susie said was that Maddy had just dropped out of sight: she might have moved away from Manchester or gone abroad. These girls were all pretty shiftless, with no family roots, which, of course, made reading about her murder all the more shocking. It had quite taken her breath away, she had been really quite upset, because she was a nice kid really, who only wanted to get on and make something of herself. So Henry didn't know what Monty knew: about *The Imperial Hotel,* Brian the Barman and his little black book.

But Henry knew something that Monty didn't know. Western Hire Cars had supplied him with Dickie's home address, a council house in Ardwick, just behind the Asda supermarket: it had a tiny kitchen, with food still in the fridge, a small bathroom and sitting-room, with two small bedrooms. Maddy's bedroom was quite tastefully furnished, with rugs and a large brass bed, her few clothes neatly hanging in the wardrobe. Dickie's was scruffy and a mess, the bed unmade, a full ashtray beside it, socks and shirts scattered on the floor. There had been an important find. Tucked away in a copy of *Hello!* magazine, the police found a Lloyds Bank cheque book in the name of Richard Kelly, and from that they discovered that the account was in credit to the tune of £15,000. This sum of money had been deposited in cash payments at regular intervals, some of £500 each, some between £1000-£2000, all within the last four months. The last payment was made only three days before Maddy's death. So Henry's mind had begun to work, and it hadn't really been all that difficult to figure it out. Maddy had once been a prostitute. So perhaps, at the time of her murder, she was still a working girl, still leading the life, but now up a notch, more ambitious, with wealthy clients. And then she got pregnant by one of them. Perhaps she knew who the father was and perhaps she didn't. But that didn't matter. She could still put the pressure on, still play the innocent and threaten exposure, and make a tidy sum blackmailing the punters, hiding it away in Dickie's bank account. And, then, perhaps, in the end, she had gone just that bit too far, got greedy and demanded too much from the wrong man, from someone with a lot to lose. So that might be it. Here at least was a motive for the murders:

someone wealthy, perhaps a powerful man, who wasn't going to be pushed around by a hooker on the make and so took steps to silence her and her conniving brother. On that point Henry Fairest and Monty Slide were both agreed.

***

As Ben had said, there were fifteen names on Monty's "little list": initials on one side, telephone number on the other. Brian, who was now out of hospital and very keen to help, supplied the details. They'd double-checked and it hadn't taken long, just a couple of days, to be sure about the names. As Monty had guessed, they were an interesting lot. The majority were businessmen, coming up to Manchester on a regular basis – men in advertising, the building trade, computers and engineering – but there was also a solicitor working in Cheadle, a Headmaster, a barrister, a Trade Union official, and, most interesting of all, a local MP, who came up from Westminster every two weeks for his surgery on a Friday at 10 am in a local Primary School, overnighting at *The Imperial*, and travelling back to London the next day. So Monty made an appointment. He was a constituent, after all.

Twelve days after the murders, Monty, Ben and Matt drove to St Xavier's Roman Catholic Primary School. The school stands among the patchwork of houses and streets almost directly below the A 57 flyover, just visible as you travel into Manchester along the Mancunian Way. Ben and Matt stayed in the car, while Monty went in alone. He sat down to wait in a classroom just off the main corridor. He was early, so there were not many people there. two couples chatting together and a rather glum-looking individual, on his own, looking preoccupied and tense. Chairs had been placed around the wall and in the middle were six low tables with little stools neatly tucked beneath them. The walls were covered in brightly-coloured charts: for grammar, punctuation, vocabulary and spelling, about maths and money, about earth and space, rain forests and the environment and a much larger chart with cartoons of all the Kings and Queens of England. One side of the classroom displayed the children's art after a visit to the Zoo – pictures of giraffes, lions, elephants, monkeys, hippos and oistrichs – all painted in bright watercolours. Monty walked over to look at them. While he was standing there he turned to see a young mother come in with her son, aged about eight. She went to one of the little tables, brought out a colouring book and some crayons, settled the little boy down on a stool, ruffled his hair, and went to sit against the wall, waiting her turn with the others. The boy was soon absorbed in his book, his head bent over it, taking up one crayon, then another, rubbing away at the page. Monty stood over him and looked down.

'What's this then?' he asked.

'It's the Battle of Hastings', the boy replied, not turning round. 'That's William the Conqueror and that's King Harold. He's the one with an arrow in his eye.'

'That's wonderful, that really is! But you need more red round the eye. I mean if you got an arrow in your eye, there'd be blood, lots of it. Yes, that's much better, much better. More red. That's it! You've got real talent, you're doing a great job. Lovely colours, quite life-like.' Then, turning towards the boy's mother, he said again, 'He's got real talent, your son, he really has. A proper artist, he is!' The mother beamed back at him. Then he turned back to the boy, who was now looking up at him. Monty extended his mittened fingers and kneaded him gently on the shoulder.

'You should go to Hastings, my son, your really should, see the battlefield. Go on a school trip or something. I've been twice. And I bet you didn't know that Harold could have won. Oh yes, he could, if he'd played his cards right. Harold was at the top of Senlac hill and William was at the bottom; and every time the Normans tried to get up the hill, they were beaten back. Heavy armour, of course, arrows raining down. Then the Saxons did something daft. Instead of staying put, at the top, they pursued the Normans down the hill – thought they were retreating, see – and so lost their defensive position. Can you believe it? A terrible blunder, a basic mistake. They should have known better. Because when Harold's men got to the bottom – he only had infantry, no horses – the Normans were waiting for them, and they had cavalry, so of course they cut them to pieces, bodies all over the place, with the archers finishing them off. It lasted all day.'

'Mr Packer?'

'And it was a real slaughter. No prisoners, probably 6000 dead in total, with the English bodies just left to rot. Stacked in heaps they were, the grass slippy with blood, and the stench must have been….'

'Mr Packer?'

Monty turned round to see a middle-aged lady looking at him, frowning slightly, with pursed lips.

'Are you Mr Packer? Don't you have an appointment to see Mr Lockyer?'

'Oh, sorry luv, I was just talking to this little lad here. Just coming.' Monty turned to pat the little boy on the head but the boy had moved from his seat and had gone back to sit with his mother, cuddled up beside her. So Monty waved at him and then went into the next room through some double-doors. It was the school assembly hall, with high windows, a raised stage at the back and a canopied roof of wood. Chairs and desks were neatly stacked along the walls and in a corner stood a covered upright piano. Behind a table in the middle of the room sat a man in his middle forties, of clean good looks, reading through some notes. He was smartly dressed in a pin-stripped suit with a bright blue tie. As Monty entered, he stood up and extended his hand, greeting Monty with a professional smile. Monty took his hand in both of his.

'Mr Packer, good morning. I'm Reginald Lockyer. Do please sit down. Now, tell me how I can help? What seems to be the trouble?'

'I'll explain that in a moment, Mr Lockyer. But may I first ask about the lady who just brought me in?'

'Oh, that's my assistant, Mrs Shaw. Don't worry about her, she's very discreet. But it helps me if she keeps notes of what is said.'

'I'm sure it does, Mr Lockyer,' replied Monty, looking round and smiling broadly at Mrs Shaw, who was sitting some distance away in a corner. 'I'm sure it must be very helpful, keeping a record. But in this particular case, I'd prefer it, if you don't mind, if I could see you alone. Because what I have to say is rather embarrassing and I'd feel much happier just telling you privately. I mean, if you think it necessary, you can always tell Mrs Shaw afterwards. I shall rely on your judgment and discretion.'

'Well, if you insist, Mr Packer'. Lockyer gave a brief nod towards Mrs Shaw, who picked up her things and left the room.

'Now, Mr Packer,' said the MP, leaning back in his chair, and placing his hands across his stomach. 'Now we're alone, I must make clear to you that everything you say to me will be treated in absolute confidence. So don't you worry. There's really nothing to be nervous about, nothing at all. So tell me, what's the problem?'

Monty leant forward in a confidential manner, furtively looked round the room, and asked in a slightly hesitant voice, 'Have you ever heard of Monty Slide?'

'Well, as a matter of fact, I have heard of Monty Slide, although I've never met him. We move, I think, in rather different social circles. But I believe that one or two of my colleagues in the House have had dealings with him. Quite a power in the land, I'm told.'

'That he is, Mr Lockyer, that he is. And I say this because nobody knows Monty Slide like I know Monty Slide. Absolutely nobody. And all I can say about him is that he is a totally honest man in all his business dealings, his word is his bond. If he says a thing will be done, it's done. You can absolutely trust him on matters of business. He always, absolutely always, tells the truth. I've never known him tell a lie.'

'Well, I'm glad to hear it, Mr Packer. An honourable man, obviously, which is nice to know. But I'm not sure where this is getting us. Would you be a little bit more specific about your problem?'

'Of course, Mr Lockyer. There I am rabbiting on, with other people waiting outside. So let me say, first of all, that when I say that Monty Slide always tells the truth, I must also tell you that today, right now, this instant, is an exception, the only one I know of, believe me. Because I have to confess that my name is not Packer. No, it's... well, it's Slide. Yes, I am the afore-mentioned Monty Slide.' Here Monty rocked back in his chair, grinned, smoothed back his white hair and adjusted his pony-tail.

'You are Monty Slide?' asked Lockyer, clearly puzzled and frowning slightly. 'I'm sorry, I don't understand. Why come here using a false name?'

'It all has to do with leakage, Mr Lockyer. I wanted absolutely nobody knowing that I was coming to see you. I mean, if the Press got hold of it...Well, I mean it would be a disaster.'

As soon as Monty mentioned the Press, Reginald Lockyer's manner changed. He sat upright in his chair, cocked his head to one side and raised an eyebrow. 'Why a disaster?' he asked, his eyes narrowing

'Oh, Mr Lockyer, I haven't made myself clear. Certainly a disaster, a real career stopper. But not for me. For you!'

'For me? Why for me?'

'Well, I'll come straight to the point, Mr Lockyer, I shan't beat about the bush. I owe you that much. But please remember what I said just now: that I'm a man of my word. So. You have been a Member of Parliament for seven years, and my friends in Westminster – and I have lots of them there – tell me that one day you may well be in the Cabinet. I believe them. So you are a man after my own heart, Mr Lockyer, you really are, a gentleman of ambition and intelligence, and I like that. You live in London, at No.14 Bouvery Street in Wandsworth, a nice Victorian detached house. Must be worth a bomb now, what with London prices being what they are. You are a married man, married to your wife, Jean, for 16 years. You have two children: Sammy, aged 14, and Ginny, aged 12. Both educated privately. You yourself are not a wealthy man, but your wife is a wealthy woman. Father was in shipping. So on the face of it, all seems hunky-dory, the very picture of domestic bliss. But that's not quite true, is it, Mr Lockyer? I wish it were, because I respect family values, but it isn't, I'm sorry to say. Because, when you think about it, something must be lacking, because from what I hear you have certain... how shall I put it?...needs...needs that you don't find at home. So you find them elsewhere, outside the nest. And I know this because whenever you come up to Manchester you always stay at *The Imperial Hotel*; and because, before you arrive, you always contact the barman, Brian his name is, and Brian sets you up with a girl called Maddy. And she's expensive, Mr Lockyer, very expensive Maddy is. Her basic rate is £500 an hour, and that's not including extras. And I bet you don't put that on your Parliamentary expenses. And this has been going on for some time, you travelling up on a Friday night and seeing young Maddy at *The Imperial Hotel*.'

Reginald Lockyer had turned to stone.

'And you might well ask me how I know all this. If I was in your place, I'd wonder too. "How on earth does Monty Slide know all this?" That's what I'd be asking myself: "How'd he find all this out then?" Well, the answer is simple. You weren't the only one making out with the ladies at *The Imperial Hotel*. Oh, no There were others besides yourself, quite a few in fact, respectable gents just like you, engaging in a bit of extra curricula. And managing all those lovely girls – you must have seen them, all dolled up at the bar – running them must have been a complicated business, a real nightmare, I shouldn't wonder. One bloke wants to see Lorraine, another wants Desireé, and you wanting Maddy. So Brian, not to get muddled, not to get confused with all these special arrangements, keeps a little black book. You can't blame him really, I'd do the same – kept it under the bar he did, in an ice-bucket to be exact – and in this book was a list, with names and telephone numbers. At the top of the page was the girl's name, and below that were the punters' numbers. And let me tell you, these men are an interesting lot, wealthy with reputations, most of them much better off than you, with their own money, not having to make do on an MP's salary. I know all this, Mr Lockyer, because Brian's book, by a very circuitous route, which I won't bore you with, has come into my possession. It's now *my* little black book.'

Reginald Lockyer still did not speak, but his face was pale, now glistening with a fine sheen of sweat, as if dipped in varnish.

'But what makes your case, Mr Lockyer, so very, very special – what elevates it above all the others – has to do with our poor Maddy. I have to say that for a short time Maddy was in my employ. I can't say that I remember her exactly – I have quite a large work-force – but nevertheless there was a personal connection, not with her, but with her brother, Dickie. Dickie, I have to say, was a lovely lad, and he worked for me as my driver. Drove me about, he did. So it would be true to say that both of them – both Maddy and Dickie –

had, at one time or other, worked for yours truly. And I was fond of that boy, Mr Lockyer, I really was, admittedly not too bright, if you get my meaning, but quiet and sensible. Well, you can imagine how I felt when I heard about the terrible tragedy up at the Newtown Estate. Both murdered. Of course no need to tell you, Mr Lockyer. What happened was plastered all over the place, the news, the telly. And it must have given you a bit of a shock to see such a familiar face looming up at you from the front pages of *The Daily Telegraph*. It was a shock for us as well, I can tell you. We were all absolutely gutted, we couldn't believe it! I mean, who would want to do such a thing, to such a nice young couple like that? It beggars belief! What is the world coming to? It's a descent into chaos, that's what it is! But then I said to myself, I said: there must be a reason for all this. So I thought about it. And you know what? I came up with an answer, Mr Lockyer. It's one of Maddy's punters who did her, that's what I reckoned. It's one of her gentlemen-friends. Not personally, of course. I mean, I don't think it was actually one of her clients that actually did the deed. It was probably somebody else, put out to tender, as it were. But, then, from my point of view, that's all beside the point because I don't care one way or the other. I don't care who did it. And I'll tell you why I don't care. I don't care because I'm a man of business. I told you that right at the beginning, Mr Lockyer. Remember? I was honest with you. That's what I said to you right from the start. So it's business I'm talking about. So, not to put too fine a point on it, I want £10,000 a.s.a.p. or else your name will be plastered across every local and national newspaper you can think of, not to mention the radio and Channel Four News. Is that clear enough, Mr Lockyer?'

Reginald Lockyer took out a handkerchief and wiped this forehead. He tried to speak, he opened his mouth to speak, but he found himself quite unable to say anything: the words stalled in his tightening throat. He just sat there, wide-eyed, staring at Monty, paralysed, his mouth half open. Then, gathering himself together, he said in a muted, shaking voice: 'Mr Slide, you have already said that I am not a rich man. How, then, do you expect me to raise £10,000 at short notice?'

'Oh, Mr Lockyer, that's no problem. I'd be happy to lend you the money!'

Reginald Lockyer raised his eyes to Monty's smiling face and could not suppress a bitter laugh: 'I think this must be a first, Mr Slide. I'm being blackmailed, and you, the blackmailer, are offering to lend me the money to pay you. I suppose this is what they call the funny side of life!'

'Well, it would be funny if it was interest-free, Mr Lockyer. But there'll be charges, of course, not exorbitant, market rates. Nevertheless I do take your point. Yes, it's really quite amusing when you think about it, seeing it from your side of the fence, so to speak. So I understand where you're coming from, I really do, that you might find my proposal, well, a bit strange, although, between you and me, I have done it several times before. But I'll leave it on the table, just in case. It's there if you want it. But anyway, I'm sure you'll have no trouble raising the money at your bank – Barclays, isn't it? – what with you being an MP and all. Just say it's for school fees or for a conservatory in that large back garden of yours – plenty of space there. Banks are much more helpful these days, particularly to people like you and me, respectable gents with collateral.'

Here Monty Slide stood up, well pleased with himself. He thought the meeting had gone very well. He had put his cards on the table, concealed nothing, and had tried to help his MP out of what, he realized, was a very embarrassing situation. He was turning to go, when he suddenly had a thought, and went back to stand in front of Reginald Lockyer. Lockyer still sat motionless, looking down at his hands clasped together on his desk, his head bowed under an enormous weight pressing down on his neck.

'I almost forgot,' said Monty. 'There is just one other thing. We can't delay over this. I mean, I'll have to have the money fairly soon. I say this because of one little detail that I have to admit is slightly worrying – not to me, of course, but certainly to you. As you know, the police are very occupied with this case and they've put their top man on it. Personally, I don't take to him, I think he's unpleasant and a bully, a bloody nightmare if you want to know; but I have to say that he's very professional, with a big reputation. Henry Fairest is his name, you may have heard of him. So unless we tidy up all these loose ends quickly, he'll be on to you before you know it. So the sooner this business is cleared up, the better for you and the better for me.'

Monty Slide turned to go and walked casually towards the double-doors marked "Exit". With unblinking eyes Reginald Lockyer regarded him as he went, watching the slight sway of Monty's hips and the bobbing of his white ponytail. Then he called out: 'Mr Slide, you don't know everything! You think you do but you don't! The girl was pregnant! Did you know that? The bloody girl was pregnant!'

That Lockyer knew what Monty knew gave Monty quite a start; but his face showed no surprise as he returned to the table and sat down again. He moved his chair forward, extended the forefinger of his right hand, tapped the desk twice, and said in a low voice: 'Well, this is a turn-up and no mistake, you knowing that. And how did you find that one out, Mr Lockyer?'

'Because Maddy told me! Because the bloody girl told me! So I'm afraid, Mr Slide, that she got there before you, her and that bastard brother of hers. But it can't make any difference now, I've nothing to lose, so I'll tell you. A few weeks back, on one of my usual Fridays – well, you know all about that, I won't go into details – I saw Maddy at *The Imperial* and she was in a terrible state, crying, sobbing, quite hysterical. She told me she was pregnant. Admittedly, she didn't say it was mine. I mean, that would have been stupid. I knew what line of work she was in, after all. She said that she wouldn't have done anything about it – that she was genuinely fond of me, after all, and didn't want to cause trouble – but that it was her brother. He was the one putting the pressure on, putting her up to it. He had debts, apparently, sounded a really nasty piece of work and just kept on pestering her, that this was too good an opportunity to miss. Well, anyway, I wasn't going to fall for that one so easily, and I didn't believe her at first, about the pregnancy. But Maddy had proof. She had a little blue card, listing her appointments at the hospital. She showed it to me. I remember she was a bit put out because it described her as an "elderly primer." Well, there was nothing I could do. So I paid up. I paid her £2000. I could just about manage that much without my…without anyone noticing. So you see, Mr Slide, you're not the first. I've already paid out on this one. And you're wrong about Dickie. He wasn't such a "lovely lad", as you put it. According to Maddy, he was a violent lout, a bit of a druggie, who would stop at nothing to feed his habit. Well, as I say, I paid her, but I knew that was just the first instalment, probably the first of many. So I paid up to gain some time, time to think about what to do next. But I knew she'd be back. But I didn't kill her and I didn't kill him, Mr Slide. I am telling you the truth. I didn't kill them, nor did I have them killed. Believe me on that, I'm not lying. I wouldn't even know how to go about it. Of course, when I heard the news, that they were both dead, I can't pretend that I wasn't relieved, hoping that was the end of the matter, that I was finally in the clear. But I was wrong, wasn't I, Mr Slide, because you've turned up.'

'Well, I have to be honest with you, Mr Lockyer,' replied Monty, leaning forward in a confidential manner. 'I did know about Maddy being in the family way, but I didn't say anything just now because, well, to be frank, I thought it quite irrelevant to the business between us, quite beside the point. I mean, all I want is to make some money and all you want is to save your neck. That's fair enough, that's our arrangement, something we both understand. But remember this, Mr Lockyer. Maddy was a hooker, a good one, I'm told, but a whore nonetheless; and all whores, all of them, love only one thing: they love the money! Take my word for it, that's all they care about. Even when a bloke's pumping away, that's all they're thinking about, not him, but the money, their hourly rates. So I'm telling you: that's what our Maddy was like, she'd be no different, just the same as all the rest, even when she was crying her eyes out, blubbing away. That's all she'd be thinking about, how much she'd get by putting the squeeze on. Don't get me wrong. She really was pregnant. I know that for a fact. But once a Tom, always a Tom. That's my view and I speak from experience. So even if she didn't know who the father was, that wouldn't have stopped her. She'd have soon been back, this time with another sob story: that she'd changed her mind and that all she wanted now was to find out who the real father was, not for her sake, of course, but for the baby's, to provide for it, to be a proper mother. So I'm telling you, the £2000 was just for starters. Sooner or later she'd have mentioned maintenance. And then, if you'd said "No", she'd have mentioned blood tests and DNA, very reluctantly of course. She didn't want to do it but you'd forced her. So it'd be your fault, not hers. And what would you have done then, Mr Lockyer? Well, we'll never know, will we? That's anybody's guess. But you weren't alone. No, our Maddy was doing the rounds, seeing all her clients with the same sad story, weeping and wailing, lying through her teeth, reeling them in, one by one, fishes on the hook. But somebody didn't buy it, Mr Lockyer. I'm telling you. Somewhere along the line she picked a wrong'un, some gent who really meant what he said, somebody who'd really had enough, had a lot to lose, and so put an end to the greedy little minx.'

'But Mr Slide, what about the brother?' asked Lockyer. 'Maddy said he was the one behind it all, threatening her unless she did something. He was the blackmailer. And somebody rumbled him and killed him. Surely that's was happened!'

'Mr Lockyer, I've been thinking about this. Don't

148

forget, I knew our Dickie, knew him quite well, and what you've said about him just doesn't stack up. Because he was a simple sort, not bright, almost monosyllabic, just loved his cars, driving me about, and he was good at it – could strip an engine in no time. But this kind of caper, I'm telling you, was way beyond him. On the other hand, he'd have done anything for Maddy, just anything, putty in her hands, he was. So I think she was lying – not about the baby, that was true – but about being the victim and blaming it all on poor Dickie. No, I think it was her all the time. I bet Dickie didn't have a clue of what she was really up to. But as I said, Mr Lockyer, all this changes nothing between us. So don't you worry about a thing, I'll see you right. I've given you my word on that and my word is my bond. Believe me, this pregnancy is a side-issue, a diversion. The only thing that matters is that I have the little list of Maddy's clients. It's me that has it, only me, and it's staying with me, going nowhere. So just you remember that, Mr Lockyer. This is just between you and me and no one else. You have nothing to worry about. It's just the two of us. Keep to our business arrangement, get me my money, and you'll be quite safe and in the Cabinet before you can say "Margaret Thatcher." Now, would you like me to call in Mrs Shaw?'

Monty Slide visited all fifteen of Maddy Kelly's clients. Each meeting was tailored to suit the individual, with the sums of money demanded depending on Monty's assessment of their financial status. Some were asked for more than Lockyer, some less; but all of them, once matters had been carefully explained to them, had paid up within the agreed period, on the clear understanding that this was a one-off payment and that nothing more would be asked of them. Monty had given them his word on this and told them he could be trusted. When all transactions were completed, Monty's profit was just over £42,000.

***

But Monty was still right to be worried about Henry Fairest. Because on the evening of Monty's meeting with Reginald Lockyer, Henry made a discovery, small in itself, that was to bring the case to an abrupt and shocking end. It was nearly midnight. Henry was in bed, with Lotte snoring gently at his feet. He couldn't sleep. Thoughts were running round in his head. So he turned on his bedside light and picked up a book. But he couldn't read, so just lay there, staring up at the ceiling. Then Lotte woke up and moved further up the bed, nuzzling her head against Henry's hip. In the morning Henry explained to Bob Bonfield what happened.

'It was all Lotte's fault. She was very restless, panting away, jumping on and off the bed. I thought she wanted water. So I got up and opened the door. She went straight to the sitting-room and sat down beside my desk. I called to her but she wouldn't budge. She just sat there, her eyebrows twitching. Well, now I was wide awake. On my desk were the case files. I took them back to bed. Lotte jumped up beside me, almost shaking with excitement. I opened the folder. I looked at the photos, the autopsy reports, the statements from Weismann and his wife. Everything. Then I came to Dickie's bank statements. I knew I'd missed something. And in the end it was so simple, Bob.'

'It was the payments. Remember how they went? There

were in two batches, regular cash deposits but of varying amounts, ranging from £500 up to £2000. It begins with the smaller payments, the £500s, and then these overlap with the larger ones, the two of them continuing right to the end, in tandem, to just before Maddy's death. We're right about them. These are blackmail-payments. She was tapping the punters. Then I saw it. Why the difference between the two payments? That was the question I asked. Why start with the smaller payments and after that run them *alongside* the larger ones? Why the *parallel* payments? I mean, if she was a greedy girl, wanting as much as possible, if she was becoming more sure of herself, soaking the punters for all she was worth, why carry on with these smaller payments at all, right up to just days before her murder? Why not up the ante and ask for more? But that's not what happened. The smaller sums just continue being paid in, right up to the end, alongside the others.'

'And then I saw why. In the old days a girl suspected she was pregnant when she missed two periods. Not now. Now she knows incredibly quickly. With a pregnancy testing kit a girl can tell on the first day of her missed period: in other words, something like fourteen to twenty-one days after conception, give or take. Now our Maddy, given her line of work, would have known all this, she was a canny girl. So my guess is that as soon as she missed her first period, she was off to the chemist and tested herself. Then she knew. Then she realized she had only a small window of opportunity, another two or three months at most, before the pregnancy would begin to show. After that, she'd be out of work, nobody would want her. Perhaps she could hide it for a few weeks but before long all her clients would drop away. So she had to make the most of things. And she didn't have much time if she wanted to make some money.'

'And there it was, Bob, as clear as daylight. We know that at the time of her death, she was three months gone. This means that the first payments, the smaller ones, were made *before she knew she was pregnant* – it's only when she knows, presumably after the pregnancy test, that the big bucks start rolling in. The dates fit. And for us, Bob, that can only mean one thing. Maddy was a blackmailer but the money was coming in not for the *same* reason – the pregnancy – but for two *different* reasons, the much larger payments belonging to the punters, to the men with the money, the smaller ones to someone else, to someone with much less to throw around. So I think I'm right. The first blackmail can't have anything to do with the pregnancy. This means that whoever murdered Maddy may well have killed her for a different reason altogether.'

Then Henry Fairest explained what he was going to do. 'If I'm right about this, then our murderer knows nothing about Maddy's pregnancy. So let's tell him, put it out there in the Press and TV. Let's tell him that it wasn't just Maddy and her brother he murdered but also her unborn child. That might get his conscience working, be something he can't live with. I've seen this happen before, a crime too heavy to bear. Just imagine how he'll feel when he learns the truth. He never saw himself as a monster but as a victim. Maddy and her brother were the casualties of their own greed. Killing them was justified. He can make excuses. But this? Maddy's baby? Can that be washed away? Then perhaps his conscience will begin its work, haunt his nights. Then something might give.

That's all we can hope for. We want the guilt to work its way through, to have its caustic effect. So let's see what happens. All we can do now is wait.'

★★★

The next morning Henry Fairest had a meeting with Jock Pringle, the Chief Constable; and in the afternoon a statement was issued by The Manchester City Police. It appeared in some of the later editions; but it wasn't until the next day – and so fourteen days after the murders – that it received full coverage in all the national papers. It read as follows:

> *The Manchester City Police wish it to be known that there have been significant developments in the case of Richard and Maddy Kelly, the brother and sister murdered on the Newtown Industrial Estate. Extensive enquiries have established that Ms Kelly was a prostitute working in the Manchester area, the subsequent autopsy of whom has also confirmed that she was three months pregnant at the time of her death. It is now believed that Ms Kelly's condition has direct bearing on the tragedy that occurred – a line of enquiry that the police are now actively pursuing. If any members of the public have any information regarding this case, please contact the police immediately. All information received will be treated in the strictest confidence.*

When Monty Slide read the announcement in *The Daily Mail*, under the headline "Sensation in Manchester

Murders", he turned to Bob and Matt and wagged his finger. 'Remember what I said, boys? I told you, didn't I, I told you Fairest would get there pretty quick. This is all him, this story, it's got his fingerprints all over it. He's stuck, don't you see, so he's gone fishing, fishing for Daddy. Flushing him out he is. Ha! Ha! What a man! You can't help admiring him! He's got balls he has! But he's too late, much too late, 'cos Monty got there first. So how'd you two fancy a week in Madeira, spending our ill-gotten gains? It's nice at this time of year.'

William Weisman had also seen the announcement, reading the newspaper over lunch in the University canteen. He immediately rang Marietta to tell her the news, about the dead woman being a prostitute and pregnant. Then, being a Thursday, he told her not to wait up. It was a long programme at the *Duke of York's* – a double bill of two John Wayne movies, the early *Stage Coach* and one of William's favourite films, *The Searchers*. So he'd be late. Just put something in the fridge, he said, and he'd be fine.

After a light lunch of soup and strong coffee Marietta went down to the Post Office to buy stamps and envelopes. She also bought a copy of *The Guardian*. There it was, right enough, the news about the murders, tucked away on page two, a short item, just the bare facts. The rest of the morning she spent tidying the house and writing letters. Then she walked back to the Post Office. That done, she felt restless and went for a walk. She walked along St. Anne's, crossed St Mary's and entered the wide expanse of Heaton Park, walking past the Pavilion and the Animal Centre, then along beside the Hall, then climbing up to the Temple, then back down to the Boating Lake. Here she sat on a bench and watched the ducks. There were a few people about – mums with toddlers, couples together, dogs with their owners. Marietta sat there for over an hour. She was hardly conscious of time passing. Then she looked up at the sky and realized that the light was fading, that it was getting chilly. Stupidly she had come out without a coat. So she walked briskly back. She got home quite late, around 7.00. By then it was getting dark and a cold wind was blowing. She was happy to get indoors, back into the warm. Then she prepared William's dinner. She wanted to cook him something special. She looked through her cookbooks and decided on a salad of asparagus, celery and leek, with one of William's favourite puddings to follow: the Italian *Crema di Limone e Limoncello*, which was always easy to do. She realized that she didn't have enough asparagus or any mascarpone and so drove off to Waitrose to get them. She was back by 8.30 and then started cooking. That done, with William's dinner in the fridge, she watched the Nine o'clock news, eating nothing herself. There were items about economic green shoots, a football transfer, dreadful things happening in Afghanistan, and a forthcoming bye-election down south in a safe Conservative seat. All this bored her. Towards the end of the broadcast there was a short item about the Newtown murders and the recent police announcement. A spokesman said that the investigation was continuing and that the police believed they were close to a breakthrough. Marietta switched off the TV. She now felt very tired. So she went upstairs and ran herself a bath.

8

Marietta

I sometimes meet people who are quite willing to admit their mistakes, how their lives went wrong. I remember a middle-aged woman coming to see me quite regularly. She must have been very beautiful in her youth. In her twenties she went out with a theology student. They adored each other, were quite inseparable, but she was very insecure, the only child of a bad marriage. She thought he would never marry her. Perhaps she was right. Then along came a wealthy man, who seduced her with his large house and impressive address book. Well, she was star-struck and not very bright. So she married him. Within months she realized her terrible mistake but she had nowhere to go, no qualifications of any kind. So she was stuck with him for fifteen years and had three children. In the end they divorced: he thought she was intellectually beneath him and she knew she was. Now she lives alone in a small flat with her children visiting occasionally. She told me she thinks of her student constantly, she can't get him out of her head. She wonders what happened to him, but she doesn't really want to know. She doesn't want to find him happy and successful, with a loving family and her forgotten. And the worst of it is that she can remember the exact moment when her life changed. She was alone in her bedsit and the phone rang. It was him, her rich admirer. He invited her out to an expensive restaurant. She hesitated. Then she thought, "Why not? Georgie will never marry me. So why not have some fun?" So she went, and that was the end of that. She's now a haunted woman, who drinks too much and is on anti-depressants.

Then you meet people who never admit their mistakes. My father told me about a patient of his, a solicitor, a really brilliant man, always quick to take offense and always ready to point out the mistakes of others. My father said his right hand should have been cut off at birth. Because the worst of it was he wrote scalding letters. He didn't cool down, he just sent them off without thinking. And the trouble was that these letters often contained a grain of truth, were well-written and often funny. Well, it ruined him. He was someone prepared to crawl through the gutter to reach the moral high ground.. He became unemployable and lost all his friends. But he never admitted his mistakes, never thought for a moment why he'd ended up in a rural backwater, helping old ladies with their Wills. He still saw himself as the crusader of rectitude. But then I suppose it's a definition of the self-righteous that they never admit they were wrong.

But I don't think the majority of failures are like this. These are the ones who can't put their finger on some poor decision or flaw. So they're always asking "How did I end up here?" But it's not down to anything they've done. Somebody gets ill or a job turns sour or a friend lets them down. They were always hoping for the best, that something will turn up. But it never does. And then they look at other people and that makes it worse. These others are no different, no more talented or better liked; but there they are, sitting on the heights. They're at the top looking down, not at the bottom looking up. Perhaps they're just born differently, under a lucky sign.

But I can't say this of me. I knew what I was doing. I wish I could say that I was just carried along by a strong current. In my case I could have acted differently, I needn't have drowned. I could have saved myself but instead I plunged right in. So I have nobody to blame but myself. I was conscious and clear-eyed and well aware of where I was heading, and that was down.

This, then, is the record of my descent.

★★★

It all started with my dreams, two dreams to be precise, both recurring. I had the first dream for about ten weeks, on and off. I can't call it a nightmare exactly and it didn't happen every night, but it was sufficiently disturbing to wake me up. The loss of sleep made me feel edgy and irritable.

I am driving along a country road at night. There are no stars and the clouds are heavy above me, thick and oppressive. It is raining hard, really pouring down. My headlights are on and I am leaning forward, clenching the steering wheel. But despite the poor visibility, I am going fast, steadily increasing my speed. I know I'm being reckless. But I don't care. The more it rains, the faster I go. But I know this road. This is a journey I've done many times before. But where am I going? Am I expected? Is there somebody there, waiting for me? I can't say. All I know is that I'll know I've arrived when I get there. I'm not worried or anything. I'm just in this desperate rush.

The road is a country lane, quite narrow. The beam of my headlights picks out the dark shadows of the high winter hedgerows on either side, leaning inwards, their tall leafless branches creating a long straight tunnel of light. Then, in the distance, I see two more lights. It's another car, coming towards me at speed. That's when I panic. There's only just enough room for the two of us, and the slightest mistake will be fatal. All I have to do is turn the wheel just a little – a slight shift of my hand – and we'll crash into each other, head-on. And the really terrible thing is that I am tempted to do it and I know that he's tempted to do it. There's this horrible fascination about what it would be like. Would I hear anything, feel anything? Or would it just be a sudden blank and nothing at all? It's a temptation difficult to resist. So who will give way first? I wait to see. But what should take a couple of seconds, no more than that, takes an age. He's still going faster and faster, coming nearer and nearer, but we never seem to meet. Then suddenly I'm blinded by the light, try to steer away, but I'm paralysed and we crash. Then there's a terrible screeching sound and the smell of burning rubber, and I'm falling, somersaulting down, my body turning head-over-heels, into a blackness that is cold, damp and bottomless. That's when I wake up.

My second dream is more of a nightmare. I know this because afterwards I wake up violently, thrashing about. I have had it two or three times now, always on the night following my first dream. I call it my "desert dream".

Oddly, I used to have the same nightmare in my teens. My mother always took it as a warning-sign, dosing me up next morning. I am standing in a landscape covered entirely by yellow sand, my feet shifting slightly as they do on a beach. The sky is also yellow. This means I can't tell where the sand ends and the sky begins. So there I am, I cannot move, I'm stuck in this sand. But I'm not worried, not unhappy or distressed in any way. I'm really quite content. The heat is tremendous, the sun beating down. Then the dream changes. Far off I see a small dot – a black mark so tiny it's easy to miss. It is exactly placed between the yellow sand and the yellow sky: it divides the two and so gives me an horizon. I am reassured by that. But then I look around and what I see makes me uneasy. I am quite alone in the middle of a vast desert, an ocean of sand completely featureless, without any points of reference – no dunes or rocks or plants of any kind – just an enormous blank canvas of yellow, void of shade, stretching out on all sides of me. I look back at the dot to get my bearings. I look closer, screw up my eyes, and see that it has slightly changed. It has grown, is growing as I look, puffing up, transforming into a quite definable shape, into something that I realize, to my horror, is alive, that has a heartbeat throbbing beneath its skin. I still can't move but whatever this thing is, it is getting larger all the time, becoming something more sinuous. It even has a head. And still it comes on and still I can't move. I begin to feel incredibly hot and thirsty. I become desperate for a drink. I can feel my tongue swelling in my mouth. And then, as it gets closer, right up to me, it divides, multiplying into many bodies and many heads, filling the whole yellow sand and yellow sky with whirling black tendrils, engorged and mottled with red. These living and pulsating veins are now circling about, twining together like snakes all heaped together, each moving in a different direction, touching me, suckering around my head, clinging to my arms and pushing upwards between my thighs. I see their faces, their dark eyes and gaping mouths, and breathe in their rancid breath. I am suffocating. I beat at them, fight them, struggle to tear them off, but they are pulling me down, this heavy weight on my chest making me sink deeper and deeper. Then, with a great heave, both hands pushing upwards, I release myself towards the light, and sit up in bed panting and drenched with sweat.

I was brought up to interpret my dreams. Papa encouraged my mother and me to keep notebooks by our beds, to jot down our thoughts after sleep. Sometimes I showed him what I had written, and his remarks were always illuminating. A lot rubbed off, of course, and in the end, without much help, I could look at my own dreams and read them in an informed and intelligent manner. I didn't know it at the time, but this ability to look within myself, to analyse character in a technical way, proved extremely useful in my later career.

My two dreams are not difficult to unravel. The first dream incorporates several well-known motifs, almost exclusively to do with death. Here I move inexorably towards a destination that is familiar and inevitable, that is both aim (*telos*) and end (*finis*). This transition from one state to another – of departing on a journey – is one of the best authenticated symbolisms of death, seen in the equally familiar images of boarding a train, crossing a bridge or rowing across a lake – from the time of the Greeks "water" has been a particularly potent death symbol. In my dream I pass through clear images of decay – e.g., the leafless branches of the hedgerows – and move at speed towards my final destination, an arrival illumined by light. This is all straightforward. What makes the dream more interesting is, of course, my reckless behaviour. Despite the narrowness of the road, the weather and the on-coming car, I throw caution to the winds and go as fast as I can. So I am tempting fate. Am I exhibiting latent suicidal tendencies? This I doubt, given what I know of my own temperament. I may be wrong, of course – for all I know, these tendencies may be there but buried deep below the unconscious layers of defensive mechanisms. No, I think my dream points elsewhere, not to a celebration of death but more to a celebration of life. My recklessness makes my journey more perilous and so more exhilarating. I am like a tightrope-walker, intoxicated by the height as I balance along the wire. This interpretation is supported by another dream of mine. I'm standing on a high cliff. I look down and see huge waves lashing against rocks. There are warning signs everywhere not to get too close to the edge. But I stride on. Now people are shouting at me. I ignore them and walk faster, going as far as I can. The wind is howling and I can feel my body being buffeted this way and that. I stand right on the cliff's edge. It is difficult to describe my feelings at this moment, when a sudden gust could so easily carry me away, down to my death. All I can say is that, standing there, my entire body is suffused with a warmth of overwhelming happiness. I feel totally exhilarated and wonderfully alive as I sway in the wind.

There are two elements in this second dream that are particularly significant. The first is that it is a dream of adolescence, of enhanced erotic awareness, and so awash with fairly crude sexual symbols. These images are classic expressions of libidinal desire and the need for possession. To begin with, my innocent life is at peace with itself, the dream itself associated with my mother's care and by memories of happy days on the beach, playing on the yellow sand. These feelings of security and well-being are soon disturbed by the appearance of the sexual predator, whom I at first scarcely notice. His advances are therefore masked. To begin with I accept him as a friendly support, as a fixed point in an otherwise blank and lonely landscape, giving me a sense of place (the required "horizon") and thus of security. These feelings, however, quickly disappear when, to my horror, the mask drops and the predator is revealed, metamorphosing into the rapacious snake of many heads, whose twirling tendrils seek to violate me in the clearest possible symbol of rape: it seeks to open my thighs. My reaction to this assault is threefold. At first I feel a terrible thirst and my tongue swells up; then I struggle with the monster as he pulls me down; and then, with a final effort, I fight my way to the surface and the nightmare is broken. The sexual symbolism of this is, as I say, straightforward and unremarkable.

The second significant thing about my "desert dream" is its chronology: it occurs on the night after my first dream. This is not fortuitous. For there is a bridge between them, coupling the first dream of death (in maturity) with the second dream of sexual desire (in immaturity). This connection is the linking symbol of "falling", the well-known symbol of seduction. Both dreams end in this way, with this image, except that in the first the falling is perpetual – I fall into a bottomless pit and continue falling – whereas in the second there is a resolution: I fall but then struggle upwards and so obtain release. It is this motif of seduction that provides the key to the interpretation of these dreams. For once this sexual component is laid bare, the dreams come together, not as two *separate* psychic events but as a *sequence*, in which the permanent and unresolved desire to be possessed in the one points towards the reality of possession in the other. What has been wished for takes place: sexual union has occurred. As with all dreams, therefore, the wish has now become *active* – one never dreams the wish but always dreams the act, the embodied wish – a wish now described as the completion of a hazardous journey, towards "the light". However, the two dreams have different outcomes, one in which I tumble down, the other in which I reach up. This is highly significant. For in the use of the light-symbol – the most commonplace image of fulfilment and revelation – we find a *reversion* or *displacement*. Under normal circumstances, it is not the experienced adult that is sexually unfulfilled – who continues to "fall" – but rather the inexperienced teenager. But here it is the other way round. It is the sexually mature adult who dreams of seduction, and not the young adolescent, who has put dream into practice and achieved orgasmic fulfilment, albeit by violent means.

This distinction, between the sexual needs of mature and immature individuals, although familiar, is not necessarily warranted: the libidinal instinct is not always crushed by experience and sexual fantasy is not the monopoly of the young. Once this is understood, we may conflate the two dreams and so arrive at a better understanding of my inner drives. My adult desire for seduction is my desire to return, a regression, a psychic need to go back to the earlier sexual excitements of adolescence, to a time when the predator is *not* recognised, unseen at first and welcomed, although ultimately revealed to be sexually demanding and even aggressive. The youth of my "desert dream" is the embodiment of this desire. This being so, I must further conclude that this backwards projection evolves from the inadequacies of my present erotic life, from my life as it is now. For however sexually active I may have been in youth – the excitements of which I recall – this activity is now at an end, or, if not at an end, in rapid decline, this being part of the natural process of ageing. This loss of sexual power is not merely inevitable but speeding up as I journey along the precarious night-road to death. And this is precisely what I subconsciously reject. I cannot accept the inevitability of this decline. So I bind myself to my youthful self. As I travel towards the light, my immature ego is rejecting the dictates of age, and seeking, by whatever means, to be released from the impotence of maturity. Given this psychic tension, neurotic consequences were bound to occur. With the sexual impulse so dammed up, so thwarted in its needs, it was inevitable that it should seek other outlets, other channels of expression – in a word, be funnelled into symptoms. Hence their onset: in my reckless disregard for my safety, in the thrill of living on a knife's edge – these being substitutes for those excitements no longer obtained in my sexual life. In this way my "love of life" is revealed to be more precisely a "love of self", that is, a form of narcissism. What I embrace in the exhilarations of danger is myself renewed, now asserted as a forceful ego throwing down the gauntlet and challenging nature. Thus standing on the cliff's edge is both a reminiscence of how I once was and a display of what I wish to become: a being of dominant will, possessed of a power so potent that it can reverse the processes of time.

It is sometimes said that dreams have a predictive power. This is untrue. Dreams are built on the past and present and nothing else. Indeed, to believe that ideas or desires, whether transmitted asleep or awake, can somehow adjust what is to come, change a reality that has yet to occur, is itself a symptom of neurosis: what Freud calls the "omnipotence of thoughts". It is on the same primitive but not uncommon level as that of a man believing that danger can be avoided by the meticulous washing of hands. Yet we dismiss these dream-messages at our peril. They provide, as it were, a road-map of our instincts and so tell us, through the decoding of signs and symbols, what things we should seek and embrace and what things we should guard against and avoid. My journey was not therefore unguided. I had been warned. There could be no excuse. I had to hand a catalogue of my unconscious wishes, of where my impulses might lead.

★★★

Those were my dreams. Understandably I was very disturbed by them. Unravelled they had disclosed a deep-seated sexual need: that I would risk everything, including my life, to attain the release of a final embrace. But what disturbed me most was that this was a personality I scarcely recognized. Was this really me? I had always thought of myself as an individual quite different. And I believed this because of the equilibrium achieved in my marriage, where, if anything, accepting the decline in our sexual activity was part of its success. We had reached a plateau of well-being and security. We were content. Yet my dreams were saying something else. They were telling me that our balanced life together could not be taken for granted, that there were deeper strains at work. I still found this hard to grasp. Because although we were not a couple who spent their time endlessly discussing their relationship – so digging up the plant every night and killing it off – we had nevertheless agreed why it worked for us. We knew that lovers ascribe to their loved ones perfections they rarely possess and that this illusion was essential for the dreamer's happiness. I knew all this because this was how William looked at me, with my air of self-assurance – what he called my "Dietrich-look". And the more distant I became, the more he desired me; the more unreachable – the more I preferred to be loved than to love – the more William was reduced to a permanent state of insecurity, so binding him fast. This was not a callous calculation of my part, a tawdry piece of theatre trading on his obsessive nature. It was just how our chemistry worked. Because it seemed such a perfect fit, operating both ways. I, too, had found what I needed: a man of affection and high intelligence, who was quite ready to love me more than I could ever love him, a partner ready to invest all his love in me without demands, asking for so little in return

So it was a shock to discover how wrong I'd been, that William needed so much more. He told me himself, stated as much in public, with me there. I shall never forget that lecture. But what he wanted was impossible. I could not accommodate him by changing my nature. So instead of accepting me for what I was, he belittled me, making me out to be some stunted creature, drying up inside. Of course I was outraged and humiliated. He had paraded our secrets in front of everybody. For days I couldn't bear to be near him and told him why I felt betrayed. He was hurt and surprised and said that I had misunderstood, that it wasn't about me, not about us at all. But what he said he still believed. There were individuals who would risk everything for love, even if devoured in the process. Well, I knew that already. After all, I knew William.

And then, much later, came my dreams. As I said, they changed everything. Without them I wouldn't be where I am today, of that I'm sure. Usually this isn't the case. More often dreams are quite innocent, with the mind freewheeling, the present and past all jumbled together. You test them in the light of day and there's nothing there, only the superficialities of everyday living. But my two dreams kept coming back, left me no peace, would not evaporate in daylight. So I persisted with my self-analysis and came to see that my embarrassment when listening to William was not that of an individual exposed as cold and unloving but of someone unmasked as quite the opposite: as a woman desperate to be possessed in the way William was possessed. What William had, I desired! Yes, that was it! How blind I'd been! Before I had believed that my happiness required a person emotionally subordinate, whose love for me was unconditional. This was someone who left my freedom intact, someone I had the power to leave. But this was not the figure of my dreams. There I was no longer the self-sufficient partner, the creature of alabaster, but an individual envious of the happiness sustained by William's own seemingly indestructible libido. Yes, what I wanted was to feel as William felt, felt about me! I wanted that power and focus. I wanted that gusting wind through my body, to feel the headlong fall of desire, to give everything up for it, to be humiliated by it, to become a slave to it, to be a woman who would prefer death on the rocks than a life without experiencing, just once, an all-consuming, devouring passion. I wanted to go back to what I had lost, to become again what I had been when young: a romantic, adolescent girl waiting for her lover. This is what my dreams said and I was deeply shocked, disturbed even, of what they told me about myself.

So William had been right all along – I now stood alongside Philip and Mariana. Knowing that, everything made sense. Sometimes dreams reveal desires that you do not wish to wish, desires that you'd prefer to hide away. But this was not how I felt. A beam of light had shown me what might lie ahead; and I felt as if some great subterranean river had burst its banks, the flooding water surging forward and lifting me up in its swell to new, intoxicating heights. From here I could look down across a whole vista of possibilities, with further journeys to make and a whole life yet to be lived. I was both excited and afraid. Because now I knew! I desired what William desired when he looked at me. It was my own envy that had embarrassed me. That was it! That was how it was! I wanted to feel *in* me what he felt *for* me. But this could not come through William. It was not William I wanted. That was all gone. Those feelings had died long ago and could never come back. He was not the object of my desire, not the sinuous lover who would come in the night and take me. No, no, it was not William! So I had to look elsewhere. But where? I knew that my lover would come unannounced and in disguise. This made me very anxious. How would I recognize him? Perhaps he was already out there, looking for me, going from place to place, not knowing where I was. Or he might be someone quite close, even somebody I knew, who had passed by without seeing me as his own.

I am no fool. I realized that I had replaced one set of neuroses with another. But there was nothing to be done. My dreams had reduced me to a permanent state of nervous tension. I was constantly on tenterhooks. During the day I was always out. I wanted to be in crowded places, to show myself to as many people as possible. I was always on the look-out. And the nights were terrible. All I did was lie awake waiting for the day. These were the symptoms of my neurosis. No wonder I became nervy and irritable. I also became very anxious living with William. I was constantly looking at him to see if he could see how I felt, could detect the change in me. It was all so obvious to me, how I'd altered. So surely it must be evident to someone with his quick eyes. But he said nothing, gave nothing away. Still, I had to be wary. I could let nothing slip. I spent my time watching him watching me. It was a relief being out of the house. At home I had to be so careful, could never lower my guard. I could not say or do anything that would put him on the scent. So I hid behind my mask, living my inner life of secrets, always vigilant and wide awake, a little girl again, standing at the garden gate, waiting and watching the strangers pass. Which one? Which one?

I did not have long to wait.

★★★

When we moved to Manchester I continued my clinical work in psychiatry, now employed within the Care Trust set up by the City Council. I did this for about six or seven years. After that I had a variety of jobs: supporting Youth Offending Teams, which were then quite new, later becoming part of commissioned study into the sex industry. We found that an overwhelming majority of women were addicted to either drugs or alcohol, often had a lifetime history of violence behind them, with childhood abuse a common factor. Half the women interviewed had been coerced into prostitution, either by partners, a pimp or a relative, and just under half had a criminal record and half were in debt. The Council was very concerned about the growth of the problem, particularly in areas like Moss Side, Ardwick and Gorton. Accordingly they set up centres at various locations, where women could meet together on a bi-weekly basis for support and receive guidance from a qualified psychotherapist. I was put in charge of one in the Fallowfield area of the City. Attendance was very slow to begin with; but word soon spread and after a year or so we had a regular attendance of about a dozen women. The stories they told supported our previous findings. These were girls, rarely more than twenty-five, living on the fringes of society, about eighty-five per cent of whom said they became prostitutes for the money: to pay for housing and food or day care for their children, to feed their addictions or pay off their debts.

My life with William during these years was, for the most part, secure and content. Indeed, looking back, I think we had never been happier. William was making a great name for himself and I found my work hard but rewarding. However, it was towards the end of this period that my dreams began. As I have already explained, these were very unsettling and induced a range of neurotic symptoms. I felt powerless and alone. I was clearly in a very excitable and impressionable state.

It was at one of our fortnightly meetings that I met Rowena. She was a beautiful and striking redhead, educated and well-spoken, smartly dressed, charming and self-assured. In our little group she seemed quite out of place. When it was her turn to talk about herself, she startled us with a very different story. Becoming a sex worker – she refused to call herself a prostitute – had been a positive choice on her part. She hadn't been forced into it, she could have done something else – she'd been to Grammar School, had the qualifications, A Levels and GCSEs. She had never had any trouble with any of her clients, most of whom were middle-aged husbands still hungry for intimacy, whose wives found sex an inconvenient and tedious chore. Most sex workers, she said, were not money-hungry alcohol and drug addicts but women working to support their families or give themselves a better start in life. At the top end of the business, girls could make good money and were usually canny enough not to stay too long, walking away with enough for a flat or for travel or for funding further training and education. Some girls she knew had become teachers and nurses, a couple even solicitors. One friend of hers was studying at the University to become a forensic scientist, writing her essays between clients.

This was a shock. I found it difficult to believe what she was saying – it went quite against the experiences of the other women. So, chatting afterwards, Rowena agreed to take me along one evening to see for myself. Then I would discover what went on at the higher end. She had her own apartment and usually she worked from there, advertising in the local paper; but sometimes, mostly at weekends, she worked from the bar at *The Imperial Hotel* in central Manchester, near Mosley Street. I agreed to meet her there the next Saturday night but was told to come quite early, about 8.00 pm, because the men came in around 10.00. That would give me plenty of time to meet the girls before the rush.

So I went, curious and not knowing what to expect. Around 8.00 the women started to arrive. They were slightly older than the girls at my sessions, in their late twenties and early thirties. They were casually dressed, most in jeans, each carrying a small hold-all. Someone in the Hotel had arranged everything for them: they had a private room to change in, with a little bathroom and shower. They quickly settled in and were obviously quite at home. They were a close-knit group, greeting each other with hugs and kisses, gossiping away about their families, films they had seen, clothes bought, the usual things. I was introduced and they were very happy to talk. It was just as Rowena had said. They were all in it for the money, some with children to support, some with more specific ambitions. I met Scarlet, the forensic scientist: she had to finish an essay on "Bloodstain Pattern Analysis" and had brought her books. Tania only worked at weekends and wanted to be a veterinary nurse. Lorraine was saving up to go to India and Desireé was a single mother of two. Sasha just loved doing what she did. It was all very friendly and relaxed. Watching them get ready reminded me of my days in the theatre: it seemed just the same, a change of personality before the curtain went up. Out came the hairdryers and brushes and on went the make-up – the eyeliner and foundation cream, the nail varnish and lip gloss – and then out came the clothes, all expensive: tailored silk trouser suits, white evening jackets with flared skirts, and I remember a little black dress of *crêpe de chine*. It was very discreet and tasteful and the transformation was complete. They were no longer recognizable. They emerged as young professional women, well-to-do, groomed and confident, with perfect manners and good conversation. Meeting them, you'd never guess what they did for a living.

All the girls went to the bar. I was alone. Maddy came late.

'Sorry, sorry,' she said. 'Typical me. Have all the girls left?'

She was breathless and in a rush. She was petite, vivacious and outgoing, quick in her movements. She unpacked her dress: it was of Japanese maroon silk, with a stand-up collar, stamped with little golden dragons. She immediately stripped off in front of me, quite naked, showing a slim figure, shaven, with full breasts.

'I hope you don't mind,' she said, 'but you can't wear

a bra or panties with silk – all the wrinkles show. Will you do me up? Sorry, they're terribly fiddly.'

The dress had dozens of little pearl buttons going down the back. So I stood behind her, doing them up one by one, on my knees for the bottom ones, all the time breathing in the soapy perfume of her pale skin. That done, Maddy twirled round in front of me, swinging her hips.

'What do you think?' she giggled. 'Does it fit? Will the boys like it?'

I didn't know what to say, so I just smiled and said 'Yes! Lovely!'

Then she did her make-up, bringing her pouting lips up close to the mirror. Unlike the other girls, she used very little, not wanting to spoil her complexion, which still retained the sheen of youth. Most of her time was spent on her hair, which was thick, black, with natural curls. While combing she chatted away, wanting to know all about me.

'Rowena told us you were coming. Been here long? Where'd you live? Are you married? What's he do then? Any kids?'

Before she left for the bar, I told her about our meetings and invited her along.

'Rowena's got my number. Why not come? We just talk things through, nothing special. I'm only there to help. Some of the girls have said they'll come.'

I never thought I'd see Maddy again but she came the next session. Thereafter she became a regular, a bundle of energy, always cheering up the other girls, full of news and gossip. She was very funny, warm, with a zest for life. Frankly, I couldn't see why she was there, she seemed so well-adjusted, bubbly and confident, without a care. She told me why later. She hadn't come for help or advice. She had come for me.

And that's how it all started, my first step along the downward path. I can't go into details, exactly how it happened, I am almost too ashamed to speak. As I've said already, I could have walked away because it didn't happen all at once. But I did nothing, I let things slide, and very soon I was caught on a hook. It was a gradual intoxication. I began to feel sensations never felt before, a surge of emotions completely strange to me, overwhelming, but which I nevertheless recognized from my dreams. That was the strangest thing. They led me on. Otherwise I might have controlled myself, acted differently; but they had charted my journey and I felt helpless to resist, to do anything but travel along the road ahead, a sleepwalker but aware. And the dangers were obvious enough. One half of me could look at Maddy quite dispassionately and know her for what she was; but the other half was bound to her, breathless in my excitement, with all my strength to leave quite gone. I watched her and every time I looked I saw something new. With us she never wore make-up or jewellery of any kind: she was always simply dressed. Her pale face was as smooth as marble, the colour of yellow ivory, the lightness of her skin framed by her dense black hair, sometimes piled up high or swept back behind her ears, sometimes hanging loose. Her eyes were her best feature. They were honey-coloured with an amber centre, over-sized, with lashes so thick I thought they were false. They were a barometer of her moods: when she looked at the other girls, they danced; when she looked at me they narrowed and went dull. Sometimes she avoided me altogether, preferring to chatter with anybody but me. But I knew otherwise. I knew what she was doing. Everything she did was done for me. All the movements of her body were gestures of complicity, every smile, every turn of her neck and arm, every word she said, were for me, making me aware of her and of how she felt. The barb had caught and she was reeling me in.

Was I shocked by my feelings? Not really. I had always believed what my father had once said: that when two people make love four people are present, with sexual satisfaction depending on whether the female and male sides of each partner are gloved within the act. So I wasn't surprised. It was more an unmasking of what I was. There was no doubt. I knew. Nothing was hidden. I was standing in the light. No, for me the mystery lay elsewhere. Why Maddy? What marked her out? How had she, this little slip of a thing, reduced me down to this? I tried to figure it out but failed. I would look and look but the more I looked the less I saw. In the end I gave up trying to puzzle it out. All I saw was a creature who had by some alchemical means cast her spell and caught me in her net. It was a bewitchment, a magnetic pull. My body told me this when I came near her. My breathing changed, coming rapidly in shorter bursts, I felt a constriction in my throat, my legs seemed heavy, and all my senses became more alert, my eyes more sensitive, my hearing more acute. I felt heady and slightly drunk. I was intoxicated by love, I was in love with love, loved by love. There was nothing else. It was wonderful, quite magical, this miracle coming to me so late in life. Everything else was cast into shadow in this dazzling glare. And all the time I was moving closer, nearer and nearer, quite powerless as I swayed towards the edge.

There's always a tipping point. I suppose it happens to us all, when our desires surge out and we take the risk. We stretch out a hand or say something or there's a sudden kiss. This is how it happened. Maddy was a wonderful mimic and had us all in stiches about her men and what they wanted when alone. Everything had a price: a hundred pounds for this, two hundred pounds for that. She was very explicit about what she was prepared to do if the money was right. The girls all laughed, amazed at how much she charged. That day Maddy was the last to leave. As she was putting on her coat she leaned against me, smiled up, and whispered in my ear, 'Of course, Etta, you wouldn't have to pay. It would be free for you.'

Nobody had called me "Etta" before. I almost swooned. She moved forward and pressed her stomach against mine, thigh to thigh, her arms wrapped around my waist. I couldn't move. I smelt her hair. She smothered me with kisses. She kissed my cheeks, my eyelids, my nose, my ears, my neck and then my mouth, first my upper lip, next the lower, then forcing them apart, her tongue on mine. There was nothing I could do. I slumped down, my knees up, my back against the wall. I was blinded by desire. She had known me before I knew myself. Everything became hers.

This is so difficult. I can hardly say what I have to say. From then on I thought only of Maddy. Nothing else mattered or seemed real. It was tunnel-vision. I walked around in a daze, only alive when alone with her. All week I did nothing but wait for us to be together. We met and made love whenever and wherever we could. We made love in the office, on the floor before our sessions. We made love in rooms rented by the hour. Once or twice I went on Saturday nights to the Hotel and met her there before the other girls arrived. Sometimes she caught the bus on Thursdays, William's cinema night, when he was always late, and came out to my place. Yes, even that! Yet I felt no shame. But oh, the taste of her, of musk and honey!

Most of all we went to her flat. It was a miserable little apartment in Ardwick in a modern block. I was quite shocked when I saw it. There were two tiny bedrooms, one neat, the other squalid.

'I didn't know you shared,' I said.

'It's my brother,' she replied.

'I didn't know you had a brother. You've never mentioned him.'

She told me all about him and it explained a lot.

'I'm all he's got. He's a bit of a druggie, in and out of prison, can never keep a job, sometimes gets violent, although not with me. All my money goes on him. I do what I can but it's a problem making ends meet. But what else can I do? And it's not really his fault. I blame our bloody mother. God, she was a cow. Up'd and left us when she could have helped. Bloody bitch, heartless and cruel. So there's nothing to be done, it's just the way it is. I'm stuck with him. I can't walk away. It's just the two of us. He'd be lost without me.'

We used the apartment regularly: it was the safest place. I never met the brother. Maddy arranged everything. She'd ring him on her mobile to make sure we'd be alone. I bought lots of things for the flat. I bought a new armchair and sofa, things for the kitchen and bathroom, pictures for the walls, one or two new rugs. I spent a lot of money on Maddy's bedroom: a large brass bed – she'd always wanted one – new linen, a bedside table and new curtains, inter-lined, to draw against the day. I loved giving her presents. Closing my eyes, I can see it all. Even now I could walk blindfolded around that room, my hands touching everything in its place. I have never been happier than in that tiny space, with the two of us marooned together, two lovers clasped tight. It was a universe apart and beyond that door nothing else existed, the bustling world locked out.

But I was still on my guard. I wasn't entirely reckless. My fear, of course, was William. His fixed routines helped. So my time with Maddy was easy to organise. Outwardly the pattern of our married life hardly changed. I was there when he returned from work, I was there in the evenings, cooking together, still going out to friends. Yet I was always looking for moments of escape, thinking two or three days ahead, almost drunk with waiting. But, as I say, I wasn't foolish. When I came back from seeing Maddy, I always showered and changed my clothes: I was convinced that William would smell her on me, the pungency of her body and sex. But even that wasn't enough. He might even smell her on my hair. So I had it all cut off. Maddy thought it very funny – 'You are now my proper lover-boy', she said. But William was upset.

'What have you done? I liked your Marburg curls. Why cut them off?'

'Oh, William, don't be silly. It's the latest fashion. You'll get used to it in time.'

But William wasn't happy. He looked at me with a side-long glance, his eyes darkening, and said nothing.

***

My affair with Maddy lasted for about four months. I have said how it began. I must now say how it ended. It was quite sudden. I had arranged to meet Maddy at the flat. I arrived in the afternoon, at our usual time, at 3 o'clock. She was in floods of tears, could hardly speak.

'Dickie knows and wants money. Otherwise he'll tell your husband.'

I panicked. 'How does he know about us?'

'Well, you remember that scarf you lost, the expensive one?'

'Yes, I remember – Gucci – I lost it days ago. I told you. I've been looking everywhere.'

'Well, he found it.'

'But where was it?'

'Under the bed!

'Under the bed? You're kidding me. I'm sure I looked. How did it get there, for Christ's sake?'

'How do I know, Etta? But he found it and knew it wasn't mine. Oh, Etta, I was frightened, it was so unlike him. He shouted and screamed, he wouldn't stop, and in the end I said you were just a friend. Then he said some horrid things. I told him who you were, the lady who helps the girls. He smirked at that. It was terrible. I can't tell you what he said. Then he left. He must have watched you, discovered where you lived. He's not stupid, Etta, and it didn't take him long to guess.'

'How much does he want?'

'Five hundred will shut him up.'

'That's not so easy, Maddy, we have a joint account.'

'Please try, Etta, I don't want this to end.'

'End? End? What do you mean by "end"? Why should things end, Maddy? God, tell me, don't joke, tell me what you mean?'

'Oh, Etta, of course I don't want things to stop. I love you, I really do. I want it to go on and on. I've never been so happy. But please see it my way. He's dangerous and I can't pay him off. I haven't the money, he's had the lot. You'll have to help. If you don't, he'll do something, I know he will. He'll get violent, he might hurt me.'

'I thought he never hit you.'

'It was only the once, Etta, nothing serious, just a punch. But Etta, I'm so frightened and it's all my fault. Yes, it is, it is! Don't argue! I know it is! We should never have come here. What a mistake! How stupid! We should have found somewhere else. But I've been so happy, Etta. So please, please do something or else we'll have to stop and my heart will break.'

So I paid. And the next month I paid again, then another and another. But it couldn't go on, there was a limit. I told her: I wasn't made of money. William was bound to notice. Either that or he'd get a letter from the Bank. But she wouldn't listen. I explained what William was like, that knowing about us would kill him or drive him mad. But she didn't take it in. She was too frightened to hear. So I paid again but this time said that was it, I'd had enough. Still she didn't let up. She started ringing the house, weeping down the phone. First it was her brother, how terrified she was, then it was William this and William that.

'If you don't pay up, Etta, Dickie will tell him, I know he will. Don't you care for me at all, not just a little? What will happen to me if he doesn't get his money? Do you want to see me hurt? God, what did I ever see in you? You're just uncaring, mean with money. It's a shock, it really is! I can't believe you're being so selfish and unfeeling. But, then, perhaps you don't love me anymore, is that it? Is that what this is all about? Are you getting rid of me? Is this your way out? Well, Etta, I still love you, with all my heart I do. I'm not fickle, I'm not like you. I know what loyalty means.'

Anyway, that's what she said. She was lying, of course. It was all lies. The two of them were in it together. With no more money coming in, Maddy's manner quickly changed. And she was plain enough: 'Just Pay Cash. Do that and I'll go away.' Those were her actual words. Can you believe it? It was a physical blow to the stomach. I was winded and literally doubled up, my hands clutched in. But she was merciless, bending over me, quite calm. She spelt it out. Did I think it would always be for nothing? She had a living to make. She had never felt for me what I had felt for her – she said that too. It was pure romance on my part and my imagination had done the rest. Every word dripped acid on my heart. I couldn't speak. I was mute with pain, in total shock, still crouching down. She never raised her voice. She stood over me and made things clear. I had no choice.

You'll say I should have guessed. If there were little signs, I missed them all. I was too stupefied by desire to read them right. I was blind, my eyes put out, I could not see what lay ahead, even though the night was closing in and I was rushing headlong downwards in the dark. So this was where I'd ended up, just another client, one among the others, paying for her body's use. But I couldn't will my love away. Despite her words, my whole being ached. I seemed to see her everywhere: in the street, in the park, boating on the lake, doing all the things we'd done together, repeating all the things we'd said. I tried to meet her but she was always out. I left messages at the flat but heard nothing back. I still refused to believe the truth. I couldn't take it in. I clung to hope. There must be something wrong, something I didn't know, some explanation that would make it right. I told myself: just take one day at a time and she'll return, come back to you, with a fresh start and everything where it was. I slept to escape the day, deep and dreamless. I'd never slept so well. Then, waking up, my blinking eyes quite sore, reality came back and dragged me down. I was sinking, drowning in a little box. I felt suffocated and could hardly breathe. *Luft! Luft!* That all I wanted! Air! Air! Just the slightest breeze and I'd be fine, giving me time to work things out. I studied myself in the mirror. My face seemed much the same, a little tired perhaps, with deeper lines about the mouth. I touched my skin but it wasn't me. There was nothing there. I'd been hollowed out, a husk, an echoing shell of pain. I had been betrayed and abandoned. Over all these months she had never told the truth, not once. She had deceived me with every caress and every kiss. Nothing, not one thing, had been real, only my need.

I almost came apart. My pain came in tidal waves, foam-tipped, crashing back and forth in high white walls of terror. One moment I was quite calm, the next distraught. There seemed no end to it. I thought things would improve, that tomorrow would be better, but it

184

never was. The next day was just the same, with the same grinding despair and sense of loss. I feared to be awake, so slept and slept.

★★★

Hate saved me. I would sit in the dark, not moving, and let the full horror wash over me, like a flood rising. My muscles tensed, I had palpitations, and I could feel the palms of my hands go damp. My panic increased, I braced myself as I felt it coming on. Then it was upon me, spiralling up through my body, tightening its grip in iron bands around my chest, making me feel giddy and nauseous. But I steadied my breathing, took great gulps of air, and gradually the attack subsided. Now I looked my tormentor in the face. I saw it rear up within me, emerge red-eyed and roaring. I heard it cry out in blinding shouts, tearing at the air and wailing, frothing at the mouth, howling obscenities and stamping on the ground. Rage! Rage! It was my own refracted self, distorted by an anger never known before, so fierce that it swept my despair aside. It was the searing rage of humiliation and self-disgust! How dare she! How could she? To me! To me! So it was that I fell in hate, just as once I had fallen in love. Yes, my hate saved me: it filled the void and gave me enough for life. I now had purpose and intent.

Hate is not the antithesis of love: indifference is. Hate huddles close to love, a near relation, of the same bloodline. That was why so little changed. Maddy remained the obsession of my life, but I was now passionately in hate. How odd that sounds! But that is how it was. So I fell again, another seduction, still sensuous in its heat. And, believe me, hate is a rarer thing than love. We parade our loves but we hide our hates. We fall in and out of love; but hate is a constant, it stays for ever. Poets sing of love but rarely sing of hate. Why not? They should. There is real joy in hate, passionate and fulfilling, and you hug it close. Hatred is a nourishment that keeps your old wounds green: it energizes the soul and keeps all the torments still.

If I survive all this, I shall write a book on hate. Hate is not a mental abnormality but a psychic need, albeit with all one's wishes reversed. In love one desires the health and happiness of the beloved; but in hate these things bring no joy, only pain and misery. In love one longs for contact and proximity; but in hate one is sick with loathing at the slightest touch. In love you bask in the successes of those you love; but in hate these become sources of despair, to be devalued by contempt. When hating you soon learn that what you cherished most when loving – like warmth, compassion, pride and adoration – are turned inside out and converted into hostility, harshness, derision and disgust. And all the time your hatred mounts up and up, fuelled by the memories of love's intimacies, by the heart-knowledge of the two of you together. This is the worst of all. One can take almost anything but this. Does Maddy tell stories about our love-making and our times in bed? Is every secret made public? Does she go into intimate details, about all my needs and wants? Do the other girls find her stories funny, just like they did before? Am I now the butt of their sordid jokes? This was the ultimate degradation. I just wanted to hide, to blank out the laughter ringing in my head.

But hate is creative and constructs new worlds. In bed I would lie awake and dream of Maddy's pain, endless and without relief. I saw her stripped in public, naked and surrounded by drooling men. I saw her strapped to a chair, weeping as her lovely hair was shaved off. Every night I thought of something new, delighting in her degradation. It wasn't difficult to unravel what was happening. These dreams of violence were constructs of my affronted narcissism. My self-regard had been deflated and these aggressive fantasies boosted my bruised ego. On waking, however, these fantasies quickly evaporated. In reality Maddy seemed impregnable. She would tell William if I made the slightest move. So I was trapped and it was all my fault. There was no excuse. I had blundered on, in thrall to a creature who sold her body on the streets. The risks I had taken haunted me. My remorse was overwhelming.

But gradually things began to change. Like a dammed up watercourse, the thwarted ego always finds an outlet. So it was with me. Another option opened up. My desire to hurt Maddy became subordinate to my desire to prevent hurt to William, to keep him safe from knowing. What was perceived as an unsolved problem during the day now achieved an extraordinary psychical intensity when overcome at night.. All my dreams began to concentrate on this single point: to protect William from the truth and so keep his love for me intact. What was ineffective awake became effective during sleep.

The impact on my dream-world was immediate. Quite quickly all the symbols of aggression and retribution were replaced by those of struggle and achievement, so renewing my love of self. I climbed high mountains, swam across vast lakes, walked undaunted through blizzards and storms. I rejoiced in all the risks of life and was never once afraid. Again, I felt the rush of wind through my body, with nature subservient to my needs. My damaged psyche was reinvigorated, transfused with blood. I felt redeemed. My vulnerability was forgotten and the balance between Maddy and I reversed. I was no longer passive before her power.

I remember one dream in particular, full of sunshine, another cliff-edge dream. I am walking barefoot along a coastal path, my feet hot upon the sand. The sea gleams blue, seagulls are circling white above, a perfect day. I look up and see the weather change: scudding clouds, in billowing groups, moving fast in land. Then I hear a cry, walk towards the edge, and look down. There, far below, is a woman, her black hair trailing in the wind, terrified, helpless and alone, cutting herself, bleeding, as she scrambles up the cliffs. But the water is rising, the tide is coming in. There's no way out and soon she'll drown. I sit down and watch. I see her clearly and hear her screams bouncing off the rocks. It's like watching an insect die. The water comes up and gradually covers her feet, then up and up still higher, to her waist, her face, her floating hair. Then up again until all I see are hands, fingers stretched, feeling for the sun. It's all quite slow. Then there's nothing left, just the lapping sea. I get up and resume my walk, quite unmoved. Yes, I would destroy Maddy, stamp her out. I would destroy Maddy and save William, and thereby discharge my humiliation and restore my ascendancy. William's love was now paramount, not mine for me.

This surge of power was so intense that it covered every aspect of my life, both at night and through the day. I was no longer exhausted but full of energy. I knew I had to act, and soon, because time was running out. So I made my plans. I lay in bed, listening to William through the wall. I would get up to see when his light went out. Then in the darkness I surrendered to my schemes, searching through a maze of plots. I hardly slept. Slowly an idea took shape. I rehearsed it all. I would walk about my room, learning all my lines, the moves and gestures, the tones of voice. By dawn I was word-perfect. Then, during the day, I would make little trips in the car to get the timings right. I took no risks. I was back on stage, the spotlight on. I felt at home again, with a part to play. And with that my happiness returned. I was reborn. I would make amends. I was exhilarated and could hardly wait. Now all I needed was the rain.

***

I shall get this over quickly. I tried to get hold of Maddy several times. I never wrote anything down – never left a message or anything like that – but rang and rang. Finally I got through. I told her that I couldn't carry on without her, that I'd do what she wanted, that I'd find the money. I just had to see her. I cast out my line: there was desperation in my voice. She didn't take much persuading. I told her I couldn't come to her, I was too tied up at home. So could she come to me? That would be the safest thing. I suggested she collect the money on Thursday, on William's cinema night. I told her to arrive late, later than our usual time.

She took the bait and arrived at 9 o'clock. I was preparing supper, tenderizing two steaks with a steel mallet. Maddy looked awful, pasty-faced and tired. She was soaking wet.

'Are you ill?' I asked. 'You don't look well.'

'It's nothing. It's the bloody rain,' she said. 'Have you got the money?

'I have, Maddy. It's all here, as agreed.'

I gave her every chance, I tell you, every chance. It was not too late, even then.

'Sit down', I said. 'You look done in. Are you sure you're all right? Want a drink?'

She sat down at the kitchen table and leaned forward on her elbows. She was shivering and exhausted. She was wearing her plastic raincoat, the water dripping on the floor, a favourite brown jumper, with a light grey dress beneath. She placed her shoulder-bag down beside her. She didn't speak or even glance up.

'Maddy,' I said, 'I'll give you the money. Don't worry, I've got it here. But first, just tell me, I want to know. Why do this? It's me, Maddy! It's me, your Etta! This can't be you! Something must have happened. Just tell me and we'll sort it out. They'll be a way. Because this can't go on. William will soon find out. I think he suspects already. And that can't happen, Maddy. He mustn't know.'

Then she looked at me, her face stretched white. 'It's not up to me. It's Dickie you have to worry about.'

'You keep on saying that, Maddy, but what's the difference? It's either you or him. But why won't you listen? I'm telling you, there's nothing left. For Christ's sake, Maddy, I've already had to sell some things. And William's beginning to wonder, I can see it in his eyes. And he mustn't know, Maddy. Do you understand me, Maddy? He must never find out! Never! I won't allow it!'

'Just get the money and we'll see about the rest later'.

'There'll be no "later", Maddy. This is it. Don't you get it? There's just no more.'

'No, you're the one who doesn't get it, Marietta. There'll be no more when I say so and not before. Look around you, look at this house with its fancy kitchen. Of course, there's more. You'll just have to sell a few more things, that's all. Just part with stuff. William won't notice, not if it's jewellery. You could claim it on insurance.'

'Stop it, Maddy, stop it! Just listen to yourself. This can't be you! Do you really mean this? Think what you're saying. Think hard. I won't ask again. Is there to be no end to this? Will you always want more? Will all this just go on and on?'

She said nothing but put out her hand, palm up. Then in a tired voice she said, 'For God's sake, just get the money. Be quick, I can't stay long. It's raining and I've a bus to catch.'

I didn't move. She stood up. 'Oh, well, have it your own way,' she said, shrugging her shoulders. She turned to go. The steel mallet was in my hand. I struck her on the back of the head, not hard. She staggered forward. Then she turned towards me, her eyes circling wide. Her mouth opened in a wordless sound. I struck her again, this time bringing my full weight to bear. I felt her skull crack and she slumped down. Blood trickled from her nostrils on to the floor. I searched her bag and took out her phone. Everything was prepared. I had bought a large plastic sheet. I took it out from beneath the sink and placed

191

it over Maddy. Then I folded her in, turning the body over and over. When wrapped up, I dragged her towards the garage doors. I was surprised how light she was, but it was still a struggle heaving her up into the boot. I placed her shoulder-bag beside her. Then I went back to the kitchen, put on some rubber gloves, and with a bottle of Domestos cleaned up the mess.

I drove out to the Newtown Estate. I had rehearsed everything, I knew the route. I stopped beside the old cars dumped along the road. The weather was perfect, heavy, unremitting rain. I opened the boot, heaved Maddy out – she was still quite warm – lay her on the ground, removed the sheet, dragged her by the feet towards the bank and rolled her down the slope. I then rang Dickie on Maddy's phone. He answered almost immediately: 'Hi, sis. How's tricks?' In Maddy's voice I said, 'Dickie, I'm at the Newtown Estate, up by the canal. Know it? Good. Come quickly. I've been hurt!' Before he could reply, I rang off. Then I reversed my car, parking it among the others, right at the back. No one would see it there. I changed quickly. I had my costume ready: it had to match. I had a plastic raincoat, like the one she always wore, with a dark jumper and dress beneath, both from M&S. I put on my wig – long, black, curly hair – and put her bag under my raincoat to keep it dry. I walked forwards to the first of the cars and got in behind the wheel. It had a dreadful, gagging smell, of mice and vomit. The rain pattered on the roof. I rang Dickie again. I shouted down the phone: 'Where are you? Where are you?' 'Don't worry,' he replied. 'I'm nearly there. Five…five minutes.'

I watched the road. I peered through the windscreen:

the glass was cracked and filthy, the rain was lashing down. I could hardly see. I leant forward to get a better look. There was nothing there! Where was he? Did he know the way? What an idiot, I should have known! Then, in the distance, I saw two lights. They were coming closer, coming fast. I wiped my hand across the misting glass. I screwed up my eyes, leaning forward. Yes, faster, faster, a car, with its headlights on. Was this Dickie? Or someone else? It came nearer, then slowed, then flashed its lights. A signal. So it must be him. I left the car and walked out into the middle of the road. The beams of light picked me out. I waved my arms. The car stopped a few feet away. I lowered my head, the hair across my face, and ran forwards, limping slightly. Dickie leant across and opened the passenger door. 'God, what's…what's happened, sis? Are you OK? I came real quick.' I got in and sat beside him. I reached back and put Maddy's bag on the seat behind.

Dickie switched on the light. Then I turned and looked at him. Then he looked at me. For a moment he couldn't take it in, you could see it in his eyes. Then he frowned and slowly something clicked. His neck bent forwards and he stared, close up, at my stranger's face. 'Who…Who are you? You're not M..Ma..Maddy! Where's Mad…dy?'

'No, I'm not Maddy,' I said. 'I'm Marietta. Remember? Remember me?'

'No! No! I don't know…know… who… But where's M..M…Maddy? She said…said …she's hurt.'

He must have seen something in my face, something fixed and set. He started shouting: 'Where is she? Have you hurt my sis!' He raised his hands and started pushing at my body, screaming out, 'Where's my sis? Where's my sis?' Then he turned sideways in his seat, grabbed my arm and started to twist it round. 'Where is she? Where's my sis?' He went on and on. I could smell garlic on his breath. He wouldn't stop.

That made it easier. It was almost self-defence. But I didn't mean to hit him with the claw-side of the hammer first, right in the eye: it gauged it out. He howled with pain and grabbed his face, his splayed fingers trying to stem the gushing blood. It was a sudden spurt, almost a solid mass: I could feel it wetting my hands and knees. He struggled again, writhing from side to side, shaking his head violently, howling with the pain. The noise was horrible, quite deafening in that narrow space. So I turned the hammer round, blunt side on, and struck him again, harder this time, with all my strength, my anger increasing with every blow. He gurgled and went quiet. I pushed him down, his head below the steering-wheel and against the door. I searched his pockets and took out his phone. Then I switched off the light.

Now came the hardest part – I hadn't banked on this. I looked at my watch. It had just gone eleven. I was there far too soon! Good God, I had almost another hour to wait! So I sat in the darkness, not looking at the body beside me but staring straight ahead. I never want to go through that again: I'll dream about it all my life. The blood was caking on my arms and hands, I could feel it seeping through my dress. The car was warming up and I began to smell a sickly sweaty scent. One or two cars drove past, but they were too early, it wasn't him. So I sat there, peering through the glass. The rain poured down, hitting the windscreen in heavy shafts. How long did I have to wait? I looked at my watch again. Any minute now. The film ended around eleven-thirty. William would soon be here, I was sure of that, with a car like his. I'd timed it myself, just the day before. But I started to panic, I couldn't help myself. Had there been an accident? Or had he, just this once, taken a different route? I tried not to think but my mind went round and round. Something had gone wrong, I was sure of it. Was there something I'd missed? Perhaps just a little thing? But what? But what?

It was an endless wait, every minute an hour's length. But I needn't have worried. Just before midnight I saw the car. The rain had eased slightly and I could see ahead. The car was white. William. Thank God. So I quickly dipped my hand in a pool of sticky blood and smeared it, cold, upon my face. I got out, ran back to the other cars and crouched down behind. I watched the road. Now for the leap of faith. I stumbled out into the road, waving my hands above my head, blinded by the light. I heard the screech of brakes, then William's voice. He shouted something I couldn't hear. I ran away. He came after me, calling out if I was hurt. I crossed the road. I couldn't let him near. Then I slumped down, head forward, my hair across my face. 'Help me' was all I said, making my voice go deep. I didn't dare say more. 'Don't worry, I'll get help. Stay there, I'll not be long.' He hurried back to his car and drove off. I knew he had no mobile, that he'd have to drive away. I parted the curtain of my hair and watched him go.

I had little time. They'd soon be here. I ran to my car and

drove home. Half-way there, I stopped the car and threw their phones down a roadside drain. I drove on. Then my mobile rang. It was William. I stopped my car: there must be no engine noise. 'Did I wake you?' he asked. 'Don't worry,' I said, 'I've only just gone to bed.' He explained where he was, with the police, what had happened, that he'd be late. I said, 'I've put some salad in the fridge. Tell me all about it tomorrow.' 'I will', he said, 'Sleep tight.' The rest was easy. On reaching home, I parked the car, cleaned it – there wasn't much to do – had a bath and then went to bed. I heard William arrive, then later heard him come up the stairs. I put on my dressing-gown and met him on the landing outside my room. 'What a night you've had, Willy. No, you didn't wake me. I couldn't sleep.' And that was that. The next morning we had breakfast as usual. Then William reported to the police. Later on I went myself, quite early, about ten-thirty. By that time William had already gone off to work. It was quickly over. I was interviewed and confirmed the time William had arrived the night before. I signed a witness statement, then left. I wasn't there long, about fifteen minutes.

You'll ask me how I felt when I got home. To begin with I felt nothing, not a thing. I had expected some reaction but in fact went numb. It was shock, of course. My nervous system had closed down. I was in a kind of dream-like condition, removed from things, obviously exhausted but in a robotic state. Stranger still, I was incapable of imagining what had happened the night before. It was all a blur, a nightmare locked away. Something had happened, that I knew, but I couldn't say precisely what it was. It was a kind of psychological

196

amnesia, my emotional detachment serving to protect my wounded psyche from the knowledge of what I'd done. But it was a strange sensation. All day I had this nagging of the mind, as if I had mislaid something important, something close to hand but which I couldn't quite place or touch. I went to Waitrose, I went for a walk, I came back home – but, truth to tell, I wasn't really there, not myself at all. I was existing without sensation, traumatised and in a semi-conscious state.

But later that night it all rushed back. It was William's doing. It wasn't his fault because how was he to know? It was after dinner and we were drinking wine. He was excited about finding this injured woman alone at night and gave me a blow-by-blow account. I had to look away, I couldn't meet his eye. He filled me in, about the murders, and I sat there, trying to show surprise. My memories flooded back. So how did I feel as he chatted on? Any remorse? No. Did I feel no guilt at all? None. Did I feel empowered, restored? Oh, yes! Because, you see, I was still so warm with hate. So what cause for shame? Why even think like that? I had achieved what I set out to do. And I had given them every chance. I could have done no more. I had warned them but they wouldn't listen. In the end, their greed had killed them. And now it was just the two of us, again together, with the road ahead, once more clear and brightly lit.

I should have known it would never last. It happened when William told me about the detective on the case. Unusually for him he was impressed – 'A very clever man', he said – and then described him in the oddest terms: as some enormous, merciless, sniffing dog, who would never give up and always pulled down his prey. You can imagine how I felt. I reeled back. I imagined this monster-man yapping at my heels, tracking me down, never letting go, his teeth tearing at my flesh. I began to have doubts. Had I missed something out, the smallest detail to put him on the scent? But it wasn't only that. That wasn't the worst of it, not by half. William told me about how they'd talked, about criminals, about lying and deceit. He remembered everything, almost word for word. So I heard it all. But really it wasn't even that. I was unnerved by something else. How can I put this? It was William's manner. It was the way he spoke. Perhaps it was just my imagination working overtime. Perhaps I was just tired and overwrought. But still…but still. I thought I detected something there, in the narrowing eyes and hollow tone of voice. William put down his glass and spelt it out. It was always the little things that gave the game away, the little gestures that unmasked the truth. The criminal was never safe. He said all this, with a chilling, staring look. Then it came to me. My God, he knows! He's always known! He knows it all! He's always known about Maddy, seen through all my lies! Even last night he knew! He'd simply waited and played his part.

It was a terrifying thought. Perhaps I was wrong but I couldn't get it out of my head. I could no longer bear his look. I had to leave the room. So I said I was tired and went upstairs to bed. I had a terrible night. I never slept. All night long I imagined he knew it all; that at any moment my door would open and there'd he'd be, standing in the light, telling me what I'd done, that there was nowhere left to hide. But I hadn't reached the bottom, nearly but not quite. There was still a little way to go. It came quite soon, next day in fact. William had been having lunch and read about it in the Press. He rang to say. 'Listen to this, Marietta. You'll never guess! The girl was a prostitute and pregnant. Well fancy that! I wonder if the killer knew?'

★★★

No, the killer didn't know, William, she never knew. Oh, Maddy, why not say? Why not tell me? You looked ill – that's all I thought – I just didn't see it, just never guessed. If only you'd told the truth, not lied. Nothing need have been, we'd have found a way. And I wonder: was it a little boy, a little girl? Would it have had your looks, your eyes, your hair? No, no, no thoughts of that, not now! Down, down, away with that! But Willy, oh Willy, it never went. It stayed attached, glued on, it never left, it nagged and nagged, and cleaved my mind in two. There's really no more to say, there's nothing else. I have reached the lowest depth, the coldest place. I want to forget and be forgotten, to see no light. Maddy's baby! Oh, dear God! Where's forgiveness for such a thing? So let me hide my face. Let me run away. I have to go, I can't stay now. But where? Not here, so somewhere else. Ah, yes! Of course, of course! Why, there it is, just over there! Look! See it, it's really not so far? Just along the narrowing track, where the trees bend in. Yes, I see it, I know it well, my road ahead. So let's be quick, I can't be late. This is where I need to be, this place beyond all tears, where no one knows and where I can't be reached. So hurry, hurry, please no delays. There's no time to lose, the sky is falling in. It'll

only take a few short steps into the darkness swelling at
my feet. Then the chilling water will rise up to cover me,
then suck me down and down, a flickering, fading light.
Oh, Willy, Willy, don't you see? You drowned me when
you told me that!

Afterword

My account of the Newtown Murders is incomplete. This is hardly my fault. Certain details were suppressed at the time, others coming to light some years afterwards. Of course, in the immediate aftermath, the Press were very active in describing events in all their lurid detail – after all, we had our murderer – and there was a lot of tittle-tattle at the time. But the complete story has remained unknown – until now that is – and what I discovered came about quite by chance.

There were, however, two immediate effects. Both of them were due to what Henry Fairest liked to call the corrosive effect of guilt, apparently a well-known phenomenon in police investigations. This is the kind of guilt that keeps you awake at night, that disturbs your sleep. Something may have happened thirty, forty years ago; but back it comes, quite fresh, as you lie in bed. Perhaps you treated somebody badly or ignored a plea for help, wrote that cruel letter or broke a heart? I know what Henry meant. With me it can get so bad that I have to put on the light and walk about. You try to forget, to push the thing away. But it's no good. Guilt, after all, is the one thing you never doubt. And guilt is not like shame. Shame needs an audience but all guilt requires is that inward turn as you remember what you were and what you did. So it's a haunting of sorts. No wonder most of us are on the run. And, take my word for it, it gets worse with age. With little future left, the past rears up and hunts you down. Only psychopaths are without guilt: they lack this inner eye, the compass of conscience.

Now escalate up. What if you feel guilty about a loss of life? Somebody died because of you. A doctor makes a mistake and the patient dies. You're driving along and for a split second you look away and hit the child. And it need not even be your fault. You were out when the call was made. You took a wrong turning and got there late. You thought your son's cough was less serious than it was. Either way, you couldn't have known, you were acting for the best. But, still, that person's dead and it's down to you. This places you on the very highest level of guilt. There are no moments of remission. The guilt takes hold in its tentacle-grip and never lets go. Your whole life is spent looking backwards, you have no future only this tormenting past. Wherever you are, whatever you're doing, whoever you are with, it shadows you about, tugging at the memory. Nobody understands, not your family, not your friends. They think you'll get over it, but you don't.

I mention all this, first, because of what happened to Henry Fairest, and second, because of what happened to Marietta Weismann. Both were the victims of corrosive guilt. Let me take Henry's case first. Nobody could have foreseen what occurred. Of course, we all felt terribly sorry for him. But knowing Henry as we did – his outsize personality, his generosity, that bellowing laugh – we thought he was too big to go under, that he'd rise above it. But he didn't. He just seemed to shrink, to become half the man he was. I never

202

want to see anything like that again. It was terrible. Bob Bonfield told me all about it, about Henry's last meeting with Weismann. He was there, taking notes.

Weismann was very matter-of-fact, clearly in control of himself, quite unemotional. Henry, it seemed to Bob, was in a much worse state, very pale and drawn, quite shaken and unlike himself. Bob thought he'd come out of it. But he didn't, not really. He retired soon afterwards. He'd had enough. Even Jock Pringle tried to cheer him up. But it was no use. He couldn't be persuaded, he just wanted out. There was really nothing to be done. We all thought him wrong, but he couldn't see it any other way. He kept on saying that it was all his fault, that he had blood on his hands and couldn't wash it off. He went over it and over it and always came up blaming himself -- that he should have delayed matters, explored other avenues, been more patient. But he'd wanted a quick result. So he made that announcement, and soon it was in all the Press, front page splashes, big features on the radio and TV. It got out of hand, really it was all too much. Well, Henry got his result all right and the case came to a rapid end. But it wasn't what he'd wanted, finishing like it did, not in that tragic way. So he left within the week, took his pension and went back to Didsbury. We didn't see a lot of him after that, sometimes at the odd reunion or dinner, but really nothing much. Yes, it was the guilt that did for Henry. The trap he laid trapped him.

At the interview Weismann was quite precise about what happened. As usual he arrived back home just after midnight – it was his Thursday night at the *Duke of York's*. There was a light on in the kitchen, with a little note from Marietta on the table: "Dinner in fridge. XXX". His supper, as always, was delicious, with a favourite pudding. He poured himself a glass of Chardonnay, went into the sitting-room, and sat down with his food on a tray in front of the TV. He just caught the end of a midnight episode of *Frasier*, which always made him laugh. Then he went back to the kitchen, washed up the dishes, and put them in the rack to dry. He went upstairs. He noticed that Marietta's door was open. He could feel the draught of cold air along the hallway. So he looked in and saw her curtains billowing in the wind. He shut the windows. When he turned round he saw that Marietta wasn't in bed. Where was she? He called out, "Marietta?" Then he saw the light under the bathroom door. He knocked. "Marietta? Are you there?" There was no reply. So he entered and saw her in the bath. She was looking at him, her head turned slightly to one side. She had washed her hair. "Oh, there you are!" he said.

When William saw the small Sabatier knife on the floor, he knew she was dead. He went up to her, knelt down and closed her eyes. Then he pulled out the plug. He watched as the rust-coloured water drained away, swirling round, slowly revealing Marietta's naked body and the deep cuts on her wrists. When the bath was empty, William decided to carry her back to her bedroom: she looked so vulnerable otherwise. With difficulty he lifted her out and lay her on the tiled floor. He dried her with a white towel. Then he stooped down, put his arms beneath her, and picked her up. He took her back to her bedroom and lay her on the bed. Her short hair was still wet. So he went back to the bathroom, got another towel, dried it off, then carefully brushed it through. Marietta looked cold. He covered her with the eiderdown and sat beside her for an hour, holding her hand. He looked around the room, at the familiar things – her clothes neatly folded on a chair, her bedside books, her bear in the corner, the photographs -- and then noticed an A4 envelope propped up on the top of the chest-of-drawers. There was a short note attached to it. "My darling Willy", it said, "I'm sorry. There was no other way. Your Marietta." William put the note in his pocket, picked up the envelope, and went downstairs. Then he phoned the police.

Weismann's statement was given almost in a monotone. Henry looked down at the document in his hand. 'And she also sent me a copy. It arrived this morning. So one for you and one for me.'

'Yes,' replied Weismann, *'Marietta's Lied'.*

'Yes,' said Henry, 'her final song. There's really nothing to add, it says it all. I am truly sorry for your loss, really more than I can say.'

'Before I go, may I ask you something, Chief Superintendent? Perhaps you'll guess what it is. My wife clearly had her suspicions about my role in this. She seemed to think that I knew all along what was going on; that, as she expresses it, I "played my part". I assure you I knew nothing, absolutely nothing. But all the same, just for the record, I'd like to know what you think.'

'What can I say to you, Professor Weismann? Your wife was clearly overwrought and in a suicidal frame of mind. In these cases, such suspicions are not uncommon. It is the fear of having the lie exposed; that somebody, usually the person closest to them, must know the truth. It is a familiar psychological condition. And remember your wife, with her psychiatric training, saw this herself, said as much. But for her it was no more than an intuition, a suspicion. She had really nothing to go on.'

'But what do you think? Do you think I've been lying?'

'You killed no one. You're innocent of any crime. Your wife was guilty. That should be sufficient.'

'Well, yes, perhaps I'm asking too much. But I'm – how can I put this? – intellectually curious. I still want to know what you think.'

'I'll tell you this – this is all I'll say. You loved your wife, of that I'm sure. But I also think you are a man capable of dispassionate action, a man who, in certain circumstances, would agree that "revenge is a dish best taken cold." So you may have known that something was up, that your wife was being unfaithful, having an affair. You may even have known about Maddy. For all I know, you may have spied on them, followed them about. Marietta always thought she knew where you were; but it might have been the other way round, with you watching her. That's a guess. I can't be sure. But even if all that were true, I ask myself: how could you have known how things would turn out? Perhaps the statement you made to me was false. Perhaps you knew very well who it was who ran out in front of your car. Perhaps you were never fooled by Marietta's disguise. But you couldn't have known how desperate she was, how far she'd go. And remember what she said. She said that it was all for you. She thought she was protecting you. She wanted you to remain innocent, unknowing; and for that she was prepared to sacrifice herself. And, then, in the end, what did she want? All she wanted was to return to you, to get back home, for her life to return to normal. That's all she desired. So by killing Maddy and her brother she wasn't leaving you: she was coming back. Nothing else mattered to her. I think she loved you more than she knew, more than you knew. And she might have got there if it hadn't been for the baby. The unborn killed her. And for that I blame myself. Her guilt is on my head, it's my guilt too. It was quite inexcusable. I should have done things differently, explored other avenues, taken more time. I'd have got there in the end, the clues were there, but I rushed things, wanted it all cut and dried. No, I'm to blame and I'll never forgive myself. But you, Professor, are innocent. You are not implicated in any crime. At the worst you are guilty of inaction, of doing nothing, of waiting to see what she would do. But that's not an offence. I just hope that others see it like that.'

'What do you mean?'

'Marietta's statement will be read out at the inquest. There's no avoiding that. And the Press will build up what Marietta says about you: they'll home in on that. You're a famous man, after all, and they love to attack people like you, with a reputation to defend. You will be implicated by innuendo. It will be trial by suspicion. So take my advice. Whatever they do, don't be provoked, never reply, don't let them drag you in, because that's what they want. In the end, they'll get tired, there'll be other stories, and you'll be forgotten. So be patient and do nothing.'

***

That was the last time they met. Later that week, William Weismann went off to the cinema – it was a Thursday, after all. But that routine didn't last for long. Three or four more visits to the *Duke of York's* and then he never went again.

Because Henry was right. The Press really went to town. It was far worse that anything Weismann could have imagined. Photographers followed him everywhere. They waited for him outside the cinema – someone had tipped them off about his Thursday nights. Journalists attended some of his lectures and interrupted him to ask questions about Marietta – there were even scuffles with the students. A film crew followed him home and someone shouted out, 'What's it like to fuck a monster?' But William followed Henry's advice and did, said nothing. He withdrew into himself. He closed the curtains and sat at home. He cancelled lectures, he took the phone off the hook, he rarely left the house and then only for short trips at night to get supplies. In the end he felt there was nothing else to do but leave for good. So he resigned from the university and disappeared. He sold up and left. His colleagues and students were very upset, of course, but he wouldn't listen. He just went. No one knew where he'd gone. It was a complete mystery. And inevitably that only increased his fame. He became a celebrity because he'd vanished without a trace. Then the myths about him began to circulate. Rumour filled in the gaps. He'd become a schoolmaster, a gardener, a hospital porter. He'd been spotted in this place and that, sometimes just round the corner, sometimes abroad. The Press tried to find him but in the end even they gave up. There were a few more stories about him but gradually these petered out. It was as Henry had predicted: he became yesterday's news. But it remained mystery, all the same, where he'd gone. It was only by chance that I discovered what had happened and that was many years later, long after Weismann's death.

I'll tell you all about that in a moment. But first, let

me skip ahead, just to round things off. I'll be brief and then come back to Weismann. You'll want to know what happened to the others. Predictably, Monty Slide went from strength to strength. He diversified and became legitimate. The gambling went, the brothels went, but the clubs stayed and he went more into the housing market and the building trade. The past was entirely forgotten – or at least passed over and ignored – and he became an upstanding member of the community, always ready to put his hand in his pocket for charitable causes. He was as good as his word with Reginald Lockyer – you'll remember him, the Member. In the end they became as thick as thieves, quite a pair, with Reggie often up at the house, making the most of the free drink and girls. He brought his well-connected friends – more celebs and politicians – and some of it rubbed off on Monty. He became quite a celebrity himself, hobnobbing with the great and good, always at the fashionable parties, at the opening of some new restaurant or gallery, a pretty girl always on his arm. Monty funded Lockyer – discreetly, of course – providing venues for meetings and political get-togethers. It paid off, it was a good investment. Lockyer rose in the ranks and became a Cabinet Minister. Then a couple of years later Monty was awarded the CBE in the New Years' Honours List. They said it was for charity work – most notably for funding two local Hospices and providing a convoy of coaches for the disabled – but by then he'd also given a lot of money to the Tories. The late-night parties continued. The neighbours never objected now. All they wanted was an invitation, to be seen with Monty and his glitzy friends. All the old houses had disappeared and been replaced by enormous mansions in Georgian or Elizabethan style.

Monty died in his late 70s. It was quite sudden: he had a seizure in the Cayman Islands. They flew his body back to Manchester. He had a big send-off in the Cathedral, the place was packed, the Bishop spoke. He left quite a fortune. The bulk of it went to the Seda Foundation, with huge annual donations to local charities. He left the house to Matt and Ben, who were the Executors of the Will. They continued to work for the Foundation until their own retirement – by then they were wealthy men in their own right. Shortly after Monty's death – he would never have approved – they took out a Civil Partnership. They adopted two Indians boys and sent them to Manchester Grammar School. They both did well: one became a proctologist, the other a solicitor.

When Lotte the deerhound died, Henry and Terence took Twinkie on a Mediterranean cruise. On their return Henry bought another dog, a little cocker called Edith. They were devoted to each other, particularly now that Henry had so much time on his hands. Then, a couple of years later, Twinkie died, and then, shortly after that, Henry himself. For his friends it was a shock but also a relief: he'd never been the same, become a shadow of himself, a haunted man, drinking in his corner at *The Sun*. Edith went to Terence, who moved down south. He lived to a great age, well into his nineties, was knighted and became a director of Tottenham Football Club.

***

Now back to William Weismann. As I said, it was anybody's guess where he'd gone. There were rumours, of course, but the truth was nobody knew. Speaking for myself, I'd lost interest. The past was past and it was all too long ago. I had other things on my mind. My *Decline and Fall* was going full steam ahead. I had decided to change the format, to make it alphabetical not chronological – I thought it more user-friendly that way, easier to digest. I'd got up to the letter "S": "S" for Sach (Amelia), Seddon (Frederick), Shelley (William), Sheward (William), Simcox (Christopher), Smedley (William), Smith (George), Smith (Madeleine), Stone (Leslie) and Swann (Emily). Still a way to go, then. But the finishing-line was in sight. Oddly, while there are quite a few murderers beginning with "T", there are surprisingly few for "W" and "Y". So there was light at the end of the tunnel. Mind you, the book still required an enormous amount of time and energy. I was travelling a good deal up and down the country, visiting various sites and libraries, and so had really little time for anything else. I think I can be forgiven, then, for forgetting all about Weismann. It was some time later that I found out what had happened and that was quite by chance.

The son of a friend of mine was studying Philosophy at University, not at Manchester but at Durham. I knew the lad quite well. Max his name was. Well, inevitably, I asked him about Weismann, told him that I'd met him a couple of times. Max got very excited. Weismann was quite a hero of his, not just because of what had happened all those years before – there was still the whiff of notoriety – but because of his philosophical significance. He soon lost me in his explanation, it was quite beyond me. Anyway, Max showed me his reading list. I was not surprised to see several books about Weismann; but the thing that intrigued me most were the books by Weismann himself. I had assumed that, with his disappearance, the work dried up. Not a bit of it. He was extraordinarily prolific, with articles and books coming out almost every year. And it was a very strange mixture. There were titles like *The Hidden Languages of the Mind, Cognitive Semiotics, Nietzsche's Signs* – on and on they went – the titles alone enough to put me off. But there were others that made me smile, knowing the man as I did: *The Life and Times of Arnold Schwarzenegger* and *J'Accuse Spielberg*. There were a whole series of articles written for various film magazines on individual actors and directors and a huge 500-page book on *Expressionism in Film*. I asked Max if there was a handy introduction to Weismann's philosophical work, something not too difficult for the amateur. He underlined two or three. I got them out of the library. Well, Max had over-estimated my abilities: they were quite impenetrable. But it was while flicking through one of them that I found my clue.

It was a volume in a series called *The Library of Living Philosophers*. It was an American publication, started in 1939, and I gather still going strong. They went far back: there were early volumes on Whitehead, Bertrand Russell and Moore, and there were many other names, all foreign to me. The format was always the same. First there was a collection of critical essays from other scholars, experts from all over the world, and then, at the end, a kind of "intellectual autobiography" by the philosopher concerned, answering those criticisms. The volume on Weismann had no Weismann reply because he had died before publication. But it was decided to publish the thing anyway. The book became a kind of memorial edition.

Leafing through it, I came across an article written by a former Weismann pupil at Manchester, a woman called

Elizabeth Anton, later herself a distinguished Professor of Philosophy. To begin with it was very technical, losing me entirely, but towards the end she included a short memoir of what it had been like to be taught by Weismann. My eye caught a paragraph beginning, 'The last time I saw Weismann...' I quote the passage in full. It's significance is self-evident.

The last time I saw Weismann occurred in the strangest way. I was in my early thirties and newly married. My husband and I had gone up to Scotland for a short holiday, staying in the Border country, at Peebles, in order to participate in the John Buchan trail organized by the John Buchan Society based there. Afterwards and making our way down south, we stayed at the small town of Langholm, intending to spend one night in order the next morning to visit the site of Telford's cottage at Eskdale – we were told it was a lovely walk. And so it was: the scenery is breathtaking. We stayed at the Douglas Hotel. After dinner in the bar we got chatting to a local man, who knew all about Telford. He suggested we visit the Telford Memorial, which we knew nothing about, and the remarkable library next to it. He asked me what I did. I told him I was a philosopher. That usually puts an end to conversation, but not in this case. He wanted to know more exactly about my areas of interest and so on. He then asked me whether I could help him out. He was the Chairman of the local Probus Club. There was a meeting the next evening at the Eskdale Hotel, which was just across the way. The guest speaker had, however, cancelled at the last minute and there was no hope of finding a replacement. So would I take his place?

All our expenses, including our extra night at the hotel, would be paid for. My husband and I could hardly refuse.

The meeting took place in the top room of The Eskdale. I was surprised to see about forty people crowded into such a small space, most of them, it seemed to me, retired men in their sixties and seventies, all quite formally dressed in jackets and ties. I was the only woman there. As I recall, my talk was entitled, "What use is Philosophy?" or something like that. I cannot remember exactly. I tried to make it quite light and amusing. The audience was very polite, but whether they enjoyed themselves I cannot say. Then our chairman – our friend from the Hotel – asked if there were any questions. One or two hands went up. The questions weren't really about Philosophy at all but much more down to earth and practical: "Which are the best universities for studying Philosophy?", "What are the job prospects like for Philosophy graduates?"

Then a hand went up at the back. "Please explain whether there are any basic beliefs that are not legitimated by philosophical criteria. If so, what are they and how is their status determined?" It wasn't the question that floored me: it was the voice. It was instantly recognizable: clipped, high-pitched and incisive. I was quite stunned. I played for time. I pretended I hadn't heard the question. Could he repeat it? Then somebody said, in broad Scots, "Stand up, Wull, the lassie canna hear ye!" And he did. It was like some terrible sea-monster emerging from the depths. Even now I see it all in slow motion: it was a gradual unbending. First up came the head with its famous quiff, the hair now quite white, then that unblinking, hypnotic stare. There was no mistaking him: it was William Weismann. He had hardly changed, thinner, more gaunt, but, as I say, instantly recognisable. Of course, he remembered me – that memory of his forgot nothing – and I thought I detected a sly twinkle in those black eyes, a slight twitch of the lips. He repeated the question. I stammered something out, I can't remember what. I confess my mind had quite seized up. Anyway, Weismann wasn't interested in my reply. It was just like the old days. He started to answer his own question. He just took off, thinking on his feet, his arms wind-milling, constantly pushing back his hair. The years rolled back: I was a student again, sitting on a hard floor. Nobody interrupted him and I guess nobody had a clue what he was talking about. He went on for some time. I wish I could remember what he said; but it was all a blank, I was still in shock. Then he sat down. The chairman lent across to me, grinning broadly. "I should have warned you about our Will. Apologies. He does go on a bit. You should have heard him the other week on Orson Welles!" After my talk I tried to find Weismann – my husband thought I was feeling unwell because I dashed out of the room as soon as I'd finished - but he'd gone. He must have left immediately. I was very disappointed. I asked the Chairman where he lived but he wouldn't say. "He keeps himself to himself" was all he said.

Well, no prizes for guessing what I did next. I drove up to Langholm the following day. I didn't know what to expect. The Anton sighting of Weismann had occurred many years before. In all probability he had left Langholm years back and died elsewhere. But it was worth a try. I had been to Scotland before, of course, as part of my research, Burke and Hare came from Edinburgh, Peter Manuel from Birkenshaw in North Lanarkshire, and Dr Edward Pritchard, the last person to be publicly hanged in Scotland, practised medicine in Glasgow. So, as I say, I'd been up there several times. The countryside round Langholm is spectacular – rolling hills and the River Esk running through – and the town itself is a typical Border mill town, uncompromising in its weather-proof granite buildings, with a spired Town Hall at the end of the High Street. Like Elizabeth Anton I stayed in the Douglas Hotel. After dinner I sat in the bar and started chatting with one or two of the locals. I casually asked about Weismann. No, they'd never heard of anybody by that name. Mind you, they'd had some Germans after the War. One of them, they remembered, had married a local girl and made violins. But it would be worth speaking to Dougie the Postman, long retired now, lives down by the river. Dougie knows everybody and might be able to help. He'll be easy to find. You can't miss him. Just ask.

Next morning I had tea with Dougie, now over eighty. 'Weismann? Weismann?' He shook his head. 'No, never heard the name.' So I described him – great head of white hair, tall, angular. Still no luck. I tried a different tack. He liked the movies.

'Oh that Will. Well, why didn't ya say? Aye, aye, I remember him, lived for years up at Bentpath, in one of those tiny cottages near the church. Can't quite remember which, but anyway in one of those white ones just below the bridge. Different people there now, of course. Aye, I remember Will, all right. Not called Weismann, though. Another name. What was it? What was it? Ah, I remember now. Anyway, always sending out his post, all over the world it went, him cycling down to town, and me taking the bigger parcels. Not much post coming back. Always thought that odd. Not talkative, like, but good tips at Christmas. Private, kept himself to himself. Very bare inside, just books and stacks of videos and DVDs. Had a huge telly, biggest I've ever seen. Took up a whole wall it did. Always watching the movies, was Will. Knew a lot. Always asking, "Had I seen this, had I seen that?" Often saw his light on late, neighbours said sometimes right through the night. It was me that found him. Stiff as a board he was. He was sitting in his kitchen, having a cup of tea. I saw him through the window. I knocked and knocked, shouted out I did, "Will, Will!" No reply. So I thought, eh, eh, something's up. Called Davie, our policeman. Went in together. Dead for a couple of days he was and it was winter, see, so almost frozen through, bloody gale blowing through the house. Must have been quick, like, never knew what hit him. Aye, quick. Heart, they said. I liked Will, often saw him about. Very active, long legs, walked everywhere. Tall, always smart. I can see him now, his white hair blowing. Used to go to all the local events – the Common Riding, the Langholm and Newcastleton shows. Loved the wrestling and the pipes and the children's races. Got quite excited, did Will, cheering on. Never spoke much. Quiet man. He's buried up at the Benty. I went. No service. Hardly anybody there. So we just popped him in, came back and drank his health.'

You can imagine how I felt. But Dougie hadn't finished.

'The house was locked up, nobody knew what to do. Rent paid until month's end. Then, a couple of weeks later, this gent arrived. American. Had a letter saying he could take the lot. Signed by Will, so nothing to be done. Just took the books and letters in cardboard boxes but left the furniture and other wee bits. Well, there was little there, not much at all. Aye, nothing really, I remember that. The telly went to one of the hotels – *The Buck* it was – and the Library got all the Videos and DVDs. Still there, I think, a lot of foreign stuff, never used. Don't know where the rest went. Probably Charity Shops. Anyway, ask Margaret Barnfather, she'll know. Lives in Buccleuch Square. Nice lass, Margaret, our librarian for years and years. She'll help you out, show you round. She's a hoarder, is Margaret, so there might be something left.'

How she knew me, I'll never know; but as soon as she opened her door she said, 'Ah, you're the gentleman asking about our Will. Come in, come in.' Margaret was a handsome woman in her seventies, silver-haired, dressed in brown brogues, a thick cardigan and a tweed skirt. I think she sensed my excitement because, bless her, she gave me a cup of tea and quickly got down to business.

'I remember the American, a university man, with a southern drawl, very polite. He had permission to take Will's things. Dick our solicitor said it was fine by him. So all above board. We emptied everything out. I helped, putting it in boxes, mostly books and files. Dougie is right. There wasn't much left after that, a few sticks of furniture, a couple of chairs and tables, some things in the kitchen. It was really quite bare, with no pictures on the walls, almost empty. I was quite shocked, Will living like that. We never knew. It was just so cold, no colour, no warmth, really nothing there. Well, as I say, we cleared it out. Somebody took over the place soon afterwards – it's a pretty cottage and lovely now. Will used to come into the Library quite often, ordering books. Then we got computers. He was always playing with them and went to evening classes. We all bought Amstrads in those days, then Apple Macs. Will and I used to compare notes: how to do footnotes, that sort of thing. Let's walk across and I'll show you what's there.'

Margaret lived twenty yards from the Town Hall. We went upstairs to a small room at the back. The walls were covered with shelves full of boxes and books. 'This is our archive,' she said. 'I was thinking there might be something left.' She dug around for a while, moving things about. Then she came to a shoe-box. 'Aye,' she said, 'I thought as much. I remember now. This was all there was, just odds and ends, but I didn't want to throw it out. Too personal for that, what with this old bear. And I always wondered about his family, whether somebody might arrive and want his things.' We looked inside. Apart from the moth-eaten animal, there were a few of old photographs – a couple on skis, a castle, some theatre tickets. There was also a woman's purse. I looked inside. There was no money in it but there were some bits of paper wedged in a side pocket. I took them out. There were four in all. At first I couldn't decipher them: they were faded and water-stained. So Margaret and I went to a desk and she turned on the light. We had a closer look. There were three poems neatly copied out in Marietta's unmistakable handwriting and her familiar turquoise ink. I didn't know any of the poems, only later discovering their authorship. The first, by Thomas Ford, was written on lined paper, from a cheap notebook of some kind, with the punched holes torn out.

> *Her gesture, motion, and her smiles,*
> *Her wit, her voice my heart beguiles,*

Beguiles my heart, I know not why,
And yet, I'll love her till I die.

The second poem was by Algernon Swinburne. I guessed that Marietta had copied this out at about the same time as the first poem. It too was on a scrap of lined paper, perhaps taken from the same notepad.

And all her face was honey to my mouth,
And all her body pasture to mine eyes;
The long lithe arms and hotter hands than fire,
The quivering flanks, hair smelling of the south,
The bright light feet, the splendid supple thighs
And glittering eyelids of my soul's desire.

The last poem was by Robert Frost. My guess is that it was copied out well after the first two poems. The ink, it seemed to me, had more colour to it and the paper was still quite crisp.

Some say the world will end in fire,
Some say in ice.
From what I've tasted of desire
I hold with those who favor fire.
But if it had to perish twice,
I think I know enough of hate
To say that for destruction ice
Is also great
And would suffice.

The last scrap of paper wasn't a copied poem. It was piece cut out of the letter page from some girly magazine – you know the sort of thing, where people write in about their love-lives, about how to get better in bed. Anyway, this lady – she herself must have been in her late fifties or early sixties – had written in about her parents, both well into their eighties, who had recently died. Under a heading, "Love Lasts", the daughter had written this:-

My parents were a wonderful couple, completely devoted and full of fun right up until the end. They were never apart and my mother died within days of my father. Not long after their deaths, I had a clear-out of the old house, where they had lived for almost their entire married life – so sixty years or more. I found this little note, written by my mother to my father, just a few weeks before his sudden death. He had evidently gone off early in the morning without telling her. "Darling Spud," it said. "Where are you? I woke up and you weren't there! Don't do this to me, you know how I ache and worry. I'm next door with Mrs Cray, you bastard. Your own Min.

Across the top of it, Marietta had written: 'This is all I ever wanted.' I can't explain it but I found this little scrap of paper very moving, much more so than the poems, knowing Marietta's history as I did. I explained a little of it to Margaret, saying nothing, of course, about the murders. I just told her that she had been Will's wife and had committed suicide. 'Poor lass!' said Margaret. 'Poor Will!' That was the only time I ever heard anyone express sympathy for Marietta. But, then, of course, Margaret didn't know the whole story.

I asked Margaret what she would do with William's few possessions. I was hoping, of course, that something might come my way. But she wouldn't let anything go. As she explained, she was still worried about relatives turning-up. Well, I wasn't going to press her. Then, just as I was leaving, she gave me the old bear. 'It's stuffing's gone and it will fall to pieces if you don't take it.' I took it home, and as I write this it is staring down at me, eyeless and shabby.

***

There was one last call to make. I went up there after lunch, before driving back down south. The weather had changed and it was now raining hard, not cold but with quite a wind – typical weather for the area, I was told. To get to Bentpath you carry along the B709 road to Eskdalemuir: it's about six miles out of Langholm. It's a turning off to the right, a short road leading to the Church, which is quite visible on the hill. I parked and walked up. Bentpath is really no more than a hamlet of about twenty houses, mostly terraced bungalows, one or two detached. Despite the rain a man was working on a tractor. I asked him about Will. Did he know him? "You mean Will the movie-man? Aye, that I did." Did he remember where he'd lived? "Aye, that I do." he said. "At the bottom. Last house before the bridge." He pointed down the road. It was pretty white cottage, quite small, with window-boxes full of flowers and a neat garden fenced off from the adjoining field. I knocked but there was no answer. I walked on over the bridge, stopped half way across, and lent over to watch the flowing river. The church was very handsome, granite-built, on a slight promontory, with a War Memorial beside it. The church was locked. So I walked further up the road which wound away to the right. I found

222

the graveyard, behind a high wall. In the middle of it stood a magnificent mausoleum with a leaded roof, surrounded by old tombstones, some ornately carved, some badly eroded by the weather. I couldn't find Weismann's grave. I must have looked at every one, walking up and down, but I couldn't find him. I gave up. I was very disappointed. Then, turning back, I noticed another graveyard. I'd missed it: it lay on the other side of the Church. I went in through a small iron gate. It was beautiful spot, enclosed within a dry-stone wall, with the hills coming down behind it and the running burn in front. It was immaculate, with a wide expanse of grass, newly mown, all the headstones standing out in ranks, some others set along the perimeter of the wall. I soon found Weismann's grave, marked by a plain block of stone with his name and dates. It wasn't his real name but the one Dougie gave me. I supposed the dates were true. I stood there for some time. I hoped he'd been happy in his last years, among these hills with his Scottish friends. But I didn't believe it. William Weismann's happiness lay dead with Marietta.

Did I have any profound thoughts? No, nothing came to mind. I just stood there, feeling rather sad. It was a peaceful spot – the green hills, the sound of water, the bracing air, everything so clean and bright, despite the wet. Anyway, I couldn't stay for long. The wind had got up and the rain was now fairly lashing down. I'd soon get soaked and I had a long, tedious journey in front of me. So I walked back up the road and drove off.

***

You'll want to know his name. I can't tell you that. It's a secret I feel bound to keep. I've dug up so many people, young and old, most of them monsters, that it's quite a novelty for me to let this one lie. And I feel better for it. All William Weismann wanted was to hide away, to withdraw from the world: he wanted no more of it, he'd had his fill. Perhaps that's why he loved the movies, the world of never-never land and make-belief, not the real world he'd known, so full of hurt and pain. Who was I, then, to disturb his peace, to show them where he rests? So I say: let the sun shine on him, the rain fall, snow's blanket cover him. Let him only hear the sound of sheep and the river and the wind. Let him get his wish and be forgotten.

But that won't happen. Weismann will always be remembered for his books. In the end, even Marietta, for all her passions and torments, will only remain a footnote on a page. So if you want immortality, write a book. I make no excuses: that's what I want for my *Decline and Fall*. Why not? It's a legitimate ambition. It's what all authors desire, if they're honest: to pass the years up there on a shelf, waiting for somebody to take them down. You're dead and gone but you've left this trace. Very few people can say as much. And thinking that quite lifted my spirits. All I wanted was to get home, to get back to my book. I was quite excited about settling back to work. Because next up was "S": "S" for Frederick Seddon, for Seddon the poisoner. There was a monster, make no mistake, cold and calculating. I shall have to give him very particular attention. But I'm forgetting. I've already told you about him and Eliza Barrow and the money and that kiss and the fly-papers dipped in arsenic and how cool he was waiting for Mr Ellis, the hangman.